Praise for Archer Mayor's Joe Gunther Series!

"I have a soft spot for quiet writers lik
suming voice and down to earth style
with a sense of integrity. The strength
come from the author's profound und
from his hero's intuitive ability to relat

there."

— Marilyn Stasio,
The New York Times

"Superb"

—Publisher's Weekly
(starred review)

"It is our good fortune that Mr. Mayor's skills are equal to the vigor of his imagination."

—The New Yorker

"Mayor's elegiac tone and his insights into the human condition make [each book] a fine addition to one of the most consistently satisfying mystery series going."

—Thomas Gaughan,
Booklist

"Archer Mayor is producing what is consistently the best police procedural series being written in America."

—The Chicago Tribune

"As a stylist, Mayor is one of those meticulous construction workers who are fascinated by the way things function. He's the boss man on procedures."

—The New York Times

"Mayor is not given to gimmicks and manipulation. There are flashier writers, but few deliver such well-rounded novels of such consistent high quality."

—Arizona Daily Star

"A fine thriller"

—Wall Street Journal

"First rate . . . Mayor has a way with white-knuckle final scenes, and he does it again in this atmospheric story."

—*Los Angeles Times*

"A powerful series, and this is only book two."

—*Kirkus Reviews*

"Lots of cat-and-mouse suspense . . . enough twists and turns to keep the reader on the chair's edge."

—*Publisher's Weekly*

"All the Joe Gunther books are terrific . . . As they say in New England, wicked good writing."

—*Washington Post Book World*

"Lead a cheer for Archer Mayor and his ability not only to understand human relationships, but to convey them to his readers."

—*Washington Sunday Times*

"Excellent . . . a dazzling tale that combines detection, compassion, small-town sociology, local politics, and personal priorities . . . How much better can Mayor get? This combination of detection and non-stop action is his best yet."

—*Toronto Saturday Star*

A deft mix of storm stories, political shenanigans, small-town procedural stuff and some pretty shocking buried secrets. One of [protagonist] Joe [Gunther]'s best."

—*Kirkus Reviews*

"This fine series offers all the elements that have captivated readers for more than two decades: solid police-procedural detail, a vivid sense of place, and wonderfully human interactions."

—*Booklist on* Paradise City

"A riveting read...Mayor writes an intelligent mystery....It's a pleasure to find a story that captures readers' attention, makes them care about the characters—and offers such dark chills."

—*Associated Press on* Tag Man

Bellows Falls

Also by Archer Mayor

Joe Gunther series

Open Season
Borderlines
Scent of Evil
The Skeleton's Knee
Fruits of the Poisonous Tree
The Dark Root
The Ragman's Memory
Bellows Falls
The Disposable Man
Occam's Razor
The Marble Mask
Tucker Peak
The Sniper's Wife
Gatekeeper
The Surrogate Thief
St. Albans Fire
The Second Mouse
Chat
The Catch
The Price of Malice
Red Herring
Tag Man
Paradise City
Three Can Keep a Secret
Proof Positive

Non-Fiction

Southern Timberman: The Legacy of William Buchanan

Bellows Falls

Archer Mayor

AMPress
Newfane, Vermont

PO Box 456
Newfane, Vermont 05435
www.archermayor.com

Cover Photo/Archer Mayor
Author Photo/Margot Mayor

Library of Congress Cataloging-in-Publication Data

Mayor, Archer.

Bellows Falls / Archer Mayor.

p. cm.

I. Title

PS3563.A965B45 1998 97-20834 CIP

813´.54—DC21

ISBN 978-0-9798122-7-9

ISBN 978-0-9798122-7-9

To Ponnie—
I love you
Thank you

Acknowledgments

In all my books, I have tried to place the story line on a realistic foundation. While the characters are always fictitious, the settings and organizations they work in are, with rare and obvious exception, rooted in the real world. This has made me gratefully dependent on a great many people, all of whom have given generously of their time and experience. It is no exaggeration to say that without them, none of these books could ever have been written.

Bellows Falls is no exception. The following list is not complete—some people have chosen to remain in the background, others have been lumped together under the name of their organization. To all of them, however, I give heartfelt thanks.

The Bellows Falls Police Department
The Burlington Police Department
The Brattleboro Police Department
The Vermont State Police
The Windham County State's Attorney's Office
The Vermont State Crime Lab
Ken Kelly
Bill Bress
The Vermont Symphony Orchestra
The Flynn Theatre
The Brattleboro Retreat
The Vermont Attorney General's Office
and many citizens, past and present, of Bellows Falls, VT

1

My desk lamp barely reached the far corners of my small, glassed-in office, leaving the squad room beyond completely dark. The lighting shrouded the whole place with an uncharacteristic intimacy, enhancing the quiet isolation I enjoyed when working after hours. The phone's sudden, electronic chirping came as a jarring intrusion.

"Gunther."

"Lieutenant, this is Marshall Smith. Pierre and I are down at the Retreat. I think we've found someone you been wanting to talk to."

"Who?"

"Jasper Morgan. One of the regulars started smashing chairs at a substance abuse meeting in the cafeteria, so they called us. When we were sorting things out, I saw Morgan trying to look invisible along the back wall."

"He still there?" I asked.

"They all are. We figured the best way not to spook him was to keep everybody put. Pierre's stalling for time right now—pretending to figure out who did what."

"I'll be right there."

I left the ancient brick building housing the police department and headed for the Retreat in my car, letting the warm summer air flush out the stale interior. Jasper Morgan was a minor drug dealer, which, given Vermont's overall activity in that field, made him pretty small fry. In addition, he wasn't currently on parole, had no warrants outstanding, and had been keeping a discreet profile. But I'd heard rumors his business had picked up lately, and was wondering why. In a town the size of Brattleboro, with some twelve thousand residents, we could still afford to focus on the vagaries of a single crook, and, given the climbing crime statistics in Massachusetts, a mere ten miles south of us, a little mild paranoia seemed like worthwhile health insurance.

If Morgan's recent prosperity was due to some change in either supply or demand, I wanted to know about it.

Not that a single conversation would be all that enlightening. Morgan was experienced enough to know who—between us and his drug business colleagues—was the bigger threat to his health. But a chat would at least remind him of our continuing interest.

The Brattleboro Retreat is one of the town's largest employers, and with some sixteen hundred acres, its largest landowner. A psychiatric hospital founded two years before Davy Crockett died at the Alamo, it began as an insane asylum, financed by a woman who took exception to a local lawyer being cured of his lunacy with an ice water immersion followed by a fatal dose of opium.

Its campus-like facility occupies a broad, mid-level plain on Brattleboro's northern edge, below the town's tree-shaded common, and above a sweeping, shallow backwater marking the confluence of the West and Connecticut rivers, called the Retreat Meadows from the days before a downstream dam turned pasture land into a lake. The Meadows form a natural magnet for the general population, luring fishermen and boaters in the summer, and providing ice fishing and skating when it turns colder. It forms a perfect sylvan backdrop to the Retreat's impressive sprawl of massive brick buildings and carefully tended trees, all of which make the place look more like a small elite college than a place for the mentally disturbed.

I left the traffic circle that cut across the front of the commons, and turned right down Linden Street, which swept down off the hill to the Retreat's entrance gate, and from which I had a brief overview of the institution's layout, attractively lit by regularly spaced iron lampposts and discreetly hidden floodlights.

There was also a police car outside the cafeteria entrance, about midway down a long string of connected buildings.

I parked behind the cruiser, walked up to its driver's window, and leaned in to kill the emergency lights. I saw no need to rile the tenants unnecessarily, especially just below its only high-security floor. Marshall Smith met me at the cafeteria's double doors.

Over his shoulder was a large, well-lit room, in the center of which were several overturned chairs and tables, a scattering of splintered wood littering the floor, and a man lying face down with his hands cuffed behind his back. Far to the rear of the room, a disparate group of silent men and women stood facing us, looking like a late afternoon crowd waiting for a bus. Pierre Lavoie was circulating among them, pad in hand, taking down names and statements.

"Where're the staffers?" I asked Smith, noticing their absence.

"It's an anonymous meeting. Staff isn't allowed inside 'cause it's open to outsiders and residents both. The residents are escorted in, and then the staff waits outside till they're all done."

Smith led me farther inside, so I could have a full view of the distant group. "I had Pierre begin to the far left to keep things slow. Morgan's over to the right."

With that, pure human instinct overrode all his careful planning. He stared directly at Jasper Morgan and began raising his hand to point. Simultaneously, between Morgan and where Lavoie was collecting statements, a door cracked open to reveal the inquiring face of one of the staffers outside.

The combination was all Morgan needed. He bolted for the door, wrenched it open, hip-checked the man beyond, and vanished from view.

"Oh, Christ," Marshall muttered, realizing his mistake. "Pierre. Get him," he shouted.

But Lavoie was already halfway through the door himself.

I pointed at the man handcuffed on the floor. "Stay with him and keep this room secure," I told Smith, breaking into a run. "And call for backup." Nearing the door, I saw the crowd beginning to shift indecisively, some backing away, others leaning toward the exit. "Nobody leave the room," I shouted, and elbowed my way through them, slamming the door behind me.

Facing me was a bright, windowless, cement-walled corridor, its walls decorated with pictures and trophy cases, its ceiling overrun with pipes. The Retreat being built on a slight incline, the first-floor cafeteria connected directly to the adjoining building's basement. The corridor was empty, except for the fading echoes of rapid footfalls upon the linoleum floor.

I ran to the first corner, rounded it at full tilt, and stumbled over Pierre Lavoie, who was rolling helplessly on the ground, holding his bleeding face with both hands.

"Shit," I said, instinctively glancing at his holster. It was empty. I grabbed the radio from his belt. "M-80 from 0-2. I have an officer down and an armed suspect on the loose inside the Retreat. Put out a mutual aid request for manpower, round up everyone of our people you can locate, and activate the Tac Team. This is only about thirty seconds old, so concentrate on locking up the Retreat grounds as tightly as possible. Also close off both ends of Linden Street and position people on the Putney Road in case he gets out and tries to reach it cross-country. Who's the on-call detective?"

"Martens," came the brisk reply.

"Have her lead the Tac Team—full combat gear. Put Klesczewski in charge of organizing the perimeter. And a couple of ambulances here—*now*."

"10-4."

I crouched near Lavoie's head. "How're you doing?"

His voice was muffled. "I think he broke my nose. Jesus, it hurts like hell."

"Are you breathing all right? Any other injuries?"

"No. I mean, yeah, I'm breathing fine. I'm okay 'cept for the nose. He was waiting when I came around the corner. Must've been holding a club or something."

I glanced around and saw a heavy book lying at some distance on the floor. "He got your gun," I said.

"Oh, Christ."

I patted his shoulder and stood up. "You stay put. I'm going to reconnoiter a bit."

"Don't do it, Lieutenant. Wait for the others."

"Stay there."

The hallway ahead was short, leading to another corner. Clearing my own gun, I approached it cautiously but with few expectations. I knew the sounds of running feet I'd heard had been Morgan's and didn't think he'd doubled back on tiptoe just to bushwhack me. Predictably, the next stretch of corridor was equally bright and empty. Outside, dulled by the thick walls, a crescendo of sirens approached.

I moved down to the next corner and stuck my head around, more careful now that I was some distance from Lavoie. I'd come to a junction of sorts. The hallway narrowed and became a ramp heading right, while opposite me, a short set of stairs led up to a closed door. It was darker here, beginning to resemble the basement it was.

Keeping my eyes glued to the far end of the ramp, I sidled over to the steps, and climbed up to try the doorknob. It was locked, as I'd hoped. Relieved, I proceeded up the ramp and risked a quick look around yet another corner. The passageway here was low-ceilinged, dimly lit, cement-floored, and lined by an almost endless row of narrow, closed doors. At its peak, the Retreat had housed some six hundred patients and an appropriately large staff. It was a notorious rabbit warren of hallways, rooms, connector tunnels, attics, and utility crawl spaces, many of them isolated behind locked doors, and many not.

Normally, I would have stopped there, not knowing which of the doors along the corridor might be hiding my frightened quarry. But a splash of light coming off the wall along which I was positioned, and a glitter of broken glass splayed out across the floor, drew me farther along.

My back against the wall, I sidestepped to the source of the light. What I found was typical of the whole building. Beyond a heavy door, its glass now shattered, lay another hallway, but in contrast to where I stood, it was as opulent as my surroundings were utilitarian. The walls were hardwood paneled, the floor thickly carpeted, antique furniture was placed along its length, and the ceiling was made entirely of lovingly maintained tin bas-relief.

I felt like a fish peering through the porthole of a luxury liner.

I gently turned the doorknob just beneath the gaping hole in the glass. It opened without a sound, but I stayed where I was. I'd been too reckless already and wasn't about to join Lavoie in a trip to the hospital.

I keyed the radio and told the others where to find me.

The next quarter hour was organized bedlam. Officers from the State Police, the Sheriff's Department, and one each from the surrounding towns of Hinsdale, Vernon, and Chesterfield, all joined us to close off the exits of the Retreat buildings. Sammie Martens, the detective on call and my second-in command, arrived in full black battle dress, complete with body armor and Kevlar helmet, leading seven other similarly outfitted members of the Special Reaction Team, or Tac Team. Finally, to help us make some sense of the facility's labyrinthine layout, the Retreat's plant manager, Ben Coven, was asked to join us with a complete set of blueprints.

The approach, unlike my wandering down the hallway, was to be run by the book. The Tac Team would conduct the search in two squads of four, each covering a separate segment of the complex. As they cleared an assigned area, a uniformed officer or two would be left behind to insure Morgan couldn't slip into their wake and hide. Communications would be over a restricted tactical channel, and geographic updates would be continuous, to ensure one team wouldn't wind up in a potential crossfire with the other. Coven and

I were to roam between the two teams, depending on where we were needed. As the plant manager ruefully pointed out from the start, the blueprints—especially where they covered the oldest buildings—were approximations only. He had more in his head than we would ever find on paper, especially where it came to the fine details.

The process, once begun, reminded me of those World War Two Navy movies, where the brass stands around a darkened communications center and listens to a battle taking place over the loudspeakers, tracking its developments by moving small symbols around a transparent Plexiglas panel. In our case, that center was the cafeteria, now empty of its first crowd, with Coven and I and a couple of runners playing the brass, surrounded by several radios, a phone, and three tables covered with blueprints. Listening to Sammie and the others exchanging terse phrases in a clipped monotone, I longed to be anywhere but where I was, standing around, fully expecting to hear gunshots at any moment.

The search was mercifully restricted to the basements, the lower floors, and the utility tunnels that ran in a tangled maze between every building on campus. Tracking Morgan by the damage he'd left behind, we discovered that while he'd tried for higher ground, he'd soon returned to where the traveling wasn't so confined by locked doors.

Corridor by corridor, section by section, we followed the progress of both Tac Teams until Sammie's group arrived under the main reception area.

"Lieutenant?"

"Go ahead, Sam."

"We've got a complication here. Looks like a low, broad cement-floor tunnel with some really old rooms off to both sides. They're all connected, like catacombs, and we can't tell how many passageways might be leading off them."

"Hold on." I looked inquiringly at Ben Coven.

He tapped his finger on the blueprint before us. "Oldest part of the complex, or near enough. It's a rat's nest."

I glanced at another map, to where the second Tac Team was searching. So far, there was no telling which one was hotter on Morgan's trail. I decided against combining forces.

"Sammie? We'll be there in a couple of minutes."

Coven grabbed the relevant blueprints and led the way out of the cafeteria and along several passageways that had already been cleared. He reached a narrow steel door at the foot of a twisting flight of stairs and pulled a jangling key ring from his pocket. Swinging open the door, he took us down into a hot, humid, dark environment filled with the restless echoes of Sammie's team muttering among themselves in a short cul-de-sac just off the bottom of the staircase.

Her face looking unnaturally pale, floating between a black helmet and vest, Sammie appeared out of the gloom. She was dripping with sweat. "Any ideas?" she asked.

I took the map from Coven and spread it out on the rough cement floor. Several flashlight beams suddenly appeared to help us see. I pointed to our location. "This is the official version. How's it compare to what you've seen?"

Sammie crouched next to Coven and me. The plant manager began moving the tip of his finger along the paper. "This is the main tunnel you described." He glanced up quickly, "Right around that corner. It's basically north-south and runs from the underground passage between Tyler Building and here to a sealed bulkhead that gives onto the service road overlooking the Meadows. The catacombs, as you called them, are on both sides—basically a series of small, dirt-floored rooms that interconnect to each other and to the central tunnel."

Sammie straightened from peering at the blueprint. "That's not so bad. I thought there might be rooms off the rooms, or maybe more tunnels we couldn't see."

Ben Coven sighed slightly, the obvious bearer of bad news. "Well, there are a few outlets that don't show up here. I wouldn't call them tunnels, exactly, but they are big enough for someone who's desperate."

"I think this qualifies," I said.

"I don't know what they're for or where they lead," Coven continued. "Maybe they're old drainage pipes. Some of them seem to be dug into the dirt, right under the cement floor, and others look like old, abandoned culverts. I always thought they were mostly dead ends, but I never bothered finding out."

"Where are they?" Sammie asked, jutting her chin toward the blueprint.

Coven sketched them out. "For sure, there're three of them, and I *think* that's it, but to me they're just something to step around so I don't break my neck. I can't swear there aren't more."

Sammie looked up at me. "You want to lead it?"

Her deferral was technically in order, since I was the ranking officer, and with her military background Sammie took whatever she was given from the top down, no questions asked. But I knew her better than that.

"It's your team, Sammie. Tell me where you want me."

I'd already borrowed a vest, but without a helmet I was correctly assigned a backup position. Ben Coven was sent back to the cafeteria after I'd cleared his passage by radio.

Sammie positioned us as if we were taking a street, house by house—in homage to the eerie layout. The Retreat's torture chambers and secret caches of human bones were common topics among the locals, born of the idiot folklore attending any treatment center for the mentally ill. But being in one of the famous cellars at last, and seeing it extend out into the gloom, with ancient brick archways, mysterious tunnels, and an inmate on the loose, it was hard not to give the tall tales some credit.

Sammie went strictly according to procedure, everybody covering someone else, flashlights either directed forward or extinguished altogether, to avoid night blindness and giving the opposition a better target. No corner was rounded without first being checked with a handheld mirror. Sammie herself operated a night vision monocular and scanned continually back and forth, watching for any surreptitious movements.

The few tunnels Ben Coven had mentioned were trickier, being too tight for more than a single, small, crawling individual. The safest bet would have been to use gas canisters and flush out whoever might be down there, but given the kind of facility we were in, that wasn't an option. What we did, therefore, harked back to Vietnam, and the tunnel-rats of Chu-Chi. One by one, again starting with mirrors, the smallest members of the team dropped down into the holes without backup and made their way to a dead end in every case.

By the time we reached the sealed bulkhead at the far end, we were drenched in sweat, our eyes were aching, and we'd built up enough nervous energy to run a generator. It was with obvious relief that Sammie announced the "all clear."

Only in the following relaxed silence did we all distinctly hear the distant, muffled sound of something in motion.

"Cover," Sammie yelled, causing us to flatten onto the ground in a circle, facing out. In the total darkness, Sammie made a slow, careful pan of our surroundings with the night scope.

"What do you think it was?" she asked, finding nothing.

"It sounded far away," I answered, "like an echo."

Ward Washburn, one of the team, muttered, "There *is* no far away, for crying out loud."

Instinctively, we all returned to total silence, straining to hear it again. Working from memory, I crawled to a spot left of the bulkhead, and to a small, jagged hole in the crumbling concrete floor. My fingers wrapped around some rebar covering the top of a caved-in drainage pipe—a barrier we'd pulled on earlier to no effect.

This time, I pushed it down instead, and the heavy mesh gave way like a swinging trapdoor. "Sammie, come here." They all joined me to stare at the tiny opening. "You're kidding," Washburn said softly.

Sammie dropped to her stomach and put her head into the pipe, the night scope in her eye. "It's open as far as I can see toward Linden Street."

The sound came again, clearer this time—something metallic dropping into place. It floated out of the twenty-inch-wide drain as from an ancient loudspeaker.

"Must be something else," a voice spoke up behind me. Sammie looked up. "You going to make that assumption?"

"No one can fit in there."

"I can," she countered.

I spoke into the radio. "This is Gunther. Somebody escort Ben Coven back here on the double."

The plant manager was by our side in under three minutes. "You know where this connects?" I asked him.

He spread out his papers doubtfully, already shaking his head. "I'd be amazed if we have it. Looks too old and too small for us to mess with."

A moment later, he straightened up. "Nope. No sign of it."

"I'm going in," Sammie announced. "I'm the only one as small as Morgan."

I laid a hand on her shoulder but looked at Coven. "Sammie thinks this runs toward Linden Street. What might it hook up with?" Coven consulted his plans again. "Utility tunnel maybe?"

I glanced over at the old bulkhead. "That wouldn't make sense. It looks more like a drainage culvert, to take away any water that might leak in through that thing."

Coven tapped a spot with his finger. "Then this is probably your best bet. It's a collection pipe for most of the drainage in this area. It's good-sized, and accessible by manhole, so you could backtrack along it and see if this connects to it."

I looked up at Sammie. "I like that idea a lot better."

Coven unlocked the bulkhead and led us into the comparative coolness of the night air. We walked along a paved service road to a manhole cover some two hundred feet to the west. He swung his arm like a pendulum, bisecting the road. "Runs in this direction, about ten feet down, angling toward the Meadows."

Two of the team members had already pried open the cover and were cautiously shining their lights down. Sammie stepped up to the hole's edge.

I poked Washburn in the side and pointed at his helmet, addressing Sammie. "I'm coming with you." Washburn handed me the helmet and I followed Sammie underground.

The cement tube at the bottom of a steel ladder was straight, clean, odorless, and big enough to walk in, stooped over.

And utterly silent.

We went up the slight incline, pacing the distance until we reached the approximate axis of the drainage pipe from the basement we'd just left. To my satisfaction, we found a rough opening, eroded by decades of runoff and rot. The tiny garden of brittle, crystalline growth that had taken root on its ragged edge had been partially scraped clean by the recent passage of something large and heavy.

I showed the traces to Sammie. "I think this just turned into a 'good-news-bad news' story." I pointed down slope. "And I bet the bad news is out there."

We retraced our steps past the manhole, to where the pipe emptied into the Retreat Meadows. There, in a narrow strip of muddy ground, right at water's edge, a fresh set of sneaker tracks headed off toward the northwest.

I used the radio to expand the cordon we'd set around the campus, asked for additional backup and some tracking dogs, and issued a statewide Be-On-the-Alert for Jasper Morgan, but I wasn't optimistic. If he'd been motivated enough to get this far, he wasn't going to be picked up in an hour downing beers at some local dive.

In any case, his escape was no longer what truly concerned me. It was the effort he'd made—and the reasons behind it.

2

Four weeks later, Jasper Morgan had all but slipped from my mind. The BOL had yielded nothing, the grapevine had remained silent, and Jasper, along with Pierre Lavoie's gun, had been put on the back burner, "pending new developments."

The spike in activity we get every spring—when the rowdier natives emerge from hibernation to wreak havoc—had subsided weeks ago, and life had returned to a predictable normalcy. As had my domestic life with Gail Zigman, my companion of many years, who had finally landed a cherished job as deputy to our local State's Attorney.

In contrast to my schedule, Gail's was awash in work, she being the lowest on the totem pole and the one with the most to learn. On the other hand, after countless months of juggling a clerkship, a correspondence course, cramming for the bar exam, and applying for jobs, even she was feeling comparatively sane. We still didn't have enough time to ourselves, but we were at last enjoying what little we could get.

I was therefore in an unguarded mood when Chief Tony Brandt appeared in my office doorway and inquired, "You have much on your plate right now? Or anyone you can spare?"

I waved a hand at the paperwork before me. "My head's above water. I don't know about the others. Why?"

He entered and sat in my guest chair, wedged between the door and a filing cabinet. "I just got a call from Emile Latour. He needs a little digging done on one of his officers."

Latour was Tony's counterpart in Bellows Falls, a small industrial-era town a half-hour's drive north of Brattleboro, just inside the northern reaches of Windham County. "Who's the officer?"

"Brian Padget. Two-year man, good record, well liked. It's a sexual harassment claim filed by some woman's husband. Emile was wondering if we could lend him someone to conduct a quick internal on it."

I made a face. The request was not unusual. If a grievance was filed against a department or one of its officers, and the outfit was too small to have its own Internal Affairs division, it was routine to ask another agency to supply an investigator. The task was usually mundane—often going through the motions to make everyone feel better. The majority were crank cases resulting in the officer involved being cleared, a happy circumstance that never helped the guy conducting the investigation—that poor bastard was always stamped a Judas before he even reached town.

I hedged my response. "I take it you'd like us to accept."

"Latour's a decent guy. It helps to be friendly."

"Have they even looked into it? Sexual harassment's a bit of a catch-all. Maybe they could handle it themselves."

Brandt shrugged. "I didn't ask. Could be they're just playing it safe."

"You give him a deadline on how many days we can spend on it?"

"Not in so many words, but I'm guessing a couple."

I flipped the pencil I was holding onto my desk. "All right, but I won't saddle anyone else with it. I'll do it myself."

Bellows Falls is a troubled community. A village swallowed whole by a cantankerous township, developmentally stalled since the Great Depression, and, reduced to being the bedroom to almost every other town within a half-hour's commute, it has a dour and pessimistic self-image out of all proportion to its size.

It is not big. The village covers a single square mile. It is also strikingly photogenic, as much for its glut of statuesque nineteenth-century mansions as for its glumly quaint, abandoned factories. Seen from the air, Bellows Falls protrudes like a pregnant stomach into the Connecticut River, forming a tight half-circle, at the apex of which is the dramatic, rocky cascade that gives the town its name. It owes its existence to that water's energy, which in the early years gave the upstart, industrially minded settlers an advantage over their more staid agrarian neighbors. For a succession of grist mills, rag-paper plants, and pulp mills, the ceaseless water became literal life blood, supplying power, spawning river, rail and road transportation, and creating other tangential manufacturing. Now, as if personifying the village's current impotence, the Connecticut's flow is controlled by a dam sluicing water down the remains of an old canal to feed the turbines of a local utility company.

Its picture postcard prettiness may in fact best represent Bellows Falls' most paradoxical irony—that while most other places proudly point to a few older buildings as standard-bearers of an earlier time, the past is about all this town has left to brag about. It is a pantheon of long vanished industrial might. Ancient red brick shells can find but a few new tenants, a once thriving railroad junction has been reduced to a single platform, and the elaborate mansions have mostly been diced up into apartments by out-of-state landlords who care little about upkeep and less about their welfare tenants.

Periodically, the village erupts with face-saving activity. Meetings are held and committees formed to identify and solve the place's underlying problems. But whether it's halfheartedness from within, or the sheer magnitude of the task, these groups never seem to last long and sink below the surface with little flotsam left behind: a few new benches on the square, a coat of paint on an old wall, a scattering of shrubs to eventually die of neglect or abuse. Another movement was afoot right now, in fact, dedicated to the usual renaissance. It seemed better organized than its predecessors, but no one I knew was placing any bets. A museum of glories past, the name Bellows Falls had become a statewide joke, solely equated with failure.

The police station, my intended first stop, was located north of the village in a modern building it shared with the fire department, and which local wags had dubbed the House of the Seven Gables for its tortured profile. But I took the southernmost of the two interstate exits servicing Bellows Falls so I could drive through downtown. I was one of those who genuinely liked the town, despite its pratfalls and ill fortune. Its mere existence spoke of the same perseverance that drove Vermont farmers to till soil that was more rock than dirt—and to dismiss it as merely "bony."

The southern approach to the village, no enhancement to its self-image, features a nondescript cluster of filling stations, pizza joints, video arcades, and one porno store; and the first building beyond the official historical marker is a bar. But the old village center, when it appears around a gentle corner, comes as a refreshing reward. A Y-shaped "square," with the Y opening toward the north, it is defined by the weathered red brick that once symbolized New England as an industrial powerhouse. Among the bas-reliefs and the odd crenelation or granite molding, the clock tower of the town hall looks startlingly like a miniature version of the same structure in Florence, Italy.

There are gaps in this facade—empty asphalt lots or tiny bench-equipped parks—which testify to Bellows Falls' most biblical of afflictions. Through the decades, with the regularity of mythic rite, fire has eaten at the village. Factories, retail buildings, homes, and a few bars have gone up in smoke, all from unrelated causes. Over time, bikers, dopers, and train-delivered New York misfits had all had their turns at stamping the town with their identities. The ceaseless fires, therefore, played in some people's minds as an eerie form of divine retribution—a viewpoint that both irritated the hard-core village boosters and occasionally left them wondering.

Currently that reputation was less lurid, sadder, and looked much tougher to cure. Bellows Falls, during the go-go eighties, had been the place to live cheaply if you worked in Springfield, Brattleboro, Walpole, or Keene. The mansions of onetime magnates went for twenty thousand dollars and rentals were plentiful and affordable. But times had changed. Values climbed, taxes kept pace, and absentee land-lords carved their holdings into ever smaller and shabbier tenements. Businesses increasingly moved out or shut down, and Bellows Falls became a welfare town, rife with domestic disputes, drinking and drug use, larceny, theft, and vandalism, and a pervading undercurrent of teenage parenthood and sexual abuse. At twenty percent, the school system had a higher percentage of "special Ed" kids than any other in the state.

For a small, low-key police department, it sometimes became quite a handful.

I'd met the BFPD's chief twice, both times only long enough to exchange greetings. Emile Latour had been described to me as a homegrown product who'd joined the force after impatiently treading water as a security guard for three years following high school. Now in his late fifties, he'd been chief for some fifteen years and was locally touted as an Eisenhower-era neighborhood cop—avuncular, available, compliant with his bosses, and maybe not the sharpest tool in the shed. Unlike most of the rest of us in Vermont law enforcement, Latour kept to himself, shunning the regional meetings and conferences we increasingly used to keep in touch, and staying outside the networking loop that had developed as a byproduct. There are only eleven hundred full-time cops in Vermont, servicing a population that barely tops half a million. Yet to the few who'd heard of him, Emile Latour, despite a lifetime in the business, had managed to remain little more than a name on his department's letterhead.

The impression was only enhanced by his appearance. As I swung out of my car in the police department parking lot and paused to enjoy the view of the broad Connecticut River across the road, a short, burly, round-bellied man with thinning white hair, a flushed complexion, and a shy smile, walked out of the building to greet me. His regulation blues fit him as comfortably as a pair of pajamas. He was a vision from a forty-year-old recruitment poster.

"Joe Gunther? Good to see you again. I'm Chief Latour. Thanks for coming up so fast."

I shook his hand, noting its blunt, dry, dormant strength, reminiscent of my long-dead father's. A farmer's hand. Despite the uniform, I instantly envisioned him on his knees in a large garden, enjoying the silky dampness of earth between his fingers.

"My pleasure," I answered. "Hope I can be useful."

He touched my elbow and gestured toward the building's front door. "Oh, that won't be a problem. I don't think this'll lead to anything."

From the outside, the House of the Seven Gables was weighted toward the fire department's needs, with a row of open bay doors revealing several gleaming trucks. Once over the threshold, I became all but convinced that the police department's tenancy had been an afterthought at best. They had a nice if compact radio dispatch room, with windows facing both the parking lot and the lobby, but beyond the inner blue door, we were faced with a cramped, ill-fitting string of narrow, short hallways, tiny rooms, and a twisting staircase. Latour's office on the second floor was tucked under the eaves, with two skylights angled so close to the one small conference table that I had to watch my head as I pulled out a chair to sit. Legend was that the building had been the first municipal project of a young architect fresh out of school, who had among other things omitted putting heat in the basement because, as he'd explained it patiently to his challengers, "Heat sinks."

Chief Latour, shorter and more used to the precarious proximity of his ceiling, grabbed the chair facing me without concern. "Did Tony Brandt fill you in at all?" he asked.

"He said it was a sexual harassment case."

The chief shook his head. "It's got to be a bum rap. The officer's name is Brian Padget. He's been with us two years. He's well liked, respected, a hard worker—probably end up going to the State Police, with my luck. The complaint is he's been pestering a married woman."

"And the husband brought the complaint?"

Latour quickly glanced at my face. I sensed that locking eyes with other people made him uncomfortable. "Right. Norman Bouch. Not one of our model citizens. That's one reason I think this whole thing is bullshit."

"He have a grudge against Padget?"

He paused while the room filled with the reverberating roar of an unseen passing truck. "I don't know that they've ever met," he said eventually.

"What makes Bouch not a model citizen?"

"Nothing we could ever prove. He pretends he's an excavation contractor. He's got a backhoe he digs holes with around town, but everybody knows he sells dope for most of his income."

I was a little uneasy with the assumptions. "He lives beyond his apparent means?"

Latour was now staring at the polished tips of his shoes, and smiled at my careful phrasing. "He's got a wife and kids, a decent house, a Harley with all the fixin's and a late-model Firebird. You figure it out."

The conviction in his voice was absolute. I shifted my approach slightly. "Tell me a little about Padget."

There was a fleeting glance at the wall. "Best officer I ever had."

Given such praise, I was surprised at its brevity. "Local boy? Married? Liked by the others?" I prompted.

Latour straightened in his seat, suddenly emphatic. "No, he's not married. But he wouldn't fool around. I told you, he's respected and admired—by everybody."

I finally sensed what was eating at him. "But you think there might be something to what Bouch is claiming."

The chief stood up, crossed the room, and resettled behind the protection of his desk.

"Are you going to interview him?" he asked.

"Not until I've finished my investigation. If I dig up anything criminal, a statement by him prior to being Mirandized will be thrown out in court—the judge'll say he was coerced into talking for fear of being fired."

Latour flapped his hand as if to shoo me away, no doubt regretting his having called Brandt in the first place. "Criminal? Christ Almighty. Bouch is just trying to bust our chops."

"Does Padget know about the allegation?"

"Sure he does. I told him. He denied it completely. I've put him on paid leave till this is cleared up."

"And he knows I've been asked to check it out?"

Latour gave a rueful half-smile. "By now, I'd say the whole department does."

"What's the general consensus?"

"They all think like I do. Bouch is just doing a number. It happens a lot, especially in this town. Do you know what they call Bellows Falls at the police academy? 'Dodge City'—I kid you not. Our crime stats are in the top four or five for the state year after year, and we're a quarter Brattleboro's size—thirty-eight hundred people, tops. Besides me, I got one sergeant, six officers, and a bunch of part-timers. My other sergeant's with the drug task force for two more years. We're sitting ducks."

"Does Bouch get much of your business?" I asked, hoping to head off more complaining.

"We've gone to his house for disturbances—domestic abuse stuff, drunk and disorderly. We've held him overnight to dry out, but no one's ever filed charges against him."

I rose and prepared to leave, my mind chasing after a dozen diverging questions. I had my doubts, however, that Chief Latour was the unbiased source I needed for answers.

I left to get my bearings—drive around, clear my head, and see the town. Latour had grumpily given me Padget's and Bouch's addresses. I wanted to check out the latter's first but took the scenic route to get there.

The geographical protuberance I thought of as Bellows Falls' pregnant belly is called the Island, although it is only the canal that has made it such. Nevertheless, that barrier has led to a wholly separate identity, consisting largely of an empty railroad yard and station, a few half-abandoned factories and warehouses, a couple of businesses, and an impressive view of the cascade and Fall Mountain beyond. It is like a failing industrial park hogging the best real estate in the area.

The next longitudinal stratum to Bellows Falls, west of the canal, is the downtown corridor I'd driven through on Rockingham Street, resolutely turned in on itself around its oddly shaped square, and—as in Brattleboro and many other older New England towns—with its back turned against the natural scenery.

Prominent above downtown is Cherry Hill, an oblong rise bisecting the village, and jammed with an assortment of schools, churches, a cemetery, and some of the town's famous and ubiquitous white clapboard housing—both pleasant Greek Revival single-family homes and several squalid three-deckers, bursting at the seams with down-and-out tenants.

Skirting Cherry Hill's western slope, Atkinson parallels Rockingham Street but is overwhelmingly lined with residential buildings.

It exposes the village's social extremes most clearly, with some of its more spectacular mansions snuggling up to the seediest flophouses. Atkinson, and the side streets extending across a narrow flat section to its west, are where the vast majority of the town's inhabitants live. It is a beehive-like neighborhood—rich, poor, elaborate, and plain—virtually crawling with people and stamped by their passage. Toys, bikes, cars abandoned and functional, swing sets, birdbaths, and assorted debris all lie scattered among the houses like yard sale rejects. More vivid than the dramatic setting, overwhelming the spectacular architecture, is the sense of people in this town. They appear to live everywhere, as on an overloaded riverboat.

Predictably, from what Latour had portrayed, Bouch had chosen this area to call home.

His house was easy to spot, being marked by a backhoe and a gravel truck, both looking the worse for wear. But it was the Harley that caught my eye—and the man working on it.

Dressed in jeans, a T-shirt, and work boots, Norm Bouch at first glance looked like any other working-class male, his head buried in a motor and his hands covered with grease. But as I drove slowly by, I noticed the precision with which he handled his tools and the perfect balance he maintained as he moved. Like a relaxing predator, he showed confidence and grace and exuded an indefinable sense of menace.

That sensation was confirmed a moment later, when a ball came soaring over the garage roof from the backyard and bounced harmlessly against the motorcycle. A screwdriver still in his hand, Bouch picked up the ball and began circling the garage, just as a small boy appeared at its far corner, running full tilt. Both of them froze in their tracks as they caught sight of each other. I could no longer see Bouch's face, but the boy's paled with fright, and he began wringing his hands with practiced intensity.

I stopped the car and continued watching, seeing the boy speaking quickly, no doubt begging forgiveness for the ball's sudden intrusion. Bouch held it up as if discovering it for the first time and turned it admiringly in his hand. Then in one fluid movement, he stuck it with his screwdriver and tossed it half-deflated at the boy's feet. The child looked down forlornly and slowly stooped to pick it up. Bouch was already heading back to the Harley, a smile on his face.

I resumed driving down the street, unnoticed—and wishing to remain that way.

I didn't want to interview Norm Bouch—not yet. Internal investigations are ticklish affairs. The cops tend to see you as a potential traitor, and the civilian complainants as a guaranteed whitewasher. So despite the pressure from both camps to come up with results, and a tradition that dictates interviewing the complainant and witnesses first before doing the peripheral homework, I tend to favor a more roundabout method. By approaching the problem from the outside, collecting knowledge on the way in, I often end up with a pretty complete picture before even meeting the primary players.

It's unorthodox, slower, and it makes twitchy officials twitchier, but it gives me a better sense of what I'm getting into.

I therefore drove past to a nearby convenience store, parked in its lot, and sat like a bird-watcher taking notes from the bushes.

The Bouch home was a two-story, ramshackle, turn-of-the century clapboard pile, probably quite tidy and small when original, now a typical cob job of artless additions and alterations. New England is dotted with such buildings, where the amendments have all but swallowed the original. Norm's was adorned with the mismatched roof lines, bare sheathing, and patched-on sagging porch exemplifying the least of such examples. The yard was a similar mess—cars, broken toys, a washing machine, and assorted jetsam all vied for space. From my vantage point, I could partially see into the backyard, where the small boy was still holding the flattened ball, but was now surrounded by several other unhappy children.

A quarter hour later, a pickup truck on testosterone pulled to the curb in a roar of doctored mufflers, and a heavyset man in a tight tank top swung out to join Bouch by the side of the Harley. Bouch greeted him with a laugh, handed him a beer from a nearby cooler, and engaged in animated conversation, still working on his bike. I didn't doubt that in the heat of a summer afternoon, variations of this scene were being duplicated a million-fold across the country.

I have long passed the point of expecting people to look their parts. Emile Latour's uniformed, round-bodied look of benevolent, innocuous authority hid an anger I'd sensed simmering just below the surface. What I was watching now, I knew, could be anything—two guys bonding over beer and the Harley mystique, or two drug dealers discussing business in a totally placid setting.

Brian Padget lived in Westminster, several miles south of Bellows Falls. But where most Vermont towns appear sprinkled across a picturesque and hilly topography, Westminster sits on a flat terrace of land, its rigidly placed buildings straddling a wide, straight, smooth stretch of road more conducive to speeding than to the leisurely enjoyment of a small, quaint village. The details of the latter are there, of course—the town predates the American Revolution. But the sturdy, classically built homes and businesses are dwarfed by the numbing, methodical way in which they were laid out, and the overall impression of Westminster remains an anonymous blur.

Padget's house was a single-story converted trailer at the edge of town, tightly wedged between two similarly built neighbors. The tiny lawn was cut and trimmed, the one bush out front neatly pruned, and the vinyl clapboards of the house looked freshly washed. I knew from Latour that Padget wasn't home—he was out of town visiting his folks for the day. As with the Bouch residence, all I was after here was a first impression of the people I was about to investigate.

Padget's home was the precise opposite of Bouch's—on the surface, it spoke of precision and attention to detail, but under that was a concern for appearances, a sense of others standing in judgment. It reflected an underlying insecurity typical of a young unmarried man, who was both relatively new on the job and eager to impress.

Bouch, on the other hand, had seemed more comfortable with himself. The self-confident blue-collar squalor of his home had been as eloquent as Padget's cautious ambition. I sensed Norm was positioned to take advantage of the world around him, whereas Brian was more dependent on the blessings of those with clout.

It made me ponder the forces that had set these two people in opposition. "Sexual harassment," like a foghorn in the night, covered a range of possibilities—from a mere disturbance to a warning of catastrophe. I didn't have Emile Latour's confidence that the former was preordained.

3

Sergeant Greg Davis had been with the Bellows Falls Police Department for seventeen years, a record broken only by his chief. Unlike Latour, however, Davis was an extrovert, stimulated and satisfied by his job. He relished the learning process, in whatever form, and made an effort to attend any conference or meeting he could to pick up pointers and make contacts. As a result, he was both well known and well liked throughout the state.

Also, for the moment, he was the department's sole sergeant, standing alone between the chief's office and the rank and file. It was for this reason, along with my general respect for the man, that I sought him out following my reconnaissance. Organizationally, he and I occupied middle rungs on the ladder, a connection I hoped would stand me in good stead.

Since Davis was on duty, he'd told me he'd swing by the police department parking lot to pick me up. It seemed like driving around Bellows Falls was going to be my first day's primary activity.

"Sorry we're meeting again under these circumstances," he said after I'd settled into his passenger seat and exchanged greetings.

"What do you make of all this?" I asked him.

His answer was understandably guarded. "Suppose anything's possible."

I looked out the side window at the parade of passing houses, and rephrased something I'd asked Tony Brandt. "Back home, we get a sexual harassment charge, we check it out first ourselves. It's only after we think it's real that we bring in an outsider."

There was a long pause. Davis pulled into one of the side streets and headed west. "What did the chief say?"

The question brought back Latour's defensive reaction when I'd asked him about Padget's culpability. "He made hopeful noises that it was smoke with no fire."

Davis snorted. "Don't I wish."

"He also said a few uncomplimentary things about Norman Bouch."

This time, the other man laughed. "Doesn't *he* wish. Latour's been grinding his teeth about Bouch for years. But he's never been able to lay a finger on him."

"He made it sound more personal than that."

"Now that his fair-haired boy's in a jam? You bet."

I chose from among several questions triggered by that response. "Was it Bouch's drug dealing that had him so worked up before, or something else?"

Davis continued negotiating the back streets of the village, his eyes taking in alleys, parked cars, pedestrians, the doors and windows of residences and businesses. With the warm weather, the car's air conditioning was on, but both windows were rolled down. Veteran cops did that sometimes—it allowed them to be comfortable, but without cutting off the sounds and smells from outside, two extra vital signs a good patrolman learns to appreciate.

"Everybody likes Bouch," Greg Davis answered. "He makes sure of it. That drives Latour nuts, plus the fact that Bouch goes out of his way to irritate the Old Man. He'll have some of his teenage rat pack commit minor offenses, knowing we can only slap them on the wrist. Or he'll slug his wife and get away with it 'cause she refuses to squeal on him. It's not all calculated—he is a bad guy. But it is a way of gaining him prestige with the people he wants to control."

"Tell me about the rat pack," I asked.

"I shouldn't have made it sound that organized. They hang around his house a lot, though, and I know goddamn well they run errands for him...It's just another thing we haven't been able to prove."

Davis slowed the car to a crawl, watching a group of kids huddled together under a basketball hoop, with no ball visible. The kids looked up as we drew near and sullenly dispersed.

"I guess it's like a basic morality issue. Latour was brought up on the straight and narrow, and people like Bouch piss him off. The Pied Piper angle gets to him, too. These kids have a slim enough chance as it is."

"You said Padget was Latour's fair-haired boy."

Davis hesitated, but only momentarily. "Padget's a rising star—everything Bouch isn't, and probably everything the Old Man wished he'd been. He's smart, ambitious, good-looking, idealistic, nice to be around. And not too goody-two-shoes, either, although he won't drink even when he's off duty. A lot of rookies have to strut their stuff, you know? Bust bad guys, put on an attitude, wear those short black leather driving gloves, supposedly so their hands won't get messed up when they start pounding the shit out of people."

I laughed at the sadly familiar image.

Davis joined me briefly. "Right. Well, Padget's not quite a rookie by now, but he's not too far from it, especially to an old fart like me. But he never pulled that crap. He can be high-strung, and he's always on the gallop to bring law to the streets, but there's nothing juvenile about it. He's one of the true believers."

"So maybe he's a little hard to take?"

The sergeant allowed a rueful smile. "He can wear you down, but that's probably more my fault than his. I get tired, depressed sometimes. Brian just keeps charging ahead."

"Even now?"

Greg Davis had been wearing dark glasses. At that, he pulled to the side of the road and pushed them up on his forehead so he could look me straight in the eyes.

"No. He definitely felt this one. He's not talking about it, but he's been stunned."

Which brought me to the one question everyone seemed to be skirting. "So the charges against him aren't just smoke?"

Davis looked at me a moment longer, and then gave me another non-answer, dropping his glasses back into place. "I guess that's why you're here."

I wondered if I'd presumed too much from my friendly acquaintance with this man, or if he was merely stalling while he decided whether to trust me. We left the neighborhood west of Atkinson and slowly drove to the top of Cherry Hill, where the Episcopal church and its small, pretty cemetery crowned the village. From the narrow road among the headstones, the view of Fall Mountain was pastoral and beautiful—the one looking down on the square precipitous.

"How did this first come to the PD?" I asked.

"Jan Bouch called me at work. Said Brian'd been bothering her—watching her house, following her when she went shopping, talking to her when she wanted to be left alone."

"Sounds like stalking."

"No, no—'He's been sexually harassing me,' were her exact words, like they'd been rehearsed." He paused, and then, as if suddenly relieved of a burden, he added, "To be honest, the harassment angle was a surprise, but not his hanging around her. Word had already leaked out about that. This town has a grade-A grapevine, and they'd been seen together, though not the way she was saying—I'd heard it was consensual."

"I thought her husband filed the complaint."

Davis looked a little embarrassed. "Yeah. I dropped the ball there. Knowing what I did about Brian and the girl, I let things slide a couple of days, thinking they'd probably just had a spat and she was getting back at him. That's when Norm Bouch called the chief. Latour chewed me out about it—Bouch whined about how he was worried that, since he'd been in trouble with the law before, Padget and his cronies might frame him for something. Get him sent to jail so Brian could have a free hand with his wife. My inaction supported that scenario. It was a total crock, of course, but Norm played it well and got the chief nervous enough to order an outside internal right off the bat."

"Did he know about the rumors?"

Davis hesitated. "I asked him. It just made him madder. But he never really answered, so I think he did. Probably didn't want to admit his chosen boy had clay feet."

That assessment mirrored some of my own misgivings about Latour. "Tell me about the chief."

"I think he's burned out and can't let go," Davis said bluntly. "He's a good guy—don't get me wrong. I like him. But he's sort of gotten buried behind that desk, like an old mole backing more and more into his hole."

We'd reached the square east of Cherry Hill, and were proceeding along Rockingham Street toward one of the bridges heading out to the Island. Davis waved his hand at the buildings around us. "Which in my book says as much about Bellows Falls as about the chief. This town can get to you if you don't watch out. People who were born and brought up here bad-mouth this town like it was the birthplace of root canal, and then they give you shit if you join in, saying it's talk like that'll doom the place forever. It's a textbook love-hate thing—like being Polish and telling all the worst Polack jokes.

"I think Latour joined the PD 'cause he thought he could help turn things around, and over time it's just ground him down. And he's especially bitter now, seeing Bouch do a number on Brian, and Brian having been dumb in the first place."

I was impressed at the depth of the analysis, and at its probable accuracy. It bolstered my opinion of Davis, but it also begged an obvious question. "Why've you hung on so long?"

He laughed and pulled into a parking lot facing the canal and the back of the Windham Hotel. "I like it here. It's not the cheeriest place in the world, but if you're into what makes people tick—or at least chew on each other—this is like a science lab. I know several twenty-eight-year-old grandmothers. I can trace family trees of people who intermarry and remarry and breed with their own kin. Any day of the week, I deal with manias, phobias, and flat-out craziness. People steal from each other, fight with each other, sleep with each other. They shift alliances, trade partners, bring up each others' babies. This is like a ghetto—a parking place for the down-and-out.

"But," he continued with a shake of the head, "at the same time it's beautiful. The river, the old buildings, the mountain, just the feeling of some kind of huge missed potential…I really sympathize with the town boosters who're always trying to fix the place up. Maybe I even believe they'll finally make it. I guess the answer for me—crazy as it sounds—is that in the middle of all the crime and poverty, I can't shake the feeling that there's hope in the air. It's like a family to me—too big and dysfunctional—but something I'm used to."

Davis paused and sighed. "Maybe the chief and I aren't all that different. He's just got twenty years on me… . Think that qualifies me for the rubber room?"

"I wish I had you on my squad back home."

The cement-bordered slab of water moved by us without a ripple, a smooth runway of solid slate. As discursive as it had been, Davis's portrait had allowed me to form a context for whatever might come next in this investigation. And the more I heard about the cast of characters, and their unusual interactions, the more background I felt was needed. History was showing through here—dark and complicated—and I wanted to be privy to as much of it as I could get.

"Okay, let's go back to Norm and Jan Bouch. What's the skinny on them?"

Davis sighed. "He's a flatlander. She's local. He's about thirty-three. She's eighteen. He came from Massachusetts in the eighties, when the housing here was cheap and the market was going crazy. He was a renter at first, like most everybody in town, and we didn't have him on our radarscope for the first couple of years. Then his name started showing up—stuff like, 'I was at a party at Norm's,' 'I was doin' some work for Norm,' 'Norm can vouch for me . . .' Bouch was making friends, hanging out in the right places with the right people, and for all the wrong reasons. He started to bloom socially, too, dating lots of girls, getting a couple of them pregnant. You been by his house yet? See all those kids?"

I nodded.

"They're his, by maybe three or four different women. Jan's the latest, and the only one he married. Two of the kids are hers. That's how we know him officially—for fighting with those women. We'd get a noise complaint and go charging over. Sometimes you couldn't tell who'd started it or even who'd won, but nobody would ever file. We'd read 'em the riot act, maybe toss him in the drunk tank, and retreat till the next time."

"When did the drug business kick in?" I asked.

"Hard to say. You know how Vermonters do business—little bit of this, little bit of that. Things get done without real money changing hands. People on welfare all of a sudden have a used car when they couldn't buy food the week before. If there was a crime involved, it's almost impossible to find, much less prove. Somehow or other, Norm started climbing up in the world—a pickup, an odd-job business, the backhoe you saw, finally he bought the house. The man's a hustler, I'll give him that. He doesn't sit around on the couch waiting for favors to roll in. He's a body in motion, all the time."

Davis put the car back into gear and eased out of the parking lot, driving past the railroad station toward the Island's outer shore, where the Connecticut had spent centuries carving a fifty-foot gorge, the steepest along the river's entire length from Canada to the Atlantic coast.

"Also," Davis continued, "he's smarter than your average bad guy. He takes his time, plans ahead, learns about the opposition." He laughed suddenly. "'Course we say he's smart 'cause we haven't caught him yet. Anyhow, he's definitely gotten to know the movers and shakers in town—lawyers, landlords, even the cops—but he's just as comfortable with the Genesee beer crowd."

He reflected on this last comment for a moment and then added, "He's a bit of a chameleon, showing different shades of himself to different people. Women find him seductive, kids think he's cool. I smell a lot of anger behind all that—and a wicked need to control."

We were driving on a narrow dirt road, sandwiched between the steep, rocky riverbank and an old, abandoned, curved-wall factory of impressive proportions. Davis saw me craning my neck out the window to take the building in.

"That's the old creamery. Used to fill up fourteen railroad cars of milk a day before the bulk-shipping laws changed and gutted the business. I guess the times changed, too...Anyway, we got wind of Norm's dabbling in drugs through the usual grapevine—some guy would get busted in Burlington or down in your town, and talk about how Norm was part of a drug highway. Or we'd bust a local kid who'd then try to cop a plea by squealing on Norm, 'cept he didn't have anything we could work with. Stuff like that—lots of noise in the woods but no clear shot."

We came to a stop at Bridge Street, which crossed the river from the Island into New Hampshire on a massive, double-arched concrete span whose central column was buried in an immense granite outcropping. Davis waited for the traffic to pass and then nosed the cruiser into an overgrown dirt track on the other side. He parked it some fifty feet farther on.

"Ever see the petroglyphs?" he asked, swinging out of the car. I joined him at a gap in the shrubbery and followed him down a well-worn steep embankment to the top of the rock cliff lining the river's edge like a huge sluiceway. Far below us the water coursed by peacefully, wending its way around countless jagged boulders and swirling over smooth, kettle-shaped holes carved by thousands of years of turbulence. The view, coming as it did after being hidden by the bushes, was abrupt and dizzying. I felt pulled forward by the void before me and was acutely aware of the steep angle at my feet.

"They're over here," Davis said lightly, traveling across the smooth rock face like a billy goat. He paused by a shelf and pointed. At his feet was a cluster of round carvings in the stone, each looking exactly like a surprised smiley face, with its smile replaced by an oh. Some of the heads were adorned with antennae, and all were grotesquely outlined in modern yellow paint, apparently so they could be seen from a distance.

"Weird, huh? Nobody knows where they came from or how old they are. They look like they're from outer space."

I glanced above and over my shoulder to where we'd started out. "I take it this isn't always so peaceful."

Davis began heading back. "That's no lie. Right now, the water's being diverted down the canal to the power station. If we get a good rain up north, though, or during the spring thaw, they open the dam's taintor gates and this place looks like a tidal wave hit it. Anything falls in then, it's good-bye Charlie."

We paused again at the top to survey the peaceful scene. Even knowing there was no danger at the moment, I felt the threat of calamity lingering, like a growl in the throat of a restless beast.

"Fifteen years I've been looking at this—still knocks me out," Davis admitted.

I picked up the thread we'd dropped several minutes ago. "If Norm's as dirty as you think he is, doesn't the Southern Vermont Drug Task Force have something on him?"

The other man shook his head and headed back up the embankment to the car. "Not that I've heard, and we're in a position to know. Our other sergeant, the guy who normally shares the shift supervision with me, he's on assignment with them, has been for over half a year now. We talk all the time, and he's never said a word about it. I guess they either don't consider Norm a big enough fish, or they just haven't got to him yet."

We returned downtown in the cruiser. After mulling it over a while, Davis added, "'Course, it might also have something to do with his coming from here. Could be the task force doesn't want to waste its time."

I glanced over at him, seeing his neutral expression. Even Greg Davis, who despite his demeanor was obviously a town enthusiast, shared the dismissive, self-deprecating, pessimistic trait that so deeply stamped the citizens of Bellows Falls.

Brattleboro was considerably larger than this town, as was its welfare population. But it was also a feisty, combative, opinionated urban hub, which took its social woes in stride. Bellows Falls, by contrast, seemed resigned to living off table scraps, wondering when someone or something from the outside would appear to make everything better.

This was interesting sociology, but I had a more pertinent motive in pondering it. It made me think about Norman Bouch, and how and why he'd chosen this particular piece of real estate on which to settle down. A contractor's haven it was not. On the other hand, given its population, its attitude, and its proximity to one of Vermont's two interstates, it did seem a custom fit for Norm's other supposed source of income.

All of which made for some curious ingredients in what Emile Latour was hoping would be a cut-and-dried case.

4

Anne Murphy glanced up at me, a wary, beleaguered expression on her tired face. Dressed in slacks, sneakers, and a blue work shirt, she didn't look like a typical nurse. But then she didn't have the typical nurse's job. Employed by Vermont's Department of Health, she spent half her time on the road, visiting patients at their homes—generally places the police also knew all too well—trying to inform them about nutrition, child-rearing, battering, and drug abuse. It was a taxing, sometimes dirty and dangerous job, not to be performed in a tidy white uniform.

She was in her office right now—a small, bland cubicle in a Springfield building shared with other state employees—and didn't seem in a receptive mood. "You the one who called?"

I nodded and extended a hand in greeting. "Yes—Joe Gunther."

Ignoring me, she waved to a chair opposite hers. "I heard of you. Sit."

I looked around quickly. The walls were white cinderblock, the lighting antiseptic, the floors easy to clean. The windows, as they always seem to be in state and federal buildings, were placed above where you could see out of them from a sitting position. She'd done her best to soften the tone—a bunch of flowers were on her desk, and several posters on the walls depicted soothing, pastoral scenes.

"What do you want?" she asked.

She sat as if recovering from a long hike up a mountain—slightly slouched, her feet planted, her forearms resting heavily in her lap. But her face spoke of a greater weariness, her eyes especially. In combat I'd seen the same look on men coming off the line after weeks of heavy action. There was resignation added to the exhaustion, which told of damage far beyond the cure of a good night's sleep.

"I'm on delicate ground here," I started, hoping she'd appreciate the candor. "I'm conducting an investigation that involves one of your patients, at least according to Greg Davis in Bellows Falls. I know you have confidentialities you can't violate, but I was hoping you could give me some background material."

"This about Jan Bouch and Brian Padget?"

I couldn't suppress a laugh. "Boy—that didn't take long to get out."

I placed my tape recorder on the desk next to her. "I want to make sure everything stays on the record. Do you mind?"

She looked at the machine for a long moment before saying, "I guess not. I think Norm's giving them both a bum rap."

I didn't take the bait, leery of moving too fast. "Do you know what the charges are against Brian Padget?"

She smiled bitterly. "Fooling around with Jan. Everyone else does that kind of stuff, but I figure it's against some cop rule or another."

"How do you define 'fooling around'?"

Her expression turned incredulous. "Cheating on Norm with her. Does turning on that recorder make you a little hard to reach?"

"Just cautious," I answered. "Did you ever see Jan and Brian together?"

"Once. It was late at night, behind some buildings, not far from her house. They didn't see me and I left them alone."

"He was in uniform?"

"No."

"When was that?"

"A week or two ago."

"And what were they doing?"

"Kissing."

"Was she resisting in any way?"

Anne Murphy laughed shortly. "She kept her clothes on. Other than that, she was all over him."

"Did you ever see or hear anything about Brian harassing her at any time?"

She frowned. "Harassing? They were cheating on her husband. Is there a law against that?"

The question seemed genuine. "Not that I know of, but it is contrary to an officer's code of conduct. My investigation isn't criminal in nature, Ms. Murphy. Norm Bouch has filed a sexual harassment charge against Padget."

Her eyes narrowed and she sat forward in her chair. "That's total bullshit. Norm Bouch would like to fuck every woman in that town, me included. The same way he shakes a man's hand, he checks out a woman's tits and ass, and if she gives him half a chance, he makes a grab for them just to see if he gets lucky. I've been waiting for him to try that with me for years, only he's not quite that dumb. If anybody's a harasser here, it's not some wet-behind-the-ears, post-pube junior cop, it's that asshole."

I let a moment pass to clear the air, before saying, "Okay. Why is Jan Bouch a patient of yours?"

The weariness resettled on her face. "You don't expect me to answer that, do you?"

"I didn't think it would hurt to try. How 'bout some more general information? Can you tell me about the Bouches as a couple?"

She pointed soundlessly at the recorder. I leaned forward and turned it off. So much for the record.

"I'm not anti-cop," she said. "The way I look at it, we do some of the same things in different ways. The best of you try to stop wife-beaters and the child abuse and the dope dealing, and those are all the things that make my job next to impossible. But I also depend on trust to get my foot in the door. I can't be blabbing to you and expect to get anything done. I shit all over Norm just now 'cause I've done it to his face, but I don't want to jeopardize the few gains I've made in Bellows Falls, especially not to protect some dumb cop's reputation. He should've known better."

I thought in silence for a few moments. "That's fair. Could you describe the Bouches as parts of a bigger picture—without compromising confidentiality?"

"You ever hear the joke about what's the most confusing day in BF?" she asked.

I shook my head.

"Father's Day. It may not be a thigh slapper, but it cuts pretty close to the bone. Norm Bouch came up here like a lot of others, 'cause the living was cheap and the pickings were easy. He's an urban animal—from Lawrence, I think—and what he learned growing up there helps him run circles around the local yokels. People like Jan. She was unmarried when she had her first kid, she's never had a job in her life, and her mom's fifteen years older than she is. She's the product of generations of welfare-dependent women—people who wouldn't know what to do with an opportunity if it bit them on the ass. Guys like Norm can walk in out of the blue, not even bother with the usual razzle-dazzle, and sweep these girls off their feet. We shake our heads and say 'Tut-tut' when they get pregnant and hooked on drugs, but we don't do jack shit about preventing the problem in the first place. We graduate kids from high school after giving them Home Economics and watching them run around the football field, and we don't seem to care that they can barely read and write and know nothing whatsoever about contraception. Norm's original spin in this routine is that he doesn't just love-'em-and-leave-'em. He keeps the kids he fathers. Not that that's good news—he coerced every one of the girls he impregnated to give up their babies, and not because he loves kids, either—he lets welfare and Jan handle them. With him, everything is possession and/or power. Father Flanagan he's not, even if we can't prove anything."

"Jan's on drugs?" I asked, extrapolating from her generalized portrait.

That brought her up short. She stared at me in silence, her mouth still half-open, and then sat back in her chair, perhaps defeated that I'd only listened to her outburst to satisfy my own ends. "I don't guess that's a state secret. Yeah."

I ventured a guess at the source of part of her anger at Norman Bouch. "And Norm helped put her there?"

"You didn't hear it from me."

"Fair enough. She in pretty bad shape?"

"Not physically, but it takes some stamina to kick even the soft stuff, and she's got none of that. To answer your question, she's admitted to me using coke and marijuana—and booze, of course. That's always there, like oxygen."

A silence settled in the small room as we looked at each other, linked by the knowledge of a world we were both paid to travel wearing metaphorical hip boots, looking for souls to salvage.

"You ever feel you might've been at this too long?" I finally asked.

"Every day. It's becoming hard for me to believe there are normal, happy families out there. I see a father walking down the street holding his daughter's hand, and I wonder how long he's been abusing her."

I looked at her in astonishment. This was about as hard-bitten as I'd seen. And yet I shouldn't have been surprised. We expect aberrant behavior to spread inside a prison, or conservative militarism to result from an Army career. To think that someone could work year after year in Anne Murphy's job, and not become a burned-out cynic, was to expect a depth of character the likes of Mother Teresa's.

I stood up and pocketed my recorder, half hoping my next interview would be with some besotted optimist. And yet I felt deeply for Anne Murphy. She was truly one of the good guys, fighting against both the bureaucracy—and the public's perception of it—and her own clients, who had in many cases come to see resignation as a birthright.

"Thank you," I said. "I appreciate all you've done."

"Good luck," she answered. "You'll need it." But this time she shook my hand.

Bellows Falls' town manager was a round, red-faced, busy-looking man with smudgy glasses. He walked around the outer periphery of his cluttered, dingy office like a blind man looking for a way out, his hands touching piles of papers, clipboards hanging from the walls, the spines of books lining the shelves. I half expected him to duck out of sight in mid-sentence when he reached the open door.

Unfortunately, he didn't.

"When Chief Latour first told me about this situation, I was all but assured it was nothing," Eric Shippee said, passing the doorway and placing a fingertip along the edge of a framed Norman Rockwell print. "Your exact words, Chief, were, 'This is smaller than a wart on a rhino's butt.' Are you telling me something different now? Do we have a problem all of a sudden?"

Emile Latour gave me a beleaguered look and didn't answer.

"Not necessarily," I said, "but to do this investigation properly, it's going to take more than a single afternoon." I considered saying more, but I was already uncomfortable just being here and decided to keep things brief. I wasn't sure why Latour had told Shippee about the allegations so early on, while downplaying them to such an absurd degree. It seemed he was opening himself up to trouble from two sides simultaneously, when simply keeping his mouth shut would have been perfectly appropriate. I wondered if I was dealing with incompetence, stupidity, cowardice, or something more devious I hadn't yet sniffed out. It was the final possibility that made me nervous.

Shippee kept roaming, peering at me periodically from various spots around the room. Latour, predictably, returned to staring at the floor.

"You must've found out something by now," Shippee persisted.

"Was there sexual harassment or not?"

"It's too early to tell. Accusations of this sort, especially against police officers, are often suspect—a way of getting back. But they all need to be looked at carefully—"

"I know the party line," Shippee interrupted. "That's precisely why I want to hear what you've found so far, so I can prepare for any fallout. In case you haven't heard, this town is a lightning rod for trouble, and the press eats it up. We've been busting our asses lately to give Bellows Falls a better image, and I don't need my own police department sneaking around behind my back with a piece of dynamite in their hands."

I raised my eyebrows, not only at his mistrust, but at why such a supposedly mundane case should stimulate this kind of passion. "Have you heard something I haven't?"

He stopped dead in his tracks and stared at me. "What's that supposed to mean?"

I instantly regretted having spoken. "Nothing. I'm picking up information where I can find it. I was told Norm Bouch travels in all the social circles, so I was wondering if you had something I could use—even a gut reaction."

"Implying I'm not only hanging out with Bouch but holding back information as well?"

I got to my feet and headed for the door, stung by the man's paranoid combativeness. "Why don't you chew this over with Emile? I'll go back to doing what I've been asked to do, as a courtesy, and I'll report what I find to him. With any luck, we won't have to meet again."

I clattered down the noisy wooden steps of the town hall, through the ground floor lobby it shared with a movie theater, and emerged into the village square. It was ghostly gray outside, an odd mixture of ebbing daylight and glowing street-lamps. Half the stores had turned their lights on. Small clusters of teenagers drove or walked by like reconnaissance platoons looking for action. It was closing in on nine o'clock, and the weather was balmy. Experience told me it would be a busy night for the police, in Bellows Falls, Brattleboro, and elsewhere.

"Sorry about that."

I turned as Emile Latour appeared in the town hall's doorway, three steps above the sidewalk.

"You tell him everything you do?" I asked him.

He came down and stood beside me, watching the traffic go by. "Things run a little differently here. We're smaller—we don't have your department's clout. And he doesn't like surprises."

"He doesn't seem to like much of anything."

"It's just his style. He's not a great people person, but he tries to keep his ship on an even keel. He's also sucking up to this new bunch that're trying to get the town back on its feet."

I took a deep breath. I wasn't sure I wanted to hear any more about Bellows Falls' contradictory identity crisis, at least not today. But I also didn't want to call it quits with no more than the innuendos I'd collected.

"I'm going to interview Bouch and his wife tomorrow," I said. "I'd like a little more background on them. Who do you suggest I talk to? Preferably somebody without an ax to grind."

Latour's hand snuck up and rubbed the back of his neck. "Hughie Cochran hired Bouch when he first hit town—still refers work to him now and then when he's too booked. He runs an excavating business—septic tanks, in-ground swimming pools, trench work for pipelines, stuff like that. He's honest and pretty successful and he hires a lot of the same people we deal with—short term grunt labor, either working to feed a drug habit, or killing time before they get busted again." Latour sighed. "Anyhow, he's good with them—seems to know what makes 'em tick. Maybe he's what you're after."

Hughie Cochran lived between Bellows Falls and Saxton's River, along one of the thousands of dirt roads that seemingly vanish into the Vermont hills, and along which live most of the state's residents. Slowly driving in the growing darkness, I passed a farm, an antique business, several homes, including one estate with vast acreage, a couple of trailers, and a place that looked like an auto junkyard advertising itself as a garage—a string of unzoned anomalies I could have found in any one of our fourteen counties. Cochran's house, a simply built ranch-style surrounded by a well-kept lawn, was near the top of the hill, with a commanding view of the distant New Hampshire mountains—the only sign of which right now was a random sprinkling of tiny lights.

A burly man in a baseball cap and a T-shirt stepped onto the porch as I got out of my car. He was holding two mugs in his hands, one of which he handed me as I approached. "Thought you might want some coffee. My wife brewed a fresh batch after you called."

Cochran didn't offer to shake hands, nor did I. This was a type of man I'd known all my life—hard-working, conservative, intensely private, and utterly, if quietly, faithful to the triad of church, family, and flag. Hughie Cochran knew where he came from and where he was headed, and he had a pragmatic distrust of any dream that didn't come stamped on a single weekly megabucks ticket. Years from now, when he was in his seventies and in a nursing home, a victim of too much coffee, beer, and starchy food, he would look back on his life, as embodied by his children, with stoical satisfaction. And I wouldn't be one to argue with him.

He gestured to a couple of metal lawn chairs at the end of the porch. "Have a seat."

The only light came from within the house—three yellow squares that spread obliquely across the floorboards to the grass beyond. Sounds of muted conversation and canned television laughter barely made it through the walls.

Cochran took his time fitting his large frame into the chair and then carefully took a long pull from his coffee mug. "Nice time of the evening."

I followed his example and agreed. "Must be quite a view."

"It's pretty nice. We moved up here about ten years ago. My wife had a longing to get out of town."

"Bellows Falls?"

"Just outside—that's where I keep the business. She wanted to get away from all that dust and noise. Can't say I blame her, though it took me forever to make the move. I like it now, but it was hard separating from work…Gets to be a habit."

He stared contentedly out at the darkness. I knew better than to rush him.

"So—on the phone you said you're a Brattleboro policeman."

"Yeah. Helping out the locals a bit. Just a small deal, but they needed an outsider—for appearances."

I left it at that. He took another swallow. "And you want to know about Norm."

"Only what you're comfortable with. I've got to talk to him tomorrow. I was curious what makes him tick."

Cochran laughed gently. "I don't know what I could give you there. I'm no psychologist—just a dozer driver."

"Who's hired a lot of people and hasn't made too many mistakes, from what I hear."

There was a slightly embarrassed but pleased moment of silence.

"Well…I've done all right so far, I guess."

I let a moment's silence remind him of my question.

Cochran scratched his cheek. "He's a good guy—easy to get along with. He does the job you tell him to."

"And then what?"

The other man shook his head, smiling sadly. "That's the catch. When he's left on his own, I think his mind wanders to what he'd like to do, instead of what he's supposed to be doin'. But he does good work, and he's real easy-goin'. I hardly ever had trouble with him."

"He worked for you when he first arrived in the area, right? Why did he leave?"

"Wanted to go independent. A lot of them do after they get a taste for it. Most of 'em go bust, of course—the overhead, the insurance, maintaining the equipment, trying to get people to pay you for what you done. People think you dig a hole and walk away with the money, but there's a lot more to it."

"But Norm made a go of it."

Hughie Cochran frowned. "Yeah…I guess. He just does it part-time. Must've got a deal on the equipment or something, so he owns it outright, or doesn't pay much monthly. Otherwise, I don't see how he keeps hold of it, not with the few jobs he does. He's a smart man, though. He could really go places if he wanted to." He laughed suddenly. "Not that I'm going to tell him how to run me out of business."

I returned to a small point he'd implied earlier. "Was there something in the back of your mind when you said you 'hardly ever' had trouble with him?"

He shook his head. "Not really. He'd have a temper tantrum every once in a while. Things wouldn't go his way and he'd blow up. He was particular that way—calling the shots—and people learned to either get along or get out of the way. He was good enough at the job that quality was never the problem. It was more of a style thing, so I never messed with it, and it never got out of hand."

"Rumors are most of his income is from dealing drugs."

Cochran waved a mitt-sized hand tiredly. "Oh hell, I heard that, too. There might be something to it, but it could be pure bullshit. Bellows Falls catches a lot of that kind of talk. If you believed it all, that town would be like one of those South American cartels. Fact is, for the most part, welfare people don't just sit around cashing government checks and drinking beer. They got to make more than the government hands out, and they got to get it under the counter. Other people see one of them getting a car or a new washing machine or whatever, and right away it's 'They must be dealing dope.' I get sick of hearing it. Sure, some of 'em might be doing a little of that. I might, too, in their place, to put food on the table."

I didn't comment, but I knew he was right. There was a large underground economy in Vermont, and only a small portion of it involved illegal substances. Of course, on the flip side, marijuana was second only to corn as the state's biggest cash crop. "You ever see Norm socially?"

"I don't see much of anybody socially—ask my wife. I work, I come home, catch a little TV and a few hours sleep, and I go back to work.

That's about it. Besides, from what I hear, I couldn't keep up with Norm anyhow. He gets around."

There was a long contemplative pause I didn't interrupt, sensing Cochran might have more to offer. A minute later, he said, "I'd say 'bout the only problem I ever had with Norm was that he was always talking it up with everybody and anybody, especially the kids."

"Kids?" I asked, struck once again at children being linked to Norm Bouch.

"Yeah. Kids love Norm—teenagers. Maybe he gives 'em stuff their folks would kill him for—I don't know. I never had any trouble that way. My two always walked straight, but Bellows Falls does have its fair share who don't—I'll give it that. Anyhow, so many of 'em started hanging around, it got to be a problem. One of 'em almost got killed three, four years ago—ran in front of a dozer and slipped. Come to think of it, he was from Brattleboro. Still, I told Norm he had to keep 'em away after that. I didn't need a lawsuit on top of everything else."

"Do you remember that kid's name?" I asked.

"Oh, sure. I made him sign a waiver at the bottom of the accident report. I wanted my butt covered on that one, I guess 'cause I didn't like him much. His name was Jasper Morgan."

5

Gail looked up from the pot she was stirring as I entered the kitchen from the back door. "How was Bellows Falls? You didn't have dinner yet, did you?"

I crossed over and kissed her. "Weird and nope."

"Good. It's spaghetti. You want to make a salad?" Salad was one of the things she'd discovered I actually could prepare that didn't entail opening cans or boxes. My philosophy was that meals shouldn't take longer to make than they take to eat. Gail was a lacto-vegetarian who loved to build from scratch. Food wasn't something we talked much about.

"How weird is 'weird'?" she asked, breaking out a skillet from the cabinet at her knee.

"I don't know...The whole town's suffering from an identity crisis—can't decide if it's an unsalvageable dump, stuck in the past and dependent on government handouts, or if it's balanced on the edge of a comeback, depending on just the right gimmick. I heard everything from drowning the place with flowers, so it looks like a Swiss village, to renaming it Great Falls. From what I saw, it'll take a lot more than that."

"How 'bout the case? Did you get it wrapped up?"

"Not even close." I began cutting up vegetables and tossing them into a bowl. "I haven't even talked to the principal players yet."

"It was sexual harassment, right? Isn't that what you told me on the phone?"

"Supposedly. I've since found out the harasser and the harassee were probably having an affair, and that the woman's husband, who's pressing the charges, may be dealing drugs. I doubt this is going to be something they'll be able to pat on the butt and see the last of."

"It still doesn't sound too bad—maybe an unprofessional-conduct ruling against the officer, and a little bad publicity. Do you smell something else going on?"

I smiled at her mild tone, thinking back to earlier days, when we lived apart and Gail was a Realtor and a selectman here in Brattleboro. Then, she'd been very much the citizen advocate, distrustful of the legal system, and often taking the underdog's side in debates with me. Now, her sympathies had broadened and become less doctrinaire. I would have been more pleased if a violent rape hadn't been the catalyst behind this transition. But she had adapted well, and I was happy with the end result and with her obvious satisfaction with her new life.

"I do as of an hour ago," I said in answer to her question. "You know that kid we chased through the bowels of the Retreat a few weeks ago? Jasper Morgan?"

"I remember the chase. I don't know anything about him."

"We've known him from when he was in his mid-teens. His parents used to beat the hell out of one another, and he tried running a protection racket at the high school, with predictable results. Later, he dabbled in anything that could make him an illegal buck, always without getting caught. We heard he'd moved on to bigger things—getting people to do his dirty work for him—when he suddenly disappeared for no apparent reason. Anyhow, I just found out he used to hang out with Norman Bouch, the complainant's husband in this case."

"Was Jasper ever found?"

"Nope—nor was Pierre's gun. It may be pure coincidence, but it keeps gnawing at me—like I'm supposed to be hearing something I can't quite make out."

Gail was by now cooking up a steamy mess in her skillet, throwing in handfuls of ingredients and stimulating a pungent aroma. "It's a small state, Joe. People bump into each other all the time, especially if they're in the same business."

"I know. I just keep wondering why Jasper ran from us, and why he ducked underground in the first place, changing his name and conning his way into the Retreat."

"I didn't know he'd done that." She drained the water from the pot and dumped the spaghetti into the skillet, mixing the contents together.

"Yeah. Turns out years before, when he lived in Massachusetts…" I paused. "Damn, that's another coincidence. I need to find out if he and Bouch knew each other before coming to Vermont. Anyway, when he first sought out help for his addiction problem, he used a false identity, so his medical records were always under a different name from the one on file with NCIC. Clever for a kid."

"Who was also clever enough to want help," Gail commented, dishing the meal onto two plates.

"Or being instructed by someone else," I said, still driven by the possibility of Bouch's early involvement. "When he wanted to disappear here, he approached a local therapist and asked to be recommended to the Retreat, which is the standard route of admission. Having conned the first guy, he pulled the same gag on the Retreat examiners. After that, he only had to make sure his supposed cure took a nice long time to kick in."

We settled around the tile-topped island in the center of the kitchen and began eating. "I'm surprised they were all so easily duped," Gail said. "You sure Jasper didn't have some legitimate motivation? Maybe you had nothing to do with it. Maybe he wanted to kick his habit and the business both."

It was all hypothetical, of course, and it had nothing to do with a misdemeanor charge filed against a cop in Bellows Falls—at least so far—but the wheels were beginning to turn in my head. What had started as a favor from one chief to another might suddenly be becoming more interesting—and more relevant to my own department.

Sammie Martens lived on Main Street in Brattleboro, in an apartment near the Municipal Building. I'd never been there before, but I had heard the ribbing she received because of it. Where most officers sought some distance from the department, and a semblance of normalcy in a home with a lawn and an above-ground pool, Sammie had opted for the ultimate short commute. In exchange, she'd been accused of sleeping in her SRT battle gear, and having a zip-line running from her building to the office so she could slide over traffic to cut down her response time. This was usually answered with an extended middle finger.

There was no elevator, at least none I could find in the building's gloomy lobby, so I took the broad wooden steps to the top.

Sammie was waiting for me, gazing over the railing, smiling at my gradual pace. "You ought to try hopping up with your feet together."

I didn't doubt for a moment that was one of her own regular habits. "That must make your neighbors happy."

She ushered me into her apartment, which turned out to be a single enormous, high-ceilinged room, stretching from the Main Street side to a row of windows overlooking the Connecticut River on the other. One of the short walls was covered with full-length mirrors. Placed throughout the vast space, like rest stops along a marathon, were weight machines, stray pieces of furniture, a small kitchenette, and a gathering spot for several rugged looking bicycles. In all, it looked like a cross between a sports equipment warehouse and a teenager's crash pad. There wasn't a zip-line in sight.

"Cozy," I muttered.

She smiled, obviously pleased. "Used to be a ballet school. I love it here." She steered me over to a pair of mismatched chairs, choosing a stool for herself. "Want some coffee?"

I sat in an armchair. "I'm all coffeed out. I got to go back to Bellows Falls tomorrow on this internal, but I wanted to fly something by you first. Have we heard anything new on Jasper Morgan?"

"Not a word."

"Did we ever dig deep into his background—have anyone check out his Massachusetts days?"

"We backtracked to when he first used the phony ID on the therapists, but we did that by phone. Nobody actually went down there."

"Where was *there,* exactly?"

"Lawrence, I think."

The same town Anne Murphy thought Bouch had come from.

"Good. Do me a favor, then. Tomorrow, look a little harder into that, and keep an eye peeled for the name Norman Bouch. See if Jasper and Bouch ever crossed paths. Do a triangulation search if nothing pops up. Check out Bouch's known associates and relatives in Lawrence, and see if any of them show up in Jasper's background—maybe they had a mutual acquaintance."

"Who's Norman Bouch?" she asked.

"The main complainant on the case I'm working in Bellows Falls. But he's also supposed to be freelancing as a drug dealer. And I found a witness who saw him and Jasper together a few years ago. Maybe Jasper's sudden rise and fall had something to do with Bouch."

"Maybe all kinds of things," Sammie said softly, her skepticism reminding me of Gail's.

"True, but I don't like leaving a coincidence like this hanging."

Sammie didn't look pleased. "If Bouch is the complainant, that makes him the injured party, right?"

"Supposedly."

"Won't it look a little funny, you doing a quote-unquote impartial internal, while you're having the complainant investigated by another agency?"

She was right, which I only found irritating.

"Maybe we could try being discreet for once."

Not one to be cowed, Sammie merely stared at me and raised an eyebrow.

I wasn't in the right frame of mind entering my interview with the Bouches. Sammie's comment of the night before still rankled, as did the sudden reappearance of Jasper Morgan, and biased me against both Norm and Jan Bouch. By forgoing the protocol that an internal investigator should stick with the stated facts and interview the complainants and witnesses first and foremost, I'd made a mess of my own objectivity. Sammie would have disqualified herself from the Bellows Falls case. I was too stubborn for that, which irritated me even more.

Norm Bouch appeared on the other side of his screen door after I knocked, his mouth smiling and his eyes watchful. "You the guy who called?"

"That's right. Lieutenant Joe Gunther."

His eyes were those of an intelligent man—focused and analytical—but the rest of his face spoke only of the menace I'd seen reflected in the small boy's face who'd had his ball deflated. My instinctive dislike of Norman Bouch was probably triggered by the same characteristic that made other people turn toward him—his self-assurance was as palpable as the shirt on his back. But my guess was it was the cruelty I'd seen in action that fueled it—and that was a motivator I'd never been able to tolerate.

He pushed the door open but didn't invite me in. "You with the PD?"

"Not this one. I work in Brattleboro. I've been asked to look into the allegations against Officer Padget to avoid any possible conflicts of interest."

Seemingly relieved by this, the smile widened, and Bouch stepped aside. "Come in. You know Padget?"

"We've never met, no. Is Mrs. Bouch around?"

"Yeah, sure. Follow me."

He led me through a series of rooms in total tumult—clothes and toys on the floor, cheap furniture pushed helter-skelter, bare sheetrock walls with holes in them. There was an odor throughout of cat litter, stale sweat, and old food. I had been in more homes like this than I could possibly count.

We headed toward a crescendo of young screaming voices and finally entered a kitchen where a woman was standing surrounded by five children, all clamoring for a box of doughnuts she was holding above her head. The kitchen table was strewn with dirty dishes, spilled milk, and scattered clots of soft, indistinguishable food. The remains of breakfast cereal crunched underfoot.

"For Christ's sake," Norm muttered. Wading into the fray, he snatched the box from his wife's hands, walked to the back door, and threw it out into the yard. The kids vanished in a stampede, leaving silence and wreckage behind. Jan Bouch stayed rooted in place, her hand still held high, as if baffled by what had happened.

Norm returned and steered her toward one of the chairs near the table in the room's center. "Sit down—the man's got some questions." His manner toward her wasn't brutal or threatening—it had the same condescending gentility I might have used on a pet dog.

Jan Bouch had a lean, tired face framed in lank, unwashed blond hair. She looked much older than her eighteen years. Her movements were doll-like, her reactions slow and mechanical, and her eyes seemed unfocused. I had serious doubts her own breakfast had been chemical-free.

"Mr. Bouch," I began, "I wonder if I might talk to your wife alone to begin with."

She looked up at him, seeking guidance. He merely shook his head, the protective man of the family. "No. You got questions, you ask both of us." He then cracked a broad smile, reminding me of the genial good-ol'-boy I'd been hearing about. "But no need to be uncomfortable. Take a seat. You want some coffee?"

I turned down the coffee, but I couldn't argue about his presence.

I pulled out a seat, wiped the milk off it with a stray napkin, and sat opposite Jan. I placed the recorder on the table between us.

"What's that?" Norm asked, his voice flattening. "You tapin' this?"

"Just so there're no misunderstandings. We want everything aboveboard."

He sat close to his wife, who immediately slipped her arm through his, a gesture he ignored. "Okay—that's fair by me."

"Mrs. Bouch," I asked, "would you tell me in your own words the grievance you have against Officer Padget?"

Jan Bouch kept her eyes glued to the tabletop. "He's been bothering me."

"In what way?"

"He follows me when I go out, stares at me..." Her voice trailed off.

"Would you say he's stalking you?"

A small furrow appeared between her eyes. "I guess so."

"Why do the allegations specify sexual harassment?"

"He *is* harassing me."

"He's been telling her to dump me," Norm said sorrowfully. "Telling her she's wasting her talents. That she's got great tits, and that he'd really know how to give her a good time."

I kept my eyes on Jan as he spoke. She looked like she was experiencing a physical pain, deep down.

"When did he say this to you—exactly."

"On the street, last week."

"When last week, Mrs. Bouch? Did anyone else hear him address you?"

Again, she glanced furtively at her husband, who seemed stumped this time.

"What does it matter?" he joked. "Do *you* run around with a pad, writing down when people say stuff to you?"

It dawned on me then why they'd chosen sexual harassment over stalking, a weightier allegation. Stalking takes time to establish, often a prior history of the two parties being involved, and it calls into play more times for which corroborating witnesses might be located. Sexual harassment, especially involving a cop, could be a one-shot deal, if all you wanted to do was get that cop into hot water.

"Maybe you can tell me what you were doing when this conversation occurred," I persisted. "Or where you were at the time."

Her face suddenly brightened, and she looked at me hopefully. "I was walking down the street, and he drove up next to me. He rolled the window down and that's when he said it."

"Where on the street?"

She faltered slightly. "Out front...near Atkinson."

"He was driving along this street, came up behind you, and addressed you just as you reached Atkinson, is that right?"

"Right."

"No," Norm said, too late.

"Which is it?" I asked, knowing Padget would have to have been driving the wrong way on a one-way street.

Jan looked totally confused.

"He was on Atkinson and met her on the corner," Norm said, visibly struggling to maintain his composure. "She's lousy with directions."

"And roughly what time of day was this?"

Jan didn't answer. Her husband let out a deep sigh, as if he'd just realized he was holding a losing hand of cards. He tried bluffing with another big smile. "Oh, I don't know...Let's see—about noon on Wednesday. Wouldn't you say, honey?"

"Sure," she whispered.

"Did Officer Padget approach you at any other time with similar comments?" I continued briskly.

Having been ambushed once, Norm headed me off with a small burst of bluster. "Once isn't enough? How many times does he have to do it before you guys consider it wrong?"

I looked at him in silence for a few moments.

"He did it that one time," he finally said.

"Mrs. Bouch, a few minutes ago you said Padget 'follows me when I go out,' to use your words, implying this has happened several times. If that's true, we'd certainly like to know about it. If Officer Padget has acted improperly, he should be held accountable."

Still looking at the tabletop, Jan merely shook her head, as if she'd lost her way.

"The other times were too vague," Norm said. "He didn't do anything you could put your finger on."

"How do you think Officer Padget came to focus on you in the first place, Mrs. Bouch? Did you know him prior to these incidents?"

She rubbed her forehead with her fingertips, hard enough to leave small oval blanches behind. "I, uh...I don't—"

"Of course we did," Norm interrupted, his voice sharp now. "There're only about six cops in the whole town. Everyone gets to know them sooner or later." He laughed awkwardly. "And I won't deny they been here a couple of times when we got a little rowdy."

"Was Brian Padget ever among the officers who responded to those calls?"

A flash of irritation swept across Norm's face. "I don't know. You can look that up, can't you?"

"Mrs. Bouch, let me rephrase this a different way. When was the first time you ever saw Officer Padget?"

She answered quickly, "Oh, it was a long—"

Again her husband stopped her, this time with a hand laid heavily on her forearm. I noticed that when she tried to move it away, she couldn't.

"Who can tell, Lieutenant?" Norm answered with a smile. "You see a cop on the beat, you don't pay attention. It wasn't till he started coming on to her that we really noticed, and that was just recent. We reported it right off."

"Have either of you had any contact with Officer Padget since the time he drove up next to you and said those things?"

"No," Norm answered flatly, apparently tired of the game at last, and hoping to end it as soon as possible.

I decided to accommodate him. Turning off the recorder and slipping it into my pocket, I got to my feet. "I think that ought to do it for the moment. I want to thank you for your cooperation. I understand the stress you must both be under. We should be able to reach a determination on this matter within a few days. I hope you understand the process we have to follow, for the good of all involved."

Ignoring a perfect opportunity to harp on how the system takes care of its own, Norm rose with me instead and merely muttered, "Sure, sure."

I stuck my hand out to Jan. "It was nice meeting you, Mrs. Bouch. Thanks for your help."

She looked at the hand reluctantly at first, but I forced her to take it by simply not moving. My persistence paid off—her hand was hot and damp with sweat, and trembling slightly. She was a nervous wreck, and I was pretty sure why.

She didn't join us as Norm escorted me back through the house to the front door.

Norm was all smiles again but without the eagerness he'd shown earlier. "I sure appreciate your coming over, and I'm sorry about my wife. This thing has really shaken her up, you know? It's kind of a shock when a police officer pulls something like that—I mean, you don't expect it. You were really professional about it, though. That'll help her a lot."

I stepped out onto the porch and faced him. "We do what we can, Mr. Bouch. We also try to make people accountable for their actions, regardless of who they are."

The smile didn't falter, but the eyes and voice turned cold. "That's good, Lieutenant. You have a good day."

6

The convenience store near the Bouch home had a small counter with a couple of stools near its front window. I sat there, watching the street, waiting for Jan Bouch to emerge.

She rewarded me three hours later, stepping out to the sidewalk and walking toward Atkinson—the same scenario she'd painted earlier with Padget as the fall guy. She walked like someone expecting a pail of cold water to drop on her at any moment, stiff-limbed and cringing.

I left the store and followed her from the opposite side of the street, not crossing until I'd passed her house, hoping Norm didn't have his nose glued to the window.

"Mrs. Bouch," I said gently as I walked up behind her.

She whirled around to face me, her eyes wide, her hand across her mouth. "What do you want?"

I gave her a reassuring smile, falling into place beside her. "Don't be alarmed. There're a lot of questions in a situation like this. It's like packing a suitcase for a long trip. You have to think about what you need, and sometimes you have to backtrack because you forget something. It's just part of the process. You feeling okay about what I was asking at your house?"

"Sure…I guess so." She continued walking jerkily, all tensed up. We reached the corner at Atkinson Street. I stopped and looked around. "This where Padget approached you?"

Her voice was almost lost in the passing traffic. "Yes…Norm should be here."

The side street continued opposite, toward downtown. Across from us and catty-corner, were a Laundromat and a small store. "And it was about this time of day, wasn't it?"

She didn't answer. Her head was bowed and her elbows tucked in.

"Busy," I mused. "Shouldn't be hard to find several witnesses who saw an officer stop his cruiser to talk with you—kind of thing people notice. It's also the kind of thing Brian might do—stop to have a chat. He's friendly that way, isn't he?"

She nodded distractedly.

"And that's something you would know, right, Jan? Because you know Brian pretty well, don't you?"

Her eyes were fixed on the pavement, her chin pressed to her chest. She seemed wholly absorbed in disappearing within herself. The second nod she gave was barely a twitch.

"Still," I continued, "all that notwithstanding, he didn't actually stop here that day, did he?"

"Jan."

We both turned at the fury contained in the shout, and saw Norm Bouch steaming down the street at us. His wife danced from one foot to the other, wringing her hands and moaning. As I waited for Bouch to reach us, I regretted not having steered her around the corner for our conversation.

"What the hell are you doing?" Bouch demanded, his face red, all pretense at civility gone.

"My job, Mr. Bouch."

"You were waiting for her."

"She seems to have some doubts about the story you told me this morning. That does make things a little confusing."

Bouch raised his finger as if to stab me in the chest but then apparently thought better of it and pointed it in the air. "Listen, you son of a bitch. You're covering for that bastard. He did something that's against the law, and you're trying to stick us with it." He grabbed his wife's arm and pulled her to his side. "I knew you fucking cops would pull some stunt. But it's not going to work. He broke the law, and he's going to get his butt canned."

"If what you say is true," I answered levelly, despite the blood surging through me, "then he will be disciplined. Your being abusive right now won't affect that one way or the other. It might get *you* into trouble, though."

His eyes narrowed, and his grip on his wife's arm tightened to the point where she began to squirm. "Cut that out," he snarled at her. He suddenly pushed her away. "Get your ass home. *Now.*"

He turned his attention back to me. "If you ever come near her again, I'll sue you."

"For what? Talking on a public sidewalk?" It almost worked. I saw the muscles on his right arm bunch up, preparing to send me a roundhouse. But then he regained control. After a long, still moment, his body relaxed, the deceptive smile of that morning returned, and he stepped back. "No—you're right. This thing's made me crazy. You married?"

I didn't respond.

"I don't blame you—the way I came on. Look, I won't deny I'm a jealous guy. My wife's a beautiful woman—maybe not too bright—but a real eyeful. It drives me crazy when guys hit on her."

I remained silent, watching his eyes.

"I'll get out of your face," he kept talking. "And I'm real sorry. I know you got your job...I just want what's right."

He'd begun backing away, and at that turned around and walked after his wife, who I could see had reached their house in a sleepwalker's trance. I half wondered if the police department wouldn't get a call in about ten minutes for sounds of a domestic dispute.

Early that evening, I met with Emile Latour in his architecturally deformed office.

"Any luck?" he asked hopefully as I sat down across from him.

"I suppose that depends on your viewpoint. I met with the Bouches this morning, heard a cock-and-bull story about how Padget complimented her breasts from a cruiser on the corner of Atkinson and their street, and then spent the rest of the day checking it out with everybody I could find who lives, works, or frequents that corner. Nobody saw it happen."

I leaned forward and slid a thin folder at him. "That's my report so far. It also mentions that I have a witness who saw Padget and Jan Bouch making out like Romeo and Juliet in some back alley near her home a week or so ago."

"He was in uniform?" Latour quickly asked.

"No, but rumor has it that wasn't the first time. Rumor also has it you knew about it early on, which is why I was called in so fast."

Latour hadn't touched the folder, but his eyes were fixed to it. "I had heard something," he slowly admitted. "I guess I was hoping it would go away."

I didn't rub it in. My own dealings with this case weren't entirely aboveboard. "Look, for what it's worth, I think it will go away. I talked to Jan Bouch alone on the street, after she and her husband had finished their little tap dance, and she admitted she knew Padget pretty well. I was about to get her to roll over on her story when her hubby came charging down on us. But she's weak, Emile, and I think if I'd done this right the first time, and brought them both into the station for questioning, we'd be done with this by now. My guess is Norm found out what everybody else knows and tried to get Brian fired. But they make a lousy pair of liars—I think if I squeeze them a bit more, maybe let them know the penalties for false accusation, I can get them to fold."

"I hope so," he said grumpily.

"This is good news, you know," I told him.

He waved that aside and swiveled his chair to stare at a distant wall. "I know."

"You disappointed with Brian?"

He waved the notion away. "A little...How long you been a cop?"

"Thirty years, plus."

"Yeah," he sighed. "Long time. Maybe Bratt's a better place to spend that much time, but I'm starting to feel sucked dry. Did Davis tell you why we can't hold on to most of our people for more than a couple of years?"

"I figured it was the money."

He let out a short, humorless laugh. "That's true enough, but I meant the size of the patrol. One square mile. They go around and around, night after night, passing each other in the streets, picking up the same people for the same complaints. There's a lot of action, but the monotony gets to them—fast. Most of them live outside the village, so all they do is clock in at night, do their shift, and leave in the morning. They never get to see the other side—the Bellows Falls that Greg Davis and I live in during the day, with the retailers and professionals and the kids at school and all the normal things. To these young guys, this is a combat zone—a town of losers."

"They don't seem to be alone in that," I said.

"I saw you reading that notice at the town hall," he answered indirectly, "before we met with Eric Shippee—about the committee to revitalize the village."

"Changing the name to Great Falls?" I said with a smile.

"I won't deny it's been tried before. And that particular idea is a little over the top. But this new group is serious. They're not bitching about the lack of state or federal funds anymore. They're doing it themselves—coming up with the money, the manpower, the ideas. They're making real changes and they're not working in a vacuum, either—there's been a turnover in the high school leadership, a few rich people have gotten involved, even the various boards are showing some cooperation, although Shippee's just paying it all lip service. It may fall flat, but for the first time there's a real spirit growing."

"So why's that put you in the dumps?" I asked.

His gaze shifted to the sloped ceiling. "I'm not sure. Maybe all that enthusiasm is telling me I'm with the wrong outfit. I'm sick and tired of the morons we drag in here day in and day out. I want to be part of something hopeful. Maybe not in Bellows Falls—although that's what I'd really like—but at least somewhere I can help things grow."

He reminded me of how, when we'd met, I'd thought of his hands as belonging to a farmer.

I didn't fault him for his mood, or even for how it had probably influenced his speaking prematurely to Shippee and looking ineffectual as a result. Actually, I was flattered that despite our brief acquaintance, he'd trusted me as a sounding board. He'd seen in me a kindred spirit, in years if not in attitude, and spoken as few cops do to anyone, much less a colleague.

That trust, along with what he'd said, softened my initial skepticism about the man and made me honor his privacy. Rather than pressing him further, therefore, I rose quietly, said, "I hope it works out for you—let me know if I can help," and left him with his thoughts. I wasn't sure he noticed me leave.

Downstairs I found Greg Davis filling out a form in the dispatch room. He glanced up as I entered. "Things looking better for Brian?"

"So far so good. You pick up anything?" I added as an afterthought.

"Only that you and Norm had it out in the street today."

I made no comment, but it highlighted Latour's comment about the size of the village. "Do you have an in-house name file on your regular problem cases? People you don't share with NCIC and everybody else?"

"Sure. Over here." He led me to a computer at the far end of the counter he'd been using. He typed a few entries, set up the screen, and stepped back. "Just enter who you're after. If we got it, it should pop right up."

Discreetly, he returned to his paperwork, no questions asked. I appreciated both the access and the courtesy, neither of which he'd been obliged to render. Internal files, departmental and personal, were not quite trade secrets, but they could be jealously guarded, especially from a man who was there to investigate one of their own.

I typed in "Morgan, Jasper," and hit *Enter*. The reference instantly appeared.

"Huh," I let out, surprised at being so instantly gratified.

"Get what you were after?" Davis asked from across the room.

"Yeah. Take a look."

He came over and gazed at the screen. "Jasper Morgan. Looks like he and Norm Bouch were pretty buddy-buddy..." He leaned forward and pressed *Scroll*. "At least until last year. No arrests, but whenever things got rowdy, Mr. Morgan was nearby. Who is he?"

"Teenage doper from our neck of the woods. You must've gotten a BOL on him about a month ago. Brained one of our officers, stole his gun, and vanished into thin air."

Davis's face broke into a grin. "Oh shit. I remember that. Pierre Lavoie. I was going to bust his chops next time I saw him."

"You'll have to stand in line. So you don't know Morgan personally?"

He studied the screen again. "The only officer still here who dealt with him is Emily Doyle—twice, according to this. She's on tonight, if you want to talk with her."

Emily Doyle was short, square, and muscular, with close-cropped dark hair and a nervous tension reminiscent of a hungry dog. She sat on the edge of her chair in the upstairs officers' room, feet planted apart, elbows on her knees, her hands holding a pen like a weapon. Her eyes were fixed on my every movement.

"This about Brian?" she demanded. "'Cause we know what you're trying to do. I won't help you with that, no matter what the rules say."

I met her gaze. "You won't help me clear him?"

She smiled bitterly. "Right—clear him. That's not your job. You're the cop's cop, and a cop busts people."

"How old are you?"

She looked mildly offended, which was fair, given my tone of voice. "Twenty-one."

"Then you've got plenty of time to do your homework. Something like seventy-five percent of all internal investigations result in the officer concerned being cleared, not the other way around."

"You'd tell me anything to get what you're after. And even if it *was* true, then it means most of what they accuse us of is bullshit. But we're cops, so of course we're guilty. Not like some scumbag with a knife in his hand—we *have* to presume *he's* innocent."

It wasn't an argument I wanted to have, so I dropped it there, but my heart was a little heavier for her knee-jerk jingoism—all too common in law enforcement.

"I'm not here to ask you about Brian," I said instead. "I'm also running an investigation back home on a teenager named Jasper Morgan. His name came up in relation to Norm Bouch. I saw from the files that you know him, or at least met him. He's about twenty now, from Brattleboro, skinny, medium height, brown hair, bad complexion."

She was already nodding. "Yeah, yeah. A real knothead. Big-mouth bad guy who was always standing behind somebody else when he sounded off."

"Did you get any feel for how he and Bouch were connected?"

"He was just another of Norm's rug rats."

I resisted pointing out she had one year on Jasper Morgan. "How's that work? What's the attraction?"

"With Norm? He makes himself cool—a grown-up who talks their language. He doesn't lecture them, doesn't tell them what to do, gives them stuff to buy them off—you know, like things for their cars or a ghetto blaster…CDs—shit like that. And dope, too, of course, although we've never caught him at it."

"Latour thinks the kids might be runners." Emily Doyle rolled her eyes at the mention of her chief. "Easy for him to say. We don't have any proof, and he won't let us hunt for any."

"Is he right, though?"

Her cheeks colored. "Probably," she admitted.

"You have any sense of how Norm's organized, then?" I knew before I asked that I'd hit a stone wall. Doyle wasn't the bonehead she appeared—her posturing was mostly self-protective. But she had a lot to learn about the goals of her job and how to achieve them. Catching bad guys was an occasional activity—getting to know what made them tick and stopping others from becoming like them were more important aspects of what we did. For all the vitality in her eyes, she hadn't taught herself to see much yet.

"I guess they're bought and paid for," she guessed. "So they do what he tells them to."

Sammie Martens wasn't at her apartment this time. I found her still at the office, processing paperwork. As energized as Emily Doyle, Martens had developed into a smart, thoughtful student of human behavior. She also worked herself like a slave, candidly admitting that as a woman she had little choice, a tough point to argue since her drive had made her my second-in-command.

"Making progress?" I asked vaguely, settling into a plastic chair next to her open-ended cubicle. There were four such alcoves in the detective squad room, constructed of chin-high, sound-absorbent panels. During slow periods these were moved around regularly— feeble attempts to enliven a dull routine.

"Barely," she sighed, sitting back and stretching. "I'm trying to put some old case files into order—mostly yours, I might add. Bo*ring*."

"What'd you find out about Morgan?"

Her face brightened slightly. "He was a bad boy in Lawrence, but since he was a juvie, I couldn't get particulars. That also made digging into known associates a little tough—through channels, that is."

I smiled at her coyness. "Meaning outside of channels was slightly more productive."

"Right," she answered with a laugh. "I have an old Army buddy who works at the PD down there. He did a little digging for me and came up with Amy Sorvino—Jasper's foster mother until she was found cheating on her husband with Norman Bouch, who was named in the divorce papers soon after."

I shook my head, "Hold it. I thought Jasper lived with his parents."

"He did after they moved up here, but Massachusetts split them up a couple of times when things got rough at home. Anyhow, Amy Sorvino's at least one connection between Bouch and Jasper."

"I don't want to be dense here, but why would a woman's illicit lover and her foster child necessarily know each other?"

I could tell from her smile that Sammie had set me up. "Because they shared the same bed."

She laughed at the look on my face. "That's why the shit really hit the fan. Amy had turned Norm and little Jasper into a tag team. Guess the state goofed in their choice of foster mothers."

I thought of the little ball player of that morning, and how I'd wondered how he and his siblings were faring in the Bouch house-hold. I was getting a dose of bad news about child rearing in this case, and, given how Norm surrounded himself with teenage admirers, I didn't doubt I'd see more.

"With all these wonderful adults in control," Sammie added, reading my expression, "makes you wonder how anyone makes it past puberty."

Good point, I thought, but said instead, "I'd like to have a chat with Amy Sorvino."

7

Early the next morning I pulled into the Lawrence, Massachusetts, Police Department's parking lot, and picked up a short, compact man with a thick head of hair and a bushy mustache.

He slid into my car's passenger seat and stuck out a small, muscular hand. "Phil Marchese."

"Joe Gunther. Thanks for riding shotgun on such short notice. Sammie says she's sorry she couldn't make it."

"Good kid," Marchese said. "Made half the guys in the unit look like wimps. Take a right out of the parking lot."

Marchese was the old Army friend who had revealed Amy Sorvino as the link between Jasper Morgan and Norman Bouch.

Protocol has it that whenever a police officer goes outside his bailiwick on business, he contacts the receiving PD out of courtesy and safety. It was a reflection of Sammie's connection to this man that he'd volunteered to escort me personally rather than giving the job to some rookie. Sammie had told me that despite his youth, Marchese was in good position for a captaincy.

He guided me to a neighborhood of cookie-cutter wooden buildings, roughly World War Two vintage. Not quite down and out, it was teetering on the edge, utterly dependent on Lawrence's rallying against hard times. This was a working-class section of town, and without work it would quickly lose the thin respectability it clung to.

We stopped in front of a house largely indistinguishable from its neighbors. "What's her situation?" I asked my host.

"Single, living alone. After the shit hit the fan with Bouch, she and her husband both picked out lawyers and began circling each other. That'd been going on a few months when hubby suddenly kicked the bucket. Stupid bastard still hadn't changed his will, so she got the inheritance, along with two life insurance payoffs, one personal, one from his job. Neither one was huge, but together they set her up pretty good, even after she settled with the state for the statutory rape of Jasper Morgan. Last five years or so, she's been a party girl, more or less, I guess looking for Mr. Right."

"How do you know all this?"

"Suspicion of prostitution. We got a file on her. Never caught her at it. I don't think she's a pro, to be honest—just an amazingly horny girl on the prowl who takes favors from men."

Seeing that her car was in the driveway, we went up to the front door and knocked. The response was slow and noisy, punctuated by something heavy falling to the ground. Marchese looked at me and shrugged, and we both moved to opposite sides of the door, just in case something or someone came flying out.

There was nothing so dramatic, however. The door opened a crack and a bleary-eyed, blurry-faced woman peered out, squinting into the morning sun. "Who're you? What'd'ya want?"

Marchese showed his badge. "Police, ma'am. Are you Amy Sorvino?"

"Yeah. What's wrong?"

"Nothing. We'd just like to ask you some questions."

"Do it later. I'm sleeping."

"That's not real convenient, Mrs. Sorvino," I said. "I came from Vermont to talk to you. I'd appreciate if you could give me a few minutes. It won't take long—I promise."

She closed the one eye we could see through the crack and sighed. "All right. But wait a minute, okay? I'm a wreck. Don't go away."

She slammed the door. Marchese smiled at me. "Ah, that Vermont country charm."

I pointed to his upper lip. "I say it's the mustache."

Ten minutes later she reappeared, this time opening the door wide. I had to admit, she looked good for having obviously come off an all-nighter. She was wearing a clingy, thin-fabric caftan, a quick touch of makeup, and had brushed her hair. I could smell the toothpaste on her breath as we crossed the threshold. I guessed her to be in her early thirties and figured she divided her time between living hard and keeping fit at the gym. I wondered how long the balance would tilt in her favor.

She ushered us into a pleasant, new-smelling living room, reminiscent of a colonial-style furniture catalogue—a startling contrast to the house's working-class exterior, and a dead giveaway of how Amy Sorvino had spent some of her newfound cash. "You want coffee?"

"No, thank you," I answered. Marchese merely shook his head.

She grimaced. "Well, I do. Grab a seat."

She vanished for several more minutes, during which we heard a microwave being put into service. When she came back, a mug held in both hands, she settled into a wingback armchair, tucking her feet up under her. It made for a very attractive picture, as she no doubt realized.

"So—fire away," she said with a small laugh. "If that's not the wrong thing to say."

I was impressed by her poise. With two cops in the house, their purpose unstated, I might've been at least slightly cowed. To this woman—now that she was awake—we were obviously only a source of curiosity. "Mrs. Sorvino—"

"Call me Amy. Who're you?"

"Joe Gunther, and this is Phil Marchese. I'm from the Brattleboro Police Department. I was working on a case when your name came up—not in any bad way, but just as someone who might be able to tell me a few things."

"What about?" She took a sip of coffee, still holding on with both hands. Over the rim of the mug, she batted her eyes at me. I couldn't resist smiling. I liked this woman. She was a hard worker, if a little single-minded.

"Norm Bouch and Jasper Morgan."

I expected the smile to fade and the conversation to get chilly. Those two names were not associated with the happiest events in Amy Sorvino's life. But she merely rolled her eyes and laughed. "Oh, those two. What a pair they made."

"How so?" I asked.

She rested her hand against her stomach, flattening the fabric of her caftan and pulling it tighter against her breasts. "You're not pretending you don't know what the three of us had going?"

Despite my best efforts, I flushed slightly. "No, but it's more the relationship between the two of them that I want to know about, not so much what they were doing with you."

She stuck her lower lip out. "Gee. That's not too flattering. What kinds of things are you after?"

"Well, for starters, were they good friends? Some men wouldn't be, in that kind of situation."

"We were all friends. That was the point. I wouldn't have done it otherwise. Jasper found Norm and me one night. I guess we woke him up with all our noise. I could see he was interested—I mean it wasn't like I was his real mother or anything. So I invited him in. And Norm was real cool about it. He told him stuff, made it a whole lot easier. It was perfect 'til old George showed up on the wrong night and screwed it all up. He was such a jerk."

I didn't have to ask if George was her husband. "Did Norm see Jasper at other times?"

The frown she'd put on disappeared. "Oh sure. That's what I mean. They were pals. Norm was a much better foster father than old George, any day. They went to ball games, movies, hung out...Norm got him involved in all his schemes. It was great. Jasper loved it. He was sort of a brat when he first came, but me and Norm together settled him down pretty good."

I thought back to how Jasper had established a false identity to separate his criminal and medical records. Norm looked like a good bet for that piece of inspiration. In those terms, "settled down" took on a distinctly subversive meaning—one that Jasper probably had found very appealing. "What were these schemes you mentioned?"

She laughed again. "Oh, Norm was going to be quite the big-time bad guy. He was going to set up a kind of family, where the kids brought him what they stole and he took care of them. I used to pull his leg and call him Fagin, after the old man in *Oliver Twist*. You ever see that movie? He didn't see the humor...It was kind of the same thing, though. Anyway, he tried it out on Jasper."

"How?" I pushed, smiling to encourage her.

"He was a cute kid—small, too—could do things and go places a man couldn't, without looking suspicious. Plus if he got caught, he was a minor."

"Were these muggings or burglaries or what?"

She waved a hand impatiently. "I don't know. They conspired together like a couple of gangsters. I just had fun with them. Anyhow, what they did here wasn't the point. Norm was going to Vermont. That's where he'd been planning to do his Oliver Twist thing from the start, and where Jasper was going to be a part of it."

A pattern was forming in my mind, and with it a growing excitement. I leaned forward in my seat. "Jasper ended up in Brattleboro, back with his folks, and Norm lives in Bellows Falls. Was that something they planned?"

She smiled broadly and shook her finger at me. "Oh, you're good. Yeah, Norm wanted a bunch of people like Jasper—lieutenants, he called them—and they would run other kids in towns all over

Vermont. When old George busted things up, Norm really pushed Jasper to clean up his act, get back with his parents if he could, but at least get up to Brattleboro fast so he could set up shop, recruit some people, and start going with this thing. Norm was hot to trot—I used to laugh at him about it, he got so serious sometimes."

"And the idea was to start a burglary ring?" I tried again.

"You mean robbing people? Oh, hell no. There wasn't enough money in that. Norm told me that was just boot camp for the kid. It was drugs he wanted to get into. That's where the profits were, and he said Vermont was easy pickings—lots of yahoos hungry for dope. He kept saying, 'I'm going to fill a need, just like Henry Ford.'"

"A history buff," Marchese spoke for the first time.

She tilted her head back and glanced at the ceiling. "Yeah, he was something else."

"Did Norm mention the towns he was going to use for his network?" I pressed her.

"The two of them studied maps all the time. They had to be on the interstates, and they had to have the right kind of people. I didn't pay much attention to all that, but the ones they talked about most were Brattleboro, Bellows Falls, Barre, and Burlington. I remember because of all the Bs."

"Did you ever meet others that were supposed to work like Jasper—as lieutenants? People Norm sent to those towns?"

"No, but they talked about them. The real clever part of this thing was that only the lieutenants would know who their own people were—the kids wouldn't know each other and the other lieutenants wouldn't know them. Norm called them 'cells,' and said that that way, if one of them got blown, the others could keep on going. Smart, huh? That was about all I knew, though—stuff I heard when we were all at home. Mostly they talked where Norm worked at a garage. I never went there—I'm not even sure exactly where it was—but they had meetings all the time, with kids, just like in that movie."

"Was Norm's grand plan ready to go when George suddenly appeared?"

"I don't think so, but who knows? Our little deal getting busted up, we kind of lost touch. I know Norm and Jasper kept seeing each other, so I guess they were still hot at it."

For the first time, she appeared vaguely uncomfortable, staring at the floor and fingering the material of her caftan.

I took a wild guess. "Maybe the breakup wasn't such bad news anyhow."

She looked at me, surprised, but she took her time before answering and then said unexpectedly, "No. It was time."

I thought back to the dynamics I'd seen in the Bouch kitchen. "Because of Norm?"

She nodded. "The more that grand plan of his grew, the worse he got—pushing me around, acting like he owned the place. There was something a little scary about it, too."

I felt I knew what she meant and shared the sadness I saw in her eyes. For the first time in this case, the true impact of all I'd been collecting slipped under my defenses—and darkened my spirit.

The sexual harassment case against Brian Padget collapsed like a pierced balloon, as I'd thought it would. After leaving Lawrence, and Phil Marchese, I continued playing hooky and spent the rest of the morning in Brattleboro with my squad, suggesting we contact the towns Amy Sorvino had mentioned, to see if Norman Bouch or Oliver Twist-style teenage gangs rang any bells. I had been planning to grill the Bouches later in the day, in far more detail than the day before, but around lunchtime a phone call from Emile Latour turned that idea inside out.

"The Bouches want to come in at two o'clock and make a clean breast about Brian."

"What's that mean?" I asked.

"Norm called me and said Brian was the innocent victim of a marital spat. He wants to make a formal statement to you and put the whole thing to rest."

"Did he say the marital spat was because his wife and Brian were fooling around?"

"No—just that Brian had nothing to do with it."

I frowned at the phone. "Making Norm the only guy in town not to know?"

Latour didn't answer.

"How's Brian feel about it?"

There was a telling pause at the other end of the line, from which I assumed Brian had not been informed.

"If they do as they claim, we're not going to pursue it."

His tone of voice reminded me of when we'd both been in the town manager's office.

"What's going on?" I asked, irritated by the memory. "It's not necessarily 'we' who have anything to say in this. If Brian wants to go after them civilly, that's his right."

"We've got another situation with Brian right now."

He didn't elaborate, but I could tell it wasn't good. "What?"

"I got a call from your newspaper down there. They had a tip Brian is dirty—he's been dealing and using drugs."

I scowled at the phone. "Oh, for Christ's sake. But they wouldn't identify who tipped them, right?"

"No."

"Come on, Emile. You use a paper to smear someone, because you know they won't reveal their source. You're not actually moving on this, are you? Give the kid a break."

"I don't have any choice. If I ignore it, they'll start yelling about a cover-up. Besides, I think I got it licked. I told Brian about it, and he volunteered for a urine test and a polygraph, then and there. He's already in Waterbury, doing both at the state lab. They said they'd let me know by late this afternoon, maybe sooner. With that in my hand, I can tell the paper to piss off, no pun intended."

It was a hopefulness I distrusted. I didn't believe for a moment that Norm Bouch's conversion and Brian Padget's latest hurdle weren't connected, and I was tempted to call the paper myself to see if a little personal pressure might not yield better results. Using the press to bolster the us-versus-them mania Emily Doyle had demonstrated earlier made me furious. I didn't know Brian Padget, but I knew for a certainty that if he wasn't showing some of Emily's attitude by now, he was missing some major vital functions.

I kept such thoughts to myself, however, and told Latour I'd be at his building at two.

I opted to use the Bellows Falls Police Department's cramped, sterile interrogation room to interview the Bouches rather than Latour's more spacious office, to help drive home my dissatisfaction with the latest turn of events. Not that my opinion carried any weight, of course. If the Bouches officially withdrew their accusation, my job was over, and since the insult was against the PD, they and Padget became the injured parties, and it was up to them to file the appropriate charges. But I was angry, and I wanted to show it the only way I was officially allowed. I didn't believe in Norm's contrition. His and Jan's appearance today was to be another act, and his pretending not to know about her and Brian's affair was at the heart of it. Unfortunately, I was now a bystander—a spectator to Norm's next move.

Latour and I were already seated at the interrogation room's bare table when an officer escorted in Jan and Norm Bouch. Unsmiling, I removed my recorder from my pocket, laid it on the smooth surface between us, and, as they settled into seats opposite, I pushed the *Record* button.

"Police officers Latour and Gunther interviewing Jan and Norman Bouch in the Bellows Falls Police Department, the latter two people being here of their own free will." I checked my watch and added the time and date of the meeting.

I clasped the fingers of both hands before me and rested them lightly on the tabletop, watching our guests closely. Jan looked terrible—wan, tired, her eyes puffy and bloodshot, her hair dirty and uncombed. She sat slumped in her chair, staring into space. Norm, by contrast, was predictably pleased with himself, his head tilted back, a small smile working hard to lie still.

"It's my understanding you are here for an official retraction of allegations you previously made against Officer Brian Padget of this department. Is that correct?" I asked.

Norm unleashed his smile now—failing at a look of embarrassed guilt. "Yeah. Jan and I feel terrible about what we done. I got mad at Brian and got my wife to say things that didn't happen."

I ignored the obvious bait. "So there was no conversation between Officer Padget and your wife in which Officer Padget made disparaging comments of a sexual nature?"

"Right—nothing happened. At least not that way. Brian's been screwing around with my wife, but I guess that's our problem, and we're doing our best to sort it out. We shouldn't have done what we did, and we're real sorry we put Brian in a pickle."

I sat back and crossed my arms, knowing my face was several shades redder than it had been moments earlier. Latour sat awkwardly still as a long silence filled the room, knowing the spotlight had unexpectedly put him on center stage.

Norm Bouch had made his move. He'd ended a cock-and-bull story he'd hoped would get Padget fired but which was falling apart fast, and had rendered moot the internal investigation that had put me in his face. With the same stroke, by seemingly letting slip what he had about Jan and Brian Padget, he'd also opened a can of worms which

Latour, Padget, Shippee, and others would be forced to deal with in full public scrutiny.

And there was an additional bonus to this new strategy—if open humiliation seemed a step down from getting Padget fired, there was always that anonymous phone call the paper had asked Emile about.

Latour cleared his throat after a pause. "Mrs. Bouch, is this true, what your husband just said about you and Brian Padget?"

Still staring off into space, she barely nodded without comment.

"Speak up," I ordered roughly. "We need this on tape."

"Yes," she said softly.

"What is the nature of your relationship with Officer Padget?" Latour continued, sounding as if he'd be far happier in a dentist's chair.

"We were…are lovers."

"For how long?"

"A couple of months maybe."

"And your husband was aware of it all that time?" I asked, hoping to dampen Norm's moment of glory.

"I found out just before I accused Padget of harassment," he said quickly, cutting off his wife as she opened her mouth.

"Why did you invent the harassment story?" I persisted, more for the record now.

"I wanted to hurt Padget for ruining my marriage. I thought that would do it. I know it was wrong, but I was real mad. Later, I realized what I'd done."

"Because we were about to prove you'd made the whole thing up?"

"No, no. Because it was wrong. I'm an emotional guy, and I can fly off the handle. You seen me do that. I'm not proud of it, but that's why we're here—to set things right."

Which brought Latour back to a concern of his from the start—and a major factor in determining Padget's fate. "Mrs. Bouch, when you and Brian Padget were together, was he ever in uniform?"

I gave her that much. Jan Bouch knew the relevance of the question, just as her husband did, and she beat him to the punch. As he began to answer, she said, "No" in a strong, clear voice. Her husband's look at her was like a promise of future pain.

Things followed predictably after that. Latour and I wrapped up the bureaucratic loose ends, asking a string of formulaic questions designed solely for the tape recorder, and brought the meeting to an end about ten minutes later. Through it all, I had one thought in mind, and as we all rose to our feet, the recorder back in my pocket,

I circled the table and stopped Norm Bouch as he placed his hand on the doorknob.

"I'd like a moment alone with your wife." I was standing close to him, close enough to smell his breath, and close enough for him to feel my physical advantage over him. While older by far, I was bigger than he was, and better trained to put that advantage to use—an implication he obviously considered in making his decision.

After a telling pause, he forced a smile, stepped back, and said, "Sure. Fine with me."

I escorted Jan Bouch upstairs to Latour's office, about the only place that ensured any privacy, and sat her down in one of his guest chairs.

I hitched one leg on the edge of his desk. "Jan, is there anything you'd like to add to what was said down there—privately?"

She stared at her lap and shook her head.

"Look at me."

She lifted her face, and I fixed her tired eyes with my own. "You are not in a good situation. You know that, right?"

"Yes." Her voice was barely audible.

"How're you going to deal with it?"

Her head tilted to one side. "I don't know. Same as always...I got to get back to my husband."

"Does he ever get rough with you?"

"No."

"I don't just mean physically, Jan. I mean mentally—emotionally."

Her face remained placid, but tears welled up in her eyes. "It's hard sometimes."

"You can do something about it. There are women who do nothing but take care of other women in your situation. They'll take you in, protect you, hide you if necessary, or at least guard your location from whoever's making you miserable until something legal can be done. And they'll do the same for your kids."

"I been told," she said in a near whisper.

"Don't you think now might be a good time to do that?"

"I love Norm."

"What about Brian?"

"He cares a lot."

I tried a different approach. "Maybe a small break then, like a vacation. These women do that, too—give you shelter and enough time to think calmly about things. I'm not saying you should leave Norm necessarily, but things are pretty tense right now. A little distance might be good."

She surprised me then. Instead of answering, she stood up and walked to the door, showing more resolve than I would have credited her with. "Thank you, Lieutenant. You've been very kind."

It was like a line from a bad Civil War movie, and the irony of it hung in the air long after she'd left the room.

It was a long afternoon. I returned to my office and had Harriet Fritter, the detective squad administrative assistant, transcribe the tapes I'd been accumulating. In the meantime, I wrote a long and detailed report of the investigation, up to the one remaining detail to be addressed before I was officially rid of it—the interview with Brian Padget.

I had heard of instances in which the interview of the accused never took place—ones in which the charges were so easily dismissed, no one saw the point—but this situation was a little different. While the reason I'd been called into service had in fact disappeared, the coming public circus made following the regulations a must.

In the end I needn't have worried. At four o'clock that afternoon, I received a call from Latour.

"Thought you'd like to hear Padget's results," he said immediately, his voice flat.

I didn't admit it, but the test had totally slipped from my mind. "Yeah. What came up?"

"The polygraph was inconclusive, but the urine was positive for cocaine...I can't believe it."

Public embarrassment was going to be the least of Brian Padget's problems. I glanced at the exonerating report on my desk. "You tell him yet?"

"I just found out."

It wasn't my problem, but I was in too deep by now to willingly let go. "You better head on down here. I'll set up a meeting with the State's Attorney."

8

Jack Derby was Windham County's State's Attorney—and Gail's boss. He was youthful for a man in his forties, slightly tweedy, favoring patches on his jacket elbows and horn-rimmed half-glasses he habitually shoved up on his forehead until they were needed for reading. He exuded a friendly warmth which had made mincemeat out of his frosty, domineering predecessor, whom he'd handily defeated in the last election.

But while pleasant to work with, cuddly he was not. Derby was practical, clear-sighted, and keenly aware of the prevailing winds. The latter were not currently forgiving of drug-tainted cops.

"Tell me about the phone call from the newspaper," he said.

Latour, Tony Brandt, and I were sitting in Derby's small office. Emile was staring at his hands, Tony was merely looking interested, since he was there at my suggestion but had no idea why.

Emile looked up at the question, his mouth slightly open. "Oh. It...I mean, I got a call from the editor, Stan Katz. He's not going to run anything immediately. He was looking for confirmation."

I kept my mouth shut. Stan Katz had entered journalism as a barracuda. The prior cops-'n'-courts reporter for the *Brattleboro Reformer,* he had become its editor after the employees bought the paper. The years had softened him somewhat, or at least taught him that a steady diet of other people's throats was bad for business. We'd even cooperated now and then. But I'd never forgotten his roots, and I doubted he had either.

Derby smiled at Emile indulgently. "What did Katz actually say?"

"That his source claimed he and Brian did coke regularly at Brian's house, up to night before last, and that if anyone wanted to confirm it, they'd find Brian's stash in a waterproof bag in the toilet tank, where no dogs could sniff it out."

"First place I'd look," Tony commented. "You'd think a cop would know that."

"Did the source say where Padget got the coke?" Derby asked.

"From him—that's why he called the paper—'cause Brian stiffed him on the last delivery. Said he didn't have the cash on him. Supposedly, that had happened once before, so now he was going to get even."

"Anything else?" Emile shook his head. "That was it."

Derby sighed. "Our hands are tied on this. Normally, pissing hot could get him suspended or fired without charges or fanfare, but given how we heard about this, I don't think we can tiptoe without getting clobbered. Katz wouldn't stand for it. Also, the BFPD should stay out of this—some other agency better get the search warrant."

Emile looked alarmed. "Will he be arrested?"

I spoke before Derby could. "Depends on what's found, but I wouldn't recommend it. If you cite him for arraignment instead, it could leave him free for weeks, which might give us enough time to find out what happened. Otherwise, we get judges and lawyers and all the rest in our hair. Would that work politically?"

This last comment was aimed at Derby, who merely shrugged.

"Like you said, it depends. In theory, I don't have a problem with it."

"Who did you see running the investigation, Jack?" I asked pointedly.

He looked surprised. "The State Police is the only option, isn't it? Or the drug task force?"

I shook my head and addressed Latour, noticing Tony roll his eyes, suddenly aware of why he'd been invited here. "Emile, how tight are Brian Padget and the sergeant you have assigned to the task force?"

Latour looked up, as if startled anyone would be asking him anything. "They're best friends."

"Great," Tony muttered. "I should've known."

I turned back to Derby. "Given the sensitivity, wouldn't that almost constitute a conflict of interest?"

"Close enough," he agreed, "which leaves the State Police."

"Who don't know the players, much less what they're up to."

"Joe—" Tony began, but I cut him off, still addressing Derby.

"I'd like to run this case. I've been in it from the start, our department has a vested interest, and I could hit the ground running, instead of wasting time briefing some other agency."

Derby had picked up on Tony's misgivings. "I don't know. Cutting out the task force makes sense. A Brattleboro officer running a Bellows

Falls criminal case is stretching it. The press would make it look like a bunch of local cops were bending the rules to hide something."

"Not if that local cop was working for the attorney general's office. That would make it look sanctified by God."

A stunned silence met my proposal, allowing me to explain. "I haven't just been running an internal on Brian Padget. Early on, I made a connection between Norm Bouch and Jasper Morgan, the young doper who mugged Lavoie and stole his gun early this summer. According to a woman I interviewed in Lawrence, who knew Morgan and Bouch a few years ago, Morgan is part of a drug network Bouch has established all across Vermont, mostly run by underage teenagers. Morgan was his local lieutenant, charged with establishing an organized local cell. Our own intelligence already knew about that part—we'd heard Morgan had made serious inroads into the regional market. That was the primary reason I wanted to talk to him the night he ran. The woman in Lawrence told me Bouch planned to establish similar cells all along both interstates, specifically in Brattleboro, Bellows Falls, where Bouch himself would presumably run the show, and in Barre and Burlington—all towns big enough to have a population of eager customers."

Derby was shaking his head slightly but still hadn't formulated a response. I headed him off with more. "If all that's true, and I have no reason to doubt it, we're talking about a case that touches down in at least three different counties, more if Bouch has reached beyond the towns I mentioned. That means a different State's Attorney for each county, with different staffs, different courts, and a growing crowd of interested parties all muscling each other for room at the front, none of which would change if the State Police were running the case. The attorney general's office, on the other hand, has jurisdiction over the whole state. It's got a huge staff by comparison to yours and several full-time investigators to help build a case. Not only that, but it specializes in public corruption cases, which by definition fits what we got to a T."

"And also shows off the biggest hole in your sales pitch," Tony said, a veteran of such jurisdictional shell games. "Our case concerns Brian Padget not Norm Bouch. It's Padget who pissed hot. All Bouch did was get angry at his wife's philandering and try to get even—and that's past history."

Derby was about to add his two cents when I held up both hands. "Okay, okay. Bear with me here. It's conjecture, but if we always had absolute proof from the start, we'd be out of business, right? First off, I messed up with the internal investigation. I went at it like I do with a regular case, with my eyes and ears working like vacuum cleaners. I should have gone in focusing only on whether the charges against Padget were true or not—period—but I didn't. As a result, I learned a lot more about the Bouches than I might have, along with a few of Norm's habits, the relevant one being his manipulation of women. The Lawrence woman I mentioned started out as Bouch's lover. Jasper Morgan, then a wet-nosed teenager, walked in on them by mistake one night. The woman's admittedly a little on the randy side, so she invited Jasper to jump in with them."

I was interrupted by the expected snorts of derision. "The point is," I pursued, "Bouch not only went along, he became Jasper's teacher. That's part of his appeal to these kids—there're no taboos. He's a natural at winning them over. He used this woman, who's not complaining, to turn Jasper into a crony. My feeling is that he's using his wife right now to compromise Padget, even though she's not too happy about it."

I paused a moment to let them protest, but to my surprise no one said a word. I was gaining, I hoped. "I'm not saying Padget and Jan Bouch maybe didn't fall for each other initially. Those things happen—she's young, pretty, unhappy; he's the right age, a Dudley Do-Right, and probably given to every young cop's urge to save the world. I think Norm's first reaction—to squeal on the affair to get Padget in trouble—was straight from the gut. He was pissed off. But with this new wrinkle, with Padget's urine coming up positive, especially after he volunteered for the test himself, I smell a rat, and I bet it's Norm Bouch. I don't know how, but I'd be willing to lay down money that Bouch is still involved in Padget's problems."

"Based on what?" Derby asked.

"Bouch's attitude, mostly. First, he's madder than hell—cheated on by his wife. He gets her to file a complaint against the boyfriend. The Bellows Falls sergeant who gets that call blows it off temporarily, already knowing what's really going on and hoping it'll take care of itself. That angers Norm even more. He calls Emile here and demands action, threatening God knows what. That's when Emile calls Tony, and I get the nod to do the internal. But they flub their story— Jan blows her lines, Norm scrambles to cover up, and by the time I get the chance to corner her all alone, he knows he's dropped the ball. Faced with a false accusation charge, he beats a fast retreat, says he invented the whole thing because he was angry, and begs forgiveness, which is granted."

I leaned forward in my chair to emphasize the next point. "But it was the way he did it that got my attention. He should've been shitting bricks when he walked in to retract everything he'd said. He was the one in trouble now. The BFPD could file against him, Padget could sue him for civil damages, and maybe more important to a man like Bouch, he could lose face—which is something teenagers pay a lot of attention to. And yet he was cocky as hell, could barely keep from laughing. At the time, I thought it was because he was about to turn the tables on us, putting the affair between his wife and Padget officially on record—a maneuver that still left Padget humiliated and in trouble with his boss, and pretty much pulled the teeth on any reprisal the department might have threatened. That's why I thought he was so pleased with himself. But as soon as I heard about the anonymous tip claiming Padget was a drug user, I knew Norm was still at work. The fact that the alleged corruption involved drugs, was aimed at Padget, and came right after Bouch's retraction, convinced me that Norm had to be lurking somewhere behind Padget's current problems."

I sat back, almost done. "Every instinct I have tells me that the Padget case will lead us to Norm Bouch. It might even be the only shot we get at Bouch, who's been clever and careful enough to operate without once getting his hands slapped, except," I emphasized for effect, "when it comes to women. The only time Emile's troops have ever gotten close to nailing Norm, it's been over a woman. Padget fooling around with Jan opened a wound in Bouch's pride, and Bouch has reacted accordingly. I'm hoping he's also shown us the one weak spot in his armor."

I fell silent, drained and slightly baffled at my own enthusiasm for a plan I had only half sketched out before sitting down at this meeting.

There was some shuffling by the others. Derby was the first to break the silence. "Tony? Could you spare him for this?"

"I don't think I'll have to. This ain't gonna fly."

"But if it did," Derby pushed.

"I guess. But we'd have to play up the Brattleboro connection to satisfy the powers-that-be. Otherwise, they're going to start saying I've got enough money to staff other departments."

The SA nodded. "I could help you there." He paused, still thinking hard. "I have to admit, I like the idea. Getting a bunch of SAs to cooperate on *any* case is like herding cats, and something like this could be even tougher, assuming the teenage cell concept is accurate. Also, having heard his pitch, I don't know who besides Joe could pull it off.

Giving this to another agency would be like asking a stranger to bring up someone else's problem child. I'd have to sell the AG's office on it, of course, but if this is as big as you think it is, they might like the smell of it. Everybody loves to make headlines."

He hesitated and then asked as an afterthought, "Sound okay to you, Emile?"

Latour looked up, his face pale. "Sure. Great."

Derby stood, forcing us all to join him. "All right, then. I'll take care of that end of things. Joe, you own this for the moment. Get the warrant, find out what else Brian Padget might have leaning on him, and keep your fingers crossed that all these connections really exist. If they don't, and all we end up with is a dirty cop, we're going to have to start blowing one serious political smokescreen."

Outside, in the SA's reception area, the three of us huddled briefly like survivors of a storm. I was still slightly in shock. Despite my years on the job, I'm perpetually stunned at how often critical decisions, in a world where multiple legal systems constantly overlap, boil down to a sales pitch overwhelming either precedent or logic.

"You think he can do it?" Latour asked.

Tony looked down at him from his considerable height. "Con the AG's office? Not without Joe's help." He jerked a thumb at me. "This is one grade-A bullshitter here."

Although my little campaign would undoubtedly be causing him problems down the line, Tony was obviously pleased. He loved stirring things up and never seemed happier than in a stampede of scrambling bureaucrats and/or politicians. It was one of the contradictory things that I thought ranked him among the truly gifted police chiefs.

Latour, by contrast, wasn't happy at all. "Bad enough I had Padget fooling around with a married woman. Now we'll be the center of a statewide drug investigation. Just what Bellows Falls needs. Every newspaperman who knows how to dial will be ringing my phone."

I patted him on the back. "Maybe not." But I had a feeling he was right. "If it all comes together, you can just forward the calls to the AG."

He shrugged and we dispersed, Tony and Emile heading for their respective offices, and I returning down the hallway to give Gail a quick visit. As I crossed her threshold, she was only half visible behind a row of paper columns, stacked side by side across her desk. "You look like you're preparing for an assault." She peered over the top and gave me a weary smile. "Or being buried alive. How'd things go with Jack?"

I didn't bother asking how she knew about the meeting. In the essentially rural world of Vermont, you got used to people knowing what you were doing even before you did it. "Surprisingly well. He bought my proposal to turn a single cop's positive urine test into an AG-sanctioned, statewide investigation, with me on board."

She rolled her eyes. "God—has he got a lot to learn."

I sat on her windowsill, enjoying the contrast of the sun on my back and the central air-conditioning on my face. "I thought maybe he'd grab this for himself."

"Crooked cop cases are usually political land mines, and our boy is new yet," she said, still sorting through her files. "He just needs to be consistent right now. Not that I'm complaining. The whole staff would've been sucked into this if it got messy." She waved a hand at her workload. "This would've looked like peanuts in comparison."

She sat back suddenly and looked at me thoughtfully. "I am curious, though. Why step over the drug task force, the Vermont State Police, and the Association of State's Attorneys to go to the AG?"

For the next ten minutes, I repeated the pitch I'd just delivered up the hall.

She smiled at the end of it. "Nice snow job. It still doesn't answer the real question."

She didn't elaborate, or need to. "Why me?" I hesitated before continuing. It was a good point, one I'd rationalized to Derby in procedural terms, but which I hadn't owned up to emotionally.

"I'm not exactly sure yet," I answered slowly. "Something clicked when I saw Jan Bouch surrounded by those kids in their kitchen. It was cute on the face of it—all of them clamoring for doughnuts she was holding up high. But she wasn't having fun. She was at a loss. She couldn't sort out how to handle it. And then Norm came in, and grabbed the box and threw it outside like he was distracting a pack of dogs."

I paused again, trying to string thoughts together so they made sense. "Jasper Morgan plays into this, too. When he escaped, raising all that ruckus for no apparent reason, it bugged the hell out of me. Now that he's resurfaced, and in connection to Bouch, and there's a cop in the middle who may or may not be dirty...I just don't want to walk away from it. I want to find out what's going on. There's something inside me that needs this settled."

I'd been staring at the carpet through all this, speaking as much to myself as to Gail, and now shook my head and looked up at her. "You glad you asked?"

Her answer surprised me. "You really think Bouch's network extends that far?" she asked.

"Yes, but I better come up with some proof. The AG'll take a couple of days making a decision—listening to Derby, reading through the files, brainstorming with his Criminal Division people. It would help if I dug up a small nugget in the meantime."

I could tell I'd triggered some underlying notion with my ramblings, but apparently she wasn't ready to share it. She leaned for-ward instead, kissed me on the cheek, and said, "We better get cracking, then."

I didn't ask, but I wondered what she meant by "we."

9

Brian Padget's house looked different to me on my second visit. The concern for appearances that had struck me the first time now seemed violated by the official vehicles parked in his yard. I had asked Latour to be on hand to keep me company, and his car combined with mine threw suspicions on the house's seeming propriety.

I had also brought two of my own squad to help me. J.P. Tyler, our thin, diminutive forensics expert, and Willy Kunkle, whose withered left arm and infamous bad attitude had made him a statewide law enforcement legend.

Disabled by a sniper years ago, Kunkle had been let go, to much shared relief. But in a move most of my friends, including Gail, had considered a clear sign of dementia, I'd encouraged him to sue the department under the disabilities act and get his job back. He'd never thanked me for that show of faith, and he'd been no easier to work with afterwards, but I'd never rued the decision. For all his temperamental, unorthodox, insubordinate ways, Willy Kunkle was driven to be a cop, and while there were times everyone felt like strangling him, I knew he would get me results regardless of challenge or sacrifice. Unlike any of my other officers, Kunkle came from that slice of society that gave us most of our business—a fact that fueled him with a passion the rest of us would never share.

Tyler, by contrast, fit the scientific stereotype—scholarly, quiet, self-effacing, but also highly efficient. He alone from my squad seemed unaffected by Kunkle's manner, and perhaps for that reason Kunkle rarely gave him a hard time.

We'd all arrived without fanfare. Nevertheless, the house's front door opened before I was halfway across the lawn, revealing a broad-shouldered, medium-built young man with the short buzz cut so popular among younger male officers—an affectation I personally believed served no other function than to further alienate us from the public we were supposed to assist.

The look on his face was hard to read. In its various parts I could see surprise, anger, defeat, even disappointment. Overall, however, I was struck by a sense of fatalism, as if our arrival had been anticipated for a long time.

"Brian Padget?" I said as I approached, followed by the others.

"I'm Lieutenant Joe Gunther, of the Brattleboro Police Department. I have a warrant to search your home for illicit drugs."

A small crease appeared in the middle of his forehead as he stepped to one side of the open door. "I heard you were doing the internal."

"That's right. This is different." I turned to introduce Kunkle and Tyler. Everyone nodded awkwardly in greeting. Emile Latour hovered in the background, waiting until we'd actually entered the building.

"It's okay," Latour said from where he stood. No one looked at him, and the meaninglessness of his words floated in the air like a pall.

We crossed the threshold and split up. The warrant specified the toilet tank, or any other likely hiding place, so I went to the bathroom first, hoping to settle the issue quickly. The search would be thorough in any case, but at least the suspense would end if I found what we were after. Latour kept Padget company in the living room.

The discovery was anticlimactic. I found the bathroom between the one bedroom and the central hall, went straight to the tank, lifted its lid, and immediately saw the plastic bag in its depths, weighted down by a stone.

Tyler appeared with a small evidence kit and, wearing gloves, extracted the bag, opened it, tested its powdery contents in a small vial, and quietly announced them to contain cocaine.

"How much, do you think?" I asked him.

He knew what I was after. "It's a felony possession, Joe. Way over two and a half grams."

I left him and Willy to finish the job and returned to the living room, carrying the bag in a second plastic envelope Tyler had supplied. Padget and Latour were standing awkwardly by the window, each one silently looking in opposite directions. As I approached, Latour moved off.

I showed Padget the bag. "Recognize this?"

"No."

"It was hidden in your toilet tank. It's cocaine."

He pursed his lips. "It's bullshit. I don't know anything about it."

"We were told by a source that you're a regular user of the stuff."

"He's full of crap."

"I didn't say it was a man."

His eyes widened slightly. "Then she's full of crap."

I hefted the bag in my hand. "Listen carefully. This is a felony amount. If we stick you with it, and we're nine-tenths there, you're looking at the end of a career and jail time both. Your only way out is to come up with an explanation that'll clear you. That does not include repeating that you're innocent. Do you hear what I'm saying?"

Padget lifted both hands, palms up. "I don't know what else *to* tell you. I don't know anything about that stuff."

I took his elbow and sat him on the couch, perching myself on the coffee table opposite him, so our knees were almost touching. "You tested positive for coke, your polygraph came up zero, and now this. If you don't know anything about how all that happened, you better think of someone who does."

Fear and longing were all I could read in his face now. He was hunched forward, his hands between his knees, the paleness of his face harshly contrasting with a mild case of acne. His forehead was damp. "There is nobody else."

"What about the reason I was brought up here in the first place?"

He looked shocked at the mere suggestion. "Jan? She'd never do that."

"How 'bout her husband?"

His mouth partly opened, but what he said reflected how distracted he was. "Why did I come up positive?"

The incredulity in his voice was palpable—and believable—but I needed to keep him on track. "Who have you had over here lately? Jan?"

He blinked a couple of times. "No. My neighbors are almost in my face they live so close. We thought it was too risky."

I remembered how Anne Murphy had spotted them making out in an alleyway. They could have spared themselves the discomfort. "Where did you meet, then?"

"Cars, back streets, the woods, a motel room a couple of times. It was always real quick. We were scared we'd get caught."

"So you haven't had anybody here, in this house?"

"No, not really."

"What's that mean?"

"My parents stayed over once, and Emily's been here to pick me up when my car was in the shop."

"That's Emily Doyle, from your department?" He nodded dumbly.

"How long ago was that?"

"A couple of weeks."

"What was wrong with the car?"

"It was running rough. The garage guy said he found water in the gas, so he cleaned it out and tightened a hose fitting."

"When Emily came over, did she wait outside?"

"Not always."

"Did she ever use the bathroom?"

Padget sat back as if I'd pushed him, and stared at me as if I'd lost my mind. "Emily? No fucking way."

I answered him angrily. "Keep your eye on the ball, Padget. You're the guy with a one-way ticket to jail right now. The more you tell me what saints all your friends are, the more you look like a total chump. If you've been screwed, then somebody did the screwing. Remember who filed the sexual harassment claim against you?"

He flushed. "She was forced to by her husband."

"Would you let someone force you to get a friend fired from his job?"

He shook his head as if trying to ward me off. "He's got her under his thumb."

"What did she tell you about him?"

"Just that she wanted to be free of him. That she felt she couldn't breathe when he was around. She wanted to be with me—to run away."

I could almost hear the words in Jan's own voice, and see her face as she uttered them—pleading, desperate, clinging. They were clichés common to those who knew they carried no weight. "Did she tell you he dealt drugs?"

"Not directly. I didn't ask and she didn't say. She wanted our time together to be free of him. But I knew he did. Everybody knows. We were all dying for him to make a single mistake so we could nail him."

"Didn't it cross your mind you were sleeping with the best witness against him?" I asked harshly.

It was a mistake, of course. I was too far from his age to remember what that kind of love demanded of a person—how stupid it could make you.

He gave me a pitying look. "I wouldn't do that."

I'd blown it already, but I tried one last time. "Brian. Not everybody treats friendship the way you do."

He stood up, almost knocking me over, and retreated to the window. His frustration made him throw out his arms and shout. "I'm not a kid, okay? I know there're assholes out there. I deal with them all the time. I'm good at my job and I know how to read people, so don't give me a lecture. I don't know how the fuck that shit got in here, or in me, but I didn't have anything to do with it. Norm Bouch is who you want, not Emily or Jan. Norm Bouch has been giving us the finger since the day he hit town."

He stopped abruptly and looked around wildly for a moment. Latour, who'd been leaning against the open door, suddenly straightened and stated Brian's name.

I rose to my feet as Padget slowly settled down on his own. Both Willy and J.P. appeared from the back of the house. I glanced at them inquiringly. Both shook their heads.

"Okay, Brian," I said. "I'll leave you alone. We'll finish up here as quick as we can. You're not under arrest, since I'm assuming you'll stay put, but you'll be cited to appear for arraignment on this." I waved the bag of coke in the air. "If you can afford a lawyer, you better get one, otherwise the court will appoint a public defender. It's up to your chief to decide whether your suspension will be with or without pay."

I moved toward the door, feeling a sudden need for fresh air, stifled by my own officiousness. But I paused on the threshold. "You might line up a mental health counselor, too. The shit is going to hit the fan on this—no way around it—and you're going to feel like you're the only guy on the face of the earth before it's done. You better figure out how to deal with it. And for Christ's sake, once you've cleared the fog from your head, think about who might've done this to you. I'll do the best I can, but I'm going to need all the help I can get."

"You okay?"

I took my eyes off the star-filled skylight over our bed and looked in Gail's direction. Her hand appeared from under the covers and stroked my cheek. "You've been lying that way for over an hour."

"Sorry. Didn't mean to wake you. Can't turn my brain off."

"The case?"

"And the people in it. Along with a few thousand others I've dealt with over the years. Old ghosts ganging up, I guess."

Gail shifted around and slipped her arm across my chest. I could hear the clinical neutrality in her voice as she gently prodded. "Are they saying anything that makes sense?"

I laughed to set her at ease. "Yes, doctor. They all agree I'm going nuts."

She didn't laugh with me. "Are you?"

I moved my own arm around to cradle her head, embarrassed at trying to put her off. We'd been through a lot together. She deserved honesty when she asked for it. "No. I'm just piling on the baggage with this one. I don't know if it's a critical-mass problem or just these particular people, but I'm feeling more and more weighed down by what I'm finding."

"Like what?"

"Name it: teenage mothers on coke, a young boy in a ménage à trois, a cop probably being set up by his addict lover, a guy using kids to run a drug ring. Things're looking pretty bleak..."

"You've been wading through the dregs for decades, Joe. Some of it's got to stick."

She was right, of course. It began sticking the first year—but dealing with it was a rite of passage. Routine. From the angry, out-of-town motorist cursing your small-town rules, to the fading glance of a drug-dazed, pregnant girl who'd just slashed her wrists to get some sleep, you took it in stride. It became a spectacle occurring beyond a thick pane of glass.

In fact, I'd been noticing the accumulation of all this before I'd been asked to go to Bellows Falls. It had been catching up to me like old age itself. But it took working in that town to bring it into focus. Brattleboro was a part of me, and I'd grown to overlook what I chose to. Bellows Falls was uncharted territory, and I didn't know the shoals well enough to avoid them. Jan Bouch, Emile Latour, Anne Murphy, Eric Shippee, Emily Doyle, and my own lamb-to-slaughter Brian Padget had all come too close, sharply revealed in their despair. I'd been caught by the exhaustion, the bitterness, and the suspicion I'd been avoiding.

What was keeping me awake was the effort to recall something other than all that misery. Even the woman lying next to me was in this house we shared because a brutal rape had forced her to change her life. I had to reach back to my youth on a farm, halfway up the state, to recall a time when most of the faces around me were smiling and unfettered by turmoil.

I glanced over at Gail, to see if she was still expecting me to explain what I couldn't. Thankfully, her steady, even breathing answered for her and let me off the hook. I was once again free to peruse my catalogue of lost faces in solitude.

10

Sammie Martens looked up as I approached her desk the following morning. "You look terrible."

"You should be a doctor. What did you find out about the towns Amy Sorvino mentioned? Any Oliver Twist–style teenage gangs on the loose?"

"Burlington is a definite hit, and Kunkle's been snooping around our own backyard, trying to find out what Jasper Morgan might've been up to. You ought to talk to him. Barre I got a lukewarm—there're kids into drugs, but the PD had no sense they were more organized than usual."

"Tell me about Burlington."

"I contacted Audrey McGowen—we went to the Academy together. She checked with the juvie crime squad, who said that in general, they haven't seen any changes. There are a tiny number of kids that seem vaguely interconnected, but it's fluid, they come and go like hourly workers at a fast-food joint. And when they do bust one on possession, they can't find where the drugs came from or where they're headed—the kids pick it up and drop it off but don't make contact with buyer or seller. That's the structured part the PD noticed, 'cause it's so consistent. Surveillance might crack it open, but who's got the money, especially with so little to go on? And if all they get is a bunch of kids, the busts won't justify the overhead."

"Which Bouch knew from the start," I said softly.

Sammie nodded. "He also knows to keep it small. The numbers Audrey gave me didn't come to more'n six kids, max. 'Course, who knows? And the profit margin's huge. She told me a ten-dollar bag of coke in New York'll bring you thirty-five in Burlington. They're hungry up there."

"Did she know Norm Bouch by name?"

Sammie smiled broadly. "Yeah, and it's from an interesting angle. They've got a special unit up there—some sort of multi-jurisdictional thing…"

"CUSI," I said. "Chittenden Unit for Special Investigations. I thought that was mostly sex-related crimes."

"Exactly. That's where Bouch's name popped up on her screen. It's a little dated now—a few years at least. But his interest in minors made him a natural for them. They never caught him abusing kids or anything, but they talked to juvies who knew him well—like you were telling us about those Bellows Falls kids, he was a Pied Piper. Keep in mind, though," she emphasized, "I got the clear impression Audrey wasn't blown away by any of this. Bouch is small potatoes—one name out of thousands they have on file, and an old one at that."

I rose to my feet. "I don't mind that. I'd just as soon have this whole thing run low-key. The fewer people get interested in it, the more likely it is we get the nod to run the case for the AG. If Norm Bouch was seen as a big deal, we'd have DEA, the task force, and everybody else wanting to grab some of the action. We'll probably get a little of that anyhow. Drug busts make for happy voters and keep the grant money flowing."

Sammie stopped me as I was about to leave. "That reminds me—I got something else you might like. You must've tickled Phil Marchese's fancy, 'cause he did some poking around after you left Lawrence. Norm Bouch's NCIC records I think you already know about…" she quickly checked her notes. "DWI, check fraud, two misdemeanor possessions, and a first-degree unlawful dealing with a child, for selling beer to a bunch of minors. What doesn't appear, 'cause it was supposed to stay off the books, was that Bouch participated in a special program the Lawrence PD and the local parole board had going under a short-term federal grant. It wasn't therapy, so there's no patient confidentiality to worry about, but it involved psychologists trying to find out what makes the bad guys tick when they're out on the street, instead of when they're in jail. It was like a big brother program of sorts—or big sister in this case. It folded fast, of course—you can pick your reasons why—but Marchese found a woman named Molly Bremmer who dealt with Bouch for several months. He said she'd be willing to talk to you." She gave me Bremmer's name and number on a slip of paper.

I looked at it appreciatively. "Nice work, Sam." I hesitated a moment before adding, "Do me another favor, would you? This is off the record, so be discreet, but I'd like to find out about a Bellows Falls policewoman named Emily Doyle—as much personal information as you can find. She wasn't too thrilled to talk to me when I asked her about Padget, and I found out last night she was in a position to plant that dope at his place. I have no reason to suspect her of anything, but I am curious. When I talk to her, I'd like to know more about her than she thinks I do."

Sammie wasn't too thrilled but nodded her assent.

Harriet Fritter handed me the newspaper as I walked toward my office. "Front page," she said. "You'll find it interesting."

I took the paper and sat down at my desk. "Bellows Falls Police Officer Suspended on Drug Charge," read the headline. In smaller type underneath it continued, "Chief promises thorough investigation."

I sighed deeply. It hadn't taken long for the carnival to begin. The only good news was that since I was hearing of it just now, apparently no one had given the paper my name. I began to read carefully, hoping I was correct.

For most of its length, the article toed the line, outlining how police, acting on a tip given them through the *Reformer*, had secured a search warrant for the home of Officer Brian Padget, of the BFPD, and had discovered "several" grams of what was believed to be cocaine. Padget, who had earlier tested positive for drugs in a urine analysis, was unavailable for comment and was said to be on paid suspension while awaiting arraignment. That much was pretty mundane, although I wondered at the speed with which the paper had secured its information. The answer to that was supplied on the last page, where the article concluded, "Holding a brief press conference with Town Manager Eric Shippee, Bellows Falls Police Chief Emile Latour told reporters last night, 'We will nip this thing in the bud. There will be no dirty cops tolerated on the force. The public can expect a full and speedy accounting for this whole sorry affair.'"

I reached for the phone and called Greg Davis at his home, knowing his shift didn't start until the afternoon. "Davis," he answered on the first ring.

"It's Joe Gunther. How're the troops holding up?"

He didn't hesitate, which I hoped was a sign of trust. "Considering our fearless leader has just tried and convicted one of our own without a jury, I guess they're doing okay."

"I was afraid of that."

"Can you blame them?" he asked. "You didn't have anything to do with it, did you?"

"The press conference? No way. You know I led the search, though."
"Yeah. I can't believe this."
"How's Emily Doyle taking it?" I asked.
There was a cautious silence at the other end.
"I know she likes him," I added as explanation. "She was madder than hell at me for doing the internal."
"She's taking it hard," he said simply. "But she's not alone. You might've seen Brian as Latour's pet, but everybody liked him. He was one of the guys. The double whammy of his maybe being dirty and the Old Man throwing him to the wolves so fast has everyone pretty confused."
"And angry?"
"Yeah," Davis admitted. "And beginning to split into pro-Brians and anti-Brians, with the antis winning. That's the dark side to Brian's good standing with the chief—if Latour throws him out, the troops will too. You better know there's a lot of anti-Joe Gunther in there, too."
That came as no surprise. "What was Shippee's role in calling the press conference?"
"I don't know—he couldn't've found out about the dope that quick unless Latour made a beeline to his office. I don't much care about that part, to be honest. I'm standing between Captain Bligh and a seriously pissed-off crew all of a sudden. So I just wish to hell they'd *both* kept their mouths shut."
We chatted a few minutes longer, mostly to allow him to vent some more steam. I sympathized with his position. A police organization is heavily hierarchical and leans on the conservative notion that rank begets fealty—Davis's constant reference to Latour as the Old Man was an example of that. To have a father figure turn his back at the slightest show of adversity was serious cause for the jitters. Cops were isolated enough in society without being sabotaged from within.
It was that very isolation, however, that brought me back to something I'd sensed lurking in the background. "I hate to ask, Greg, but was there ever anything between Emily and Brian?"
"Yeah," he conceded reluctantly. "They had a thing early on. Puppy love in uniform was how I described it to my wife. It's pretty common, especially with more women joining up—you think you have so much in common just because you're both throwing drunks into jail. It didn't last long and she took it pretty hard."
"How long ago?"

"Oh, hell. Six months, more or less. She hadn't been with us for long. I suppose you're going to be asking a lot of questions like that, aren't you?"

"If I end up in charge of the case. I'll try to wear kid gloves, but if I'm going to start with the presumption of innocence, it means I'll be looking to pin the tail on some other donkey. With all your boys and girls wondering what flag to rally around, they better keep that in mind."

"I hear you," he said. "I'll try to prepare them for the rough spots."

11

I met with Molly Bremmer at the Howard Johnson's in Greenfield, Massachusetts, partway between Brattleboro and Lawrence. That arrangement was at her suggestion, and I appreciated the gesture. Before I left town, I'd received a call from Jack Derby, telling me he was meeting with the attorney general's office early that afternoon, and that if I wanted my ambitions turned into reality, I'd better show up to make the best presentation of my life. I was keeping my fingers crossed that Bremmer might supply me with a little extra ammunition.

Marchese had told her some of what I was up to, and on the phone I'd answered several questions she'd formulated as a result. She'd said she would make a few calls and check some files but wanted to tell me what she found in person. Her enthusiasm, I sensed, had been stoked by Marchese's own, which had less to do with me than with his fondness for Sammie Martens. It was a refreshingly human insight on how police work often gets done, or even why in some cases.

Molly Bremmer was middle-aged, stocky, and appeared faintly doddering until I saw her eyes. They, like her hair, were iron gray and spoke of a woman who was used to standing her own ground. We greeted one another in the parking lot and entered together to find a small table, far from anyone else, near a window looking out onto the traffic.

After ordering coffee from the waitress, Bremmer placed a pair of reading glasses low on her nose, and extracted a yellow legal pad from her briefcase. "Norman Bouch, the gentleman-thief," she said with a smile, and looked over her glasses at me. "What did you want to know?"

"Charmed you, did he?"

The smile only widened. "He tried. I merely observed. I think he's more successful further down the food chain. I interacted with him over a long enough period that he finally stowed the bullshit and opened up a little, although not enough to spill any beans. He was a man with a plan, and a do-gooder like me was purely a bureaucratic necessity he had to deal with before moving on."

"So he didn't divulge the plan?"

"No, he's arrogant and a showoff, but he's far from stupid. There are elements of the chess player in him, minus the patience. Still, I'd say it probably involved kids and abused or vulnerable women. Those are his specialties. That's not necessarily a sexual scenario, by the way—he just needs to dominate those around him. The charm is part of that, practiced on those he can't actually control. If you can't win 'em, woo 'em."

That sounded right, from what I'd seen. "What did you mean by a 'sexual scenario?'"

"Personality disorders of this type often have a sexual basis, but I don't think there's any of that here—not with the children at least. Women are another matter. But I never picked up on a single pedophilic marker. Norm just needs the dependency. It's one of those paradoxical signs of insecurity. In a weird kind of way, you could describe him as a typical co-dependent."

"Did you always meet Norm in your office?" I asked.

"No. The point of the program was to send us out into the subject's habitat. It was supposed to make them feel more at home, and allow us to see them functioning among their peers. On that level, it worked quite well. After some initial discomfort—shared by both sides—" she added with a smile, "they loosened up enough that we collected some peripheral data. Nothing of much value, however, which is why the whole thing collapsed. No one figured out that the only people who'd agree to participate would be self-servers like Norm. Maybe they thought a bank robber would invite a shrink along on a heist, purely as an observer...Still, the money was good and the experience personally valuable."

"Did Norm get chummy enough to introduce you around?"

"Oh, he played it up. I was his personal show horse, after all."

"What was he up to at the time?"

"Technically, he was a garage mechanic. Psychologically, he was an empire builder. When he looked in the mirror, he saw a leader. His only problem was finding an army who'd follow. That's where the kids and women came in."

"Was someone named Jasper Morgan one of the kids?"

She laughed. "Not even a remote chance I'd remember that, probably not even if you waltzed him in right now. I met a great many people, but in this instance my only focus was Norm."

I thought a moment. "I told you on the phone we think Norm has created that army, as you put it. My guess is he compartmentalized it into cells so it won't fall over like a row of dominoes. He has lieutenants in different towns, empowered to hire and fire on their own. It gives them autonomy and a sense of authority and makes it harder for us to track the scheme from one end to the other."

She was shaking her head slightly. "What I've been dancing around with my psycho-jargon is that Norm Bouch is a control freak. What you describe may be correct in part—the complexity of the structure reflects the man's intelligence, and I'm sure he makes his lieutenants *feel* powerful, but don't believe for a moment that he trusts anyone with autonomy. Whatever it is you're facing up there in Vermont, he's pulling the strings. You should be able to backtrack everything to him in the long run, like pulling the right loose thread. It might just take some doing, that's all."

I described the sexual harassment case that had brought me to Bellows Falls, explaining how I thought Brian Padget's subsequent troubles were based partly on Norm's irritation at having his first scheme ruined by me.

Molly Bremmer shrugged. "We all make mistakes. It could be he misjudged the harassment angle, but I'd be cautious if I were you. Remember that Norm likes to show off—to himself if to no one else, somewhat like masturbation. Your Bellows Falls officer being saddled with a drug charge may have been a back-up plan—it could also have been in the works from the start."

That possibility solved some timing problems. If Padget had been framed only after the sexual harassment charge had collapsed, Bouch hadn't had much time to put it together. Bremmer's suggestion seemed more likely and made me realize just how devious an opponent Norm might be.

Assuming Brian had been framed at all.

I was having a hard time seeing him as a drug user—much less a dealer—but the young cop's own cocaine-tainted urine couldn't just be ignored. Until I could explain it, any theories that he was set up weren't going to be very convincing.

I returned to something Bremmer had mentioned earlier. "You said you met a great many people when you were hanging out with Bouch. Were there any from Vermont?"

She again consulted her notes. "Yes. There was a young man named Lenny. I only took note of him because he was such a standout. He was slightly older than some of the others and more like Norm in his personality, which struck me as an anomaly. Norm's standard choice was the submissive type, not somebody who might stand up to him. It was the one instance where I sensed a genuine friendship holding sway over Norm's usual controlling pattern."

"No last name?" I asked.

She shook her head. "No, I only knew he was from Vermont because he called Burlington home. I sensed he was traveling to and from there to meet Norm in Lawrence."

"If I ever found a picture of this Lenny, would you recognize him?"

"Maybe. I saw him several times. It was always a social setting. I don't know what business they might have been cooking up, or even how they met in the first place, but he became a familiar face."

The tip about Lenny was hopeful—maybe. It certainly echoed what Amy Sorvino had said about Burlington and the relationship Bouch had reputedly had with Jasper Morgan. But it didn't give me anything additional to win over the AG's office. I was still, as Tony had said, totally reliant on my abilities as a bullshitter.

Disappointed, I paid for the coffee and escorted Molly Bremmer to her car, thanking her for all her help.

As I was closing the door after she'd slid in behind the wheel, however, I suddenly asked, "Given Norm's personality, is it likely his wife could've been fooling around without his knowing it?"

Her eyes widened in surprise. "My professional opinion, without knowing the wife? I'd not only say it was unlikely, but that if she was, Norm probably had a hand in it. As a manipulator, it would've been right up his alley."

I arrived back at the office fifteen minutes before my scheduled meeting with the attorney general's envoy, underwhelmed at my prospects. If my pitch to Derby had worked, as Gail had pointed out, because he'd wanted to avoid a potentially messy, labor-intensive case, it stood to reason the AG might reject me for the exact same reasons. What I'd learned since had sounded encouraging to me, but I doubted someone with a tight budget and a limited vested interest would be similarly impressed.

Sammie Martens walked briskly into my office as I was pondering my strategy, a notepad in her hand. "You got a second?"

"Just that."

"I started looking into Emily Doyle—just public access stuff, no official fingerprints—and I came up with something pretty interesting. She's from Burlington originally."

I raised my eyebrows noncommittally, but she'd grabbed my attention.

"Not only that, but when she was there, she lived in an apartment on North Street, just a few doors down from where Norm Bouch still has a place."

"Any indication they knew each other?"

"Not so far." Her smile betrayed an ambition to clear that up soon.

"How'd you find out Bouch had an address in Burlington?"

She laughed. "I called Information. He's listed. Then I got hold of public records. He's been renting for about three years."

I shook my head in wonder at how often, with our growing dependence on high-tech communications and sophisticated information gathering, we simply forgot about things like phone books. "Nice, Sam. I guess you better go town by town and see if he pops up anywhere else while you're at it."

"I got something on Jasper Morgan, too," she said as I checked my watch. "I asked Willy to snoop around Morgan's neighborhood, see if anyone had gotten more chatty now that things have cooled off. Turns out Jasper'd gotten a little cocky just before he disappeared, and maybe a little greedy. Word is he was starting to look over his shoulder. This was just before he entered the Retreat incognito, which makes me think maybe we weren't the ones he was hiding from."

"And that maybe he ran from us," I finished, "because our flushing him out turned him into a sitting duck for someone else."

"Sounds good."

I patted her on the back as I left the office. "It's been a pleasure talking with you, Sammie. I'll give the AG your regards."

The AG was personified in this case by a tall, dark-haired, tough-minded woman named Kathleen Bartlett, who for the past five years had headed the Criminal Division. The AG in Vermont was similar to the county-based State's Attorneys in terms of power, but unlike them, he had greater jurisdictional reign. Also, since his office wasn't split among fourteen counties, his staff was proportionally more impressive. For example, for all the SAs in Vermont, there were two investigators, one of them part-time. In Bartlett's division alone, there were five.

I had known Kathy Bartlett since her fledgling days as a county prosecutor and had always admired her no-nonsense, apolitical pragmatism—traits I wished were more commonplace within law enforcement. After shaking hands all around—Latour, Brandt, and Derby were also in attendance—she didn't disappoint me by dwelling on the amenities.

"Jack's briefed me on your proposal, Joe, and I've read what files he and Tony could scratch together. I won't deny I'm interested, and I even agree with some of your arguments—the risk of conflict by involving the drug task force, for example, although I know they won't like it—but I'm not convinced we're the right office for this. As things stand, people could legitimately claim you're either on a vendetta for Lavoie having his gun stolen or just on an ego trip."

"Jasper Morgan may've started this case," I began, "but since then, we've come up with Norm and Jan Bouch, Brian Padget and Emily Doyle of the BFPD, and even someone named Lenny who lives in Burlington, knew Bouch in Lawrence, and who well might be running things for him in Burlington.

"And the connections are still growing. I recently found out Doyle and Padget were once an item, before Padget fell for Jan Bouch, and that Doyle used to live in Burlington, just a few doors down from an apartment rented by Norm Bouch.

"I also just got word Jasper Morgan's old neighborhood pals are starting to think he got whacked by his boss for sticky fingers. If that's true—and it fits why Jasper was so desperate to disappear—then it certainly involves the Bratt PD in more than a simple gun theft, and it gives me a leg up as the investigator since I'm already looking into the guy we're all supposing is the boss in question."

I paused, but only briefly, for any objections. "Last but not least," I went on, "is the timing and cost effectiveness. The timing hinges on the arraignment date for Brian Padget—it would be nice to have a better idea of his guilt or innocence before he faces a judge. The cost effectiveness is that since this case plays to Brattleboro's self-interest, among others, I'll be working on salary, doing most of the legwork, without calling on too many of the AG's resources. If and when I dig up enough to fully whet your appetite, then you can jump in with little lost up front."

Bartlett frowned at that. "If we're in, we're in. We won't rubber-stamp an operation just so you can run all over the state like the Lone Ranger. I'll buddy you up with one of my guys, and I'll be expecting daily updates."

"I realize that," I countered, pleased by that show of acceptance.

"This deal would merely give you an extra investigator instead of costing you one. You'd call the shots."

She seemed mollified by that. "Jack was telling me the primary reason to exclude the State Police was both your passion for the case and your already considerable knowledge. I have to admit I agree, and the arraignment does make the timing important. Emily Doyle worries me, though. What do you think's going on there?"

"Any number of things. She could've planted the dope in Brian's home because she was pissed off at him for dumping her; she might've done it because she's in cahoots with Bouch, and Bouch saw her as the easiest way to plant the stuff; or she may be an entirely innocent victim of circumstance and coincidence."

"Which we're trained to mistrust," Tony added.

"Why are you so convinced Brian Padget was framed, especially when his own urine says otherwise?" Bartlett asked suddenly.

"I'm not," I answered. "But I do think the urine is the only solid thing against him, which is unusual."

For the first time, Latour made his presence felt, with a small, enigmatic grunt.

"The dope in the toilet speaks for itself," I explained. "It may be exactly what it appears to be, or just as easily be a plant. The involvement with a dope dealer's wife straddles the same fence. He may have been trying to lure her onto the straight and narrow, and she—with or without her husband's involvement—may have been setting him up. What sticks in my craw is the guy who squealed on Padget to the paper. He said he was pissed off because Padget hadn't paid him for drugs, not once but twice. He also said they'd done drugs together the night before he made the phone call. Now, that sounds pretty screwy to me—you don't do drugs with someone who just stiffed you on the payment. My bet is Bouch was the caller, hoping to use us to nail Padget's hide to the wall."

In the silence that followed, Kathleen Bartlett took us all in for a long moment before finally nodding her head. "All right, I'll sign off on it. I'll have to fly it by the boss, and explain things to the VSP and the head of the task force, but I'm willing to give it a shot. It would be nice to clear a cop or two, jail a bad guy, stop a source of drugs coming into the state, and protect a few teenagers all in one swoop—assuming any of this pans out."

Her last comment didn't go unnoticed, but like people circling an unexploded bomb, we all gave it a wide berth and made plans for how to structure the investigation, covering our doubts with a slightly strained optimism.

It was only then I began wondering how much of my neck I'd stuck out. Worst-case scenario, it was possible I'd chosen to deal with job-related weariness and ambivalence by committing professional suicide.

12

I met with Kathleen Bartlett again the next day in Montpelier, on the second floor of the Pavilion Building, an ornate, Georgian-influenced red brick and white-trim monstrosity with two deep wooden balconies and a broad set of porch steps that reached out to State Street like a bridge spanning a moat. Ironically, I had to circle the block to reach the AG's offices in a modern addition far to the rear. Where I ended up was disappointingly familiar—a huge room divided into partitioned cubicles, with tasteful fluorescent strips overhead and the continual chirping of tinny, distant phones in the air. There was the usual row of windowed offices corralling it all, from where the privileged few could soak in the sun or call for coffee and assistance from those occupying the wasteland to the interior.

The summons to come here, befitting the summoner, had been pleasant but crisp. Bartlett's boss had taken the bait, as she put it, so time was officially wasting. I was to pack a bag for a visit of unknown duration and get on the road ASAP.

I had no complaint with that, and not just because she was right about the time. Given the vagueness of most of the allegations I'd parlayed into a hypothetical case, I needed something solid to put my hands on.

Kathy Bartlett met me at the reception desk and escorted me down one side of the central room, eventually ushering me across the threshold of an office near the back wall. "I thought I'd start by introducing you to your partner, since the two of you will be joined at the hip from now on."

As we entered, a tall, thin man wearing old-fashioned granny glasses rose from a small conference table in the middle of the room and approached us, his hand stuck out in greeting.

"I'll be damned," I said. "Jonathon Michael. How are you?"

Bartlett smiled. "So much for breaking the ice. Jon came to us from the State Police three years ago."

"From arson investigations," I completed for her. "We worked together in Gannet, in the Northeast Kingdom—wild case."

"That it was." Jonathon Michael smiled.

"Jon's been figuring out how we can loosen some of the knots in this one. You mind starting right away, Joe? I should've offered some coffee, or at least the bathroom."

I shook my head and grabbed one of the chairs grouped around the table, already littered with papers. "No, I'm fine. Thanks anyway."

Michael sat where most of the papers were gathered. "I've been trying to split this thing into its various components," he said. "So if you'll indulge me, I'll just go from the top and run through the list. We can kick it around afterwards."

I smiled at the approach. As an arson investigator, Jonathon Michael had been more scholar than cop, always proceeding methodically, never in a rush, shyly explaining things as he went along, even when his audience already knew where he was headed, or couldn't have cared less. He'd graduated from college as an architectural engineer after seven years of intensive study and had then immediately joined the State Police with no explanation. He was unflappably easy-going, completely self-effacing, and the most private man I'd ever met. He also had a near-perfect solve rate.

He pushed at his glasses absentmindedly, sliding them up his nose. "The case on top, regardless of its true importance, is the only one actually headed for court," he said softly. "That's the Brian Padget illegal possession charge. Joe, have you come up with anything new on that?"

"No, but the more I've thought about it, the more I'm convinced both Bouches are involved, and maybe not as I'd first thought."

He nodded politely. "Right. Kathy told me a little about that. But in terms of concrete leads…"

I shook my head. "Best I can do right now is a relative shot in the dark. As far as I know, we haven't run a comparative test between the coke found in the urine sample and the stuff in the bag. Maybe that's where we'll get lucky."

Kathy Bartlett wrote a note on the pad before her. "I'll get that done."

"Okay," Michael continued. "Next up is Emily Doyle. There's nothing here except innuendo, but there are some strange coincidences. The problem with digging into them openly, though, is that if word gets out, we'll be caught in a limelight none of us wants, and Doyle may not deserve."

"Maybe we should approach it indirectly," I suggested.

He nodded. "I agree. If all this is interconnected, we'll find where Officer Doyle fits eventually. Next up is Jasper Morgan. Am I correct that not a single sighting of him's occurred since the night he gave you the slip?"

"As far as I know."

Michael pursed his lips. "That puts an ominous slant on things. When was the last time you remember a young punk keeping totally underground for more than a week?"

"So we assume he's dead," Kathy said flatly.

I agreed with her. "I'll have the Brattleboro PD grill everyone who knew him. We did that before, when we thought he was just lying low, but people are starting to talk more, supposedly because they've reached the same conclusion."

Jonathon wrote a note to himself. "Good idea."

I sat back, comforted by how things were progressing. A good twenty-five years my junior, Jonathon Michael was as easy in his supervisory role as I was with my own squad. I had been in other special units where the team leader's style had been boorish, autocratic, aloof, or downright incompetent. This was obviously to be a much more pleasant experience.

"Next up is Jan Bouch," he continued. "I decided to keep her separate, mostly because you seem to be leaning that way."

"I'm not sure one way or the other," I amended. "She could be a complete patsy—she might also have acted independently in some of this. She's obviously under her husband's control. I'd like to interview a nurse named Anne Murphy about her. We talked once, but I might be able to get her to open up more."

"Good. That would be handy." He sat back and looked at me, the overhead fluorescent lighting glinting off his glasses. "Which brings us, last but not least, to Norman Bouch. I've treated him almost like a small company and turned him into a flow chart."

He extracted two sheets of paper from a folder and handed one copy to each of us. "Under his name are six categories: 'Sources,' 'Network,' and 'Clients' being the basics of most drug operations. I've also listed 'Assets,' 'Friends,' which include employees, and 'Habits,' meaning travel routines and weekly and monthly schedules. We don't have the wherewithal to analyze each one of these, but I thought I'd highlight them to see if one stands out more than the others."

I looked over the neatly typewritten sheet. "We know nothing about his sources. They might come out of Lawrence, that being his old stomping ground, but Lowell or Boston or New York would fit, too. Same thing for clients. I think our best bet is the network. We've got an inkling of how it's run and where, and we're pretty sure Jasper Morgan was part of it, as might be Lenny in Burlington."

"Maybe the local PD's in-house computer will spit out something on him," Kathy said, "assuming he has priors."

"Assets are something else we can use the computer for," Jonathon added. "I can do that from here."

I folded the sheet and put it in my pocket. "I suppose the most straightforward approach would be to put Norm under surveillance and tap his phone line..." Both my companions' heads shot up, so I quickly added, "I know, I know—I don't think it would be a good idea anyway. Norm knows goddamn well he's put a bee up our nose with Padget. I spoke to a psychologist in Lawrence, who told me he's a control freak and a showoff, so we can assume he's expecting a reaction and maybe waiting to ambush us with something else."

Jonathon Michael examined his paperwork. "How 'bout going through Lenny? You learned about him in a roundabout way. If Bouch is playing this like a chess game, he may not even know Lenny's on the board."

I nodded. "I can also find out what happened to the void Jasper left behind. Presumably somebody's replaced him."

"I doubt that," Kathleen said, without looking up from her note-taking. "Using Jonathon's logic, if I'd whacked my regional operator, I'd lie low, especially if I had other sources of income."

"True," I agreed. "But it might work to distract Bouch. I'll dig into Lenny and have my squad chase down the Jasper angle. If I go back to Brattleboro to get them rolling, that ought to put me in Burlington in a day or so."

"You can pick me up on your way back," Michael said. He suddenly smiled at an afterthought. "It is a little weird, not doing anything about the only hard-core case we've got."

Kathy Bartlett dropped her pad on the table. "We'll be running the toxicology comparison, but I think Joe's right. Let's avoid the obvious, if for no other reason than to frustrate Norm. We can investigate Brian Padget in a few days, especially if we start feeling his dealings are separate from Bouch's. Right now," she added with a smile, "let's avoid the bait, if that's what Padget is, and work on finding out how to bite the fisherman."

Willy Kunkle shifted in his car seat and pointed through the windshield at a scrawny young girl, her long hair swinging across her back, who'd just appeared on the sidewalk and begun walking quickly away from us, down Flat Street toward the shadowy parking lots near the end of the block.

"Give her ten minutes," he said, "and I'll guarantee you we'll catch her dirty. She's like a Swiss watch."

We waited in the late night darkness, the warm breeze wafting through the car's open windows. The girl we were watching was Marie Williams, Jasper Morgan's erstwhile girlfriend, and—Willy assured me—the weak link among his old inner circle. Weak for the very reason we were here, because she had a nightly rendezvous for a supply of crack, a habit that had been escalating ever since Jasper's disappearance.

"She was a tough little cookie when I first talked to her," Willy said softly. "Told me to fuck off. 'Course then Jasper was John Dillinger on the loose, complete with a cop's stolen gun. Amazing what a little time and loneliness will do to one's self-confidence."

I glanced over at him. He would know about such things. A Vietnam vet who'd come home haunted and angry, he'd taken to the bottle and to using his wife as a target for his misery. When that sniper bullet had shattered his arm, he'd been on the threshold of being fired. Crippled, divorced, and temporarily working as the crankiest employee in the history of the municipal library, Willy had somehow rallied. Before I'd approached him with a way to come back to us, he'd already cleaned up his act. Now, as a one-armed man, he was twice what he had been, even if his personality was as maimed as ever.

"Why haven't you busted her contact, if he's so predictable?"

"Small fry. He only carries what he sells her. I haven't been able to find out where he gets the stuff. I will, though. I only tumbled to this a few weeks ago. She probably got her junk from lover-boy before. Now *that* was a tight little operation—all my poking around, I never got a look at it."

He opened his door. "You want to catch her in the act, now's the time."

We walked down the street and cut through a loading area to an alleyway near the back of a large, dark parking lot located between two building blocks and a gigantic stone retaining wall that supported Elliot Street high above us. Connecting Elliot and Flat streets was a towering, switchback wooden staircase. In the gloom of this latter structure, we saw the flare of a match and the quick reflected glow of a pale face looming over a glass pipe.

"Don't do it, Marie," Willy said sharply.

The pipe fell to the ground and broke, and someone else's feet scuffled off into the night, ignored by the both of us. Willy had produced a flashlight and was holding Marie Williams frozen like a deer in its harsh, bright halo.

"Who's there?" Marie's voice was high and frightened.

We stepped closer, so the light bouncing off her caught us as pale ghosts.

"You know us," Willy said.

She squinted into the light. "You bastards. You made me break my pipe." But her tone wasn't angry. It was plaintive, and she had tears in her eyes.

I gently took her arm and steered her around the corner to the bottom of the staircase, sitting next to her on the bottom step. After pocketing the pipe, Kunkle stood opposite us, the "bad cop" of the team.

"Marie. What're you doing?" I asked. "You know what that stuff does."

"Fuck you. What do you care?" She was looking down at her hands, clenched together between her knees.

"Enough to be here right now. You think we like seeing people like you kill themselves in slow motion, keeping a bunch of guys like that jerk in business?"

She gave me a sour look. "Oh, right. So I give you his name 'cause you care so much, right?"

"Richie Belleau," Willy said flatly.

She stared at him in surprise. "What?"

"Eleven o'clock every night, Marie," he went on. "I set my watch by you two. I liked the yellow T-shirt you had on last night better than that thing, by the way."

Her mouth opened. "You been following me?"

"Not anymore."

She slowly woke up to his meaning, and buried her face in her hands. "Oh shit, you're not going to bust me?"

I put my hand on her skinny back. "Slow down. What was I just telling you? You're in a jam. We're here to help you out of it."

"I tried that," she said in a weak voice. "I can't quit."

"You tried it alone. It's not like quitting cigarettes, Marie. You need people to give you guidance and support."

"And rip me off."

"Not a dime."

There was a long silence. Around us we could hear the familiar sounds of a town crowded in by the country—distant car engines almost covered by the gentle wind in the trees. The scratchings of small nocturnal animals foraging for urban scraps.

"You've hit bottom, Marie," I said finally, using what Willy had told me earlier. "You're panhandling, giving five-dollar blow jobs, shoplifting, all so you can sleep on a friend's floor and feed a lousy habit. You're alone, Jasper's gone, most of your old pals dump on you now that he's not around. All you eat is junk and leftovers. You're either hungry or cramped up all the time…Am I right?"

Under my hand, I could feel her weeping quietly. "We can help you."

"But you have to help us, first." Willy's voice was like a hard squeeze following a caress.

She looked up at him. Her voice shook. "Oh, right. Who'm I supposed to rat on before you make me this big gift?"

"No one," I said. "We just want to talk about Jasper."

A deep furrow creased her forehead. "Jesus Christ. You think I'd be here if I knew where he was?"

"We think he's dead," Willy said quietly.

She slid off the step and tucked her knees up into a ball against her chest.

"We want to find out what happened to him, Marie," I said. "You want to know for sure, don't you?"

She barely nodded.

"When he first disappeared, you thought he'd gone underground. You went to his standard hideaways, places only the two of you knew. Again and again."

Her voice was muffled by her arms. "He never showed."

"What was the one place you thought he'd pick over the others?"

"That old motel on Putney Road—the abandoned one near the C & S plant. He found a way to sneak in. We used to get away from everybody there."

"What room?" Willy asked.

"Nine."

I took her gently by the arms and lifted her to her feet. "Okay. We're going to take you to some people who'll help you out."

She didn't fight me, but she shook her head. "What's the point?"

I didn't answer. I figured she'd heard enough lies.

13

The motel Marie Williams had told us about dated back to the early fifties, and marked the transition between the "motor courts" of old, with their small, separate buildings, and the motels we know today, with wings stretching off to either side of a central office. This one, whose name had long ago been removed from the marquee, was a series of flat, scaling, concrete boxes squatting side by side, as if uncertain which role to play. It had been abandoned—or had looked that way—for almost as long as I could remember and before that had been a repository for the truly down-and-out. Just finding the landlord of record and securing permission to search by waiver had taken half the next morning.

With me were J.P. Tyler, complete with bulky equipment cases, and Ron Klesczewski, the fourth and final member of my squad. Ron was the least demonstrative of the bunch—quiet, self-doubting, a man who brooded unless given direction. He was a wizard at tracing paperwork and keeping large operations organized. Ironically for a timid type, Ron had been with me most often when bullets were flying. This time, however, he was along to help Tyler, having, unlike Kunkle, two good hands and no propensity to argue with any course J.P. might propose.

The motel looked as boarded up as a packing crate, all doors and windows tightly sealed with plywood sheathing. As we circled it, Ron asked the obvious question. "How did they get inside? The roof?"

I shook my head, leading them to a small shed built into the hill behind and below the motel. As Marie had told us the night before, the padlock was closed but not locked. I seized on the door and wrenched it half open, revealing a small room filled with cobwebs, dust, and piles of junk. I pulled a flashlight from my pocket and played it against the walls. Opposite me, a rusted bed frame with a wood slat bottom sat tilted up on end. I crossed over to it and twisted it on its axis, swinging it back like a door. Behind it, disguised by a grimy blanket, was a narrow door.

"I'll be damned," Ron said, and helped shove the bed frame farther out of the way.

Behind the door was a steep set of wooden steps leading up to a third and final door, this one leading into the motel's office. Except for our three flashlights, the place was as dark as a tomb, oven-hot, and smelled like a rotting septic tank.

"Now what?" Tyler asked, looking around, consciously breathing through his mouth.

"There's a breezeway out back," I explained, "running the length of the units."

I located the rear exit and stepped onto the verandah, now a dark, shuttered, musty tunnel, clotted with debris. "Number Nine should be down here."

Gingerly, still lugging J.P.'s baggage, we picked our way through the disemboweled mattresses, broken furniture, and shattered glass that littered the passageway like remnants of a battlefield. The scurrying complaints of escaping rodents were just audible above the sound of our footsteps.

The door to Number Nine was damaged but intact. Instinctively standing to one side, I turned the knob and pushed. Aside from the squealing hinges, there was nothing but silence from within.

Like a distant breeze, Ron nervously whispered, "Come out, come out, wherever you are."

I looked around the corner and shined my light into the room. As far as I could see, there was no one to come out. I crossed the threshold, motioning the others to fan out behind me.

We stood three abreast, lighting the room like a battery of search lamps. The walls were smeared, discolored, and riddled with fist-sized holes, the ceiling stained and sagging, the rug only visible in odd patches over mildewed cement flooring. The sink in the alcove near the bathroom was shattered and hanging by one bolt. All that was left of the two mirrors was a single, lightning-shaped shard leaning against a dresser with no legs. And yet, the room had been maintained, however minimally. The bed had a bare mattress, the center of the floor had been cleared with a broom, still standing in one corner, and several candles were clustered on a chair passing for a bedside table.

"Check the bathroom," I told Ron.

He carefully moved across the room and stuck his head through the door beyond the broken sink. "Clear."

Tyler approached the bed. "Looks like a bullet hole in the mattress."

"Any blood?"

He was already crouched down, opening one of his cases with a penlight held in his teeth. "Too dirty to tell in this light."

"We could tear the plywood from the windows," Ron suggested.

"No," J.P. said enigmatically. "The darker the better for the moment." From an insulated carrying case, he extracted a spray bottle much like a mister used on plants and poised it over the mattress. "Give me a little more light."

We did as he asked and watched as he lightly dampened the entire surface of the bed.

"Okay. Kill the lights."

It was like seeing a ghost take shape in the coal-black darkness. Glowing from the mattress's fabric in an amber luminescence was the clearly identifiable pattern of a stain.

"Jesus," Ron said softly.

"Luminol mixed with sodium perborate and sodium carbonate," J.P. explained. "Reacts with blood." He quickly checked under the bed with his light. "From the angle connecting the hole in the mattress to the one in the floor, I'd say the shot came from there." He pointed to where Ron was standing in front of the dresser, closer to the bathroom than to the front door.

He stepped back, spraying the luminol on the floor heading toward the door. At the entrance, he had us kill the lights again. We could clearly see glowing drops, their pattern indicating the direction of flight.

"Looks like he ran for it after he was shot," J.P. said.

Ron played his flashlight across the floor. "Why can't we see any of it?"

"It was absorbed in the filth. It's still there, though. The lab'll be able to analyze it once we collect it." He glanced out to the hallway. "But let's find out what happened first."

We worked our way slowly down the closed-in passageway, away from the office, J.P. spraying, and Ron and I alternately turning our flashlights on and off. Section by section, we followed the grisly testament of pain and suffering until we reached the room at the dead end. Its door was missing and its contents a shambles, but there was another mattress tossed on top of all the debris, crumpled against the far corner facing the entrance. Inexorably, J.P. led us straight to it. Removing the mattress, we could see there was no further need for fancy chemicals. A huge, dry, black, clotted mass of blood covered the trash on the floor like an obscene doily.

"I guess I can't complain about a lack of evidence," J.P. said sadly. Positioning himself so as not to disturb anything, he leaned far over the coagulated mess and peered at a spot low on the wall, grunting softly as he discovered what he was after. "Second bullet hole. With any luck, one of 'em will yield something we can put under a microscope."

For several hours, we stayed in that funereal location, picking through the chaos, collecting odds and ends, photographing everything. J.P. insisted on time-lapse photography to document the luminol, capturing on film the ghost of the victim's useless flight for safety.

Although I only had Marie Williams's word for it, I visualized Jasper Morgan in that role—all of twenty years old, leaving behind not a body, but only the putrid fluids he'd once contained. It was as pathetic a monument as I could imagine.

The plywood having at last been removed from the windows and doors for easier access and visibility, I finally left the motel through its lobby entrance and sat in the sun with my back against the disintegrating cement wall. Gail found me there ten minutes later.

"Don't tell me you were just in the neighborhood," I said with a smile, as she kissed me and settled down next to me.

"Hi to you, too," she answered. "Actually, my spies told me you'd finally come up for air. I can still smell that place on you."

I glanced down at my pants, dusty and streaked with God-knows-what. "Sorry."

"Did you find Jasper?"

I ran my fingers through my hair and sighed. "The lab'll tell us for sure. Whoever it was, we're pretty sure of the weapon. J.P. keeps a reference binder in his evidence kit. He had an enlargement of Lavoie's test-fired bullet. We have one made of every officer's gun. He used a field microscope to compare what we dug out of the wall to Lavoie's and he's pretty sure it's a match."

"Which tells you what?"

"Nothing specific. We figure he was shot in bed—wounded—and ran to escape in the wrong direction. He was finished off in a far room and his body removed."

"He couldn't still be alive somewhere?"

"J.P. says not according to the amount of blood he left behind."

She didn't respond, no doubt taken by the same mood that was clinging to me.

"The angle of the first shot and the fact Morgan was on the bed are suggestive, though," I added. "We entered this building the only way available and made a hell of a noise doing it, so whoever shot him was probably expected. Also, J.P. guesses the shooter was sitting on the edge of a busted dresser facing the foot of the bed. Not the standard pose of someone doing a hit-and-run."

"But no footprints or fingerprints or anything else?"

I shook my head. "We found the cartridges from the gun, but they probably have Pierre's prints on them, if that. Maybe Tyler'll find something once he sorts it all out, but I'm not counting on it. The best we can do is link the DNA in the blood to Morgan's parents and positively ID him as the victim."

I sighed and stared out at the passing traffic. Gail took my hand in hers. "It's not getting any better, is it?"

"No," I admitted, thinking of my own tangled motives in becoming involved with the case. "And I think it's just beginning."

That short, ambivalent conversation with Gail, coupled with the phone call I'd had with Greg Davis earlier, stimulated a small change of plans from what I'd told Jonathon and Kathleen. Leaving Ron Klesczewski and Tyler to wrap things up at the motel, I drove to Westminster, south of Bellows Falls, and knocked on Brian Padget's door.

As sorry as they were, it wasn't the fates of Jasper Morgan, Jan Bouch, Marie Williams, or the hundreds that had preceded them that tugged at me like weights around a swimmer's ankles. It was more general in scope than that. I was concerned with my own kind, too—Latour and Emily Doyle and Brian Padget and their ilk. The first because, after all these years, he'd run out of self-reliance and hope, the latter two because despite their best intentions, they were being blindsided by an increasingly cynical world, *and* by a support system lagging behind on its implied promises. A law enforcement career hinted at something exclusive to people who weren't used to such offers. To a high school graduate with a dubious future, it suggested a secure and supportive enough family to withstand the buffeting of a baffling world. The trade-off for low pay, social isolation, and the constant exposure to humanity's dregs was supposed to be a sense of loyalty, faith, and security.

Unfortunately, the reality was less an ideal family and more an organization as creaky and prone to error as most. While admittedly elite and proud, it was also full of prejudice, ambition, and slight, of management and union struggles, of too many people scrambling for too few promotions. The public image was to appear always perfectly unruffled, which only forced those in trouble to sometimes twist on their own, suddenly discovering the famous clannishness as more hindrance than help. Workaholic that I was, I had Gail, my books, my stints in college and in battle, and even my age to help keep me steady—and even so, I was now nagged by doubt. In contrast, shunned by the people he'd assumed would rally around him, young Brian Padget had to be lonely, confused, and increasingly bitter. In all conscience, I couldn't leave him dangling while we plotted strategy, especially since I feared Emily Doyle might soon be suffering the same fate.

Padget wasn't happy to see me. "What do you want?"

"To talk, if you got a minute."

He scowled, holding the front door as if bracing to slam it. "A minute? You're shitting me. I got nothing but, thanks to you..." He suddenly hesitated, momentarily confused. "Do I got to do this?"

"No. You can throw me off your property if you want to. I don't know why you would, though."

It was a small challenge, to test his anger, although I suspected it was early for him yet, that he was only in the confusing first stage of what would seem like an endless descent. In fact, he was still responsive to perceived authority. He stepped away from the door and muttered, "All right."

I walked into the familiar living room and took a seat on the sofa. Padget remained by the door.

"More questions?" he asked.

"Some." I waved at an armchair.

He perched on its edge, his elbows on his knees. He looked sleep-deprived. His skin was pasty, his eyes bloodshot and dark-rimmed. He didn't smell like he'd washed recently.

"It's been a few days since we found that dope in your toilet, Brian," I began briskly. "You've had a lot of time to think about how it got there—and why your urine tested positive. What've you come up with?"

He shook his head, staring at the floor. "I'm the *last* guy to ask. I don't know shit about this whole mess."

"Think back to a week before it started, further if you can. What was your routine, from when you woke up to lights out?"

"I don't know. I'm a cop. I go out on the streets. I make enemies. I'm a sitting duck."

I spoke to him sharply. "That's movie bullshit. Crooks don't make enemies out of us. They work their side, and we try to put them in jail. It's professional, not sandlot, wrestling. You're either in a jam because you screwed around with another man's wife, or because you *are* a doper. Which is it?"

He stood, his face flushed with anger. "I'm not dirty. No matter what everyone thinks."

"*Fine*," I almost shouted to quiet him back down. "So what's that leave?"

His lips compressed into a thin, bloodless line. He didn't say a word, but his eyes betrayed his confusion.

"You were used," I said gently, "by someone who went after you by turning the system against you. He knew we'd have to do what we did, and that the rest would naturally follow—the press drumming it up, the politicians covering their asses, the people you work with giving you a wide berth. You feel bad now, but it'll get worse unless we can cut it off with the truth."

"I'm not dirty," he repeated in a barely perceptible voice, sitting back down.

"Maybe I believe that. It doesn't make any difference. Not until you can help me find some proof. If you want a cliché that holds water, remember the one about cops being guilty until they're proven innocent, 'cause that's the way it is."

Padget cupped his face in his palms and rubbed his eyes hard with his fingertips. "This supposed to make me feel good?"

I took hope at that glimmer of humor. "It's supposed to get you off your ass. Right now, it looks like you committed a crime. But even though I'm the one who found the evidence, my job's not near done. I still have to look under rocks—make sure what I got is solid. I'm hoping there's something that proves what we have is bogus, and you're one of the best people I know to help me with that."

He stood up again in a frustrated lurch and stalked over to the window. "I've *been* thinking," he said, staring out at the street. "That's about all I do anymore. Jan was never in this place, and I know it wasn't Emily. You guys are definitely wrong there."

"Who says? You dumped her for Bouch's wife. That's been known to piss a few women off."

"God *damn* it," he shouted, glaring at me. "Is that how it works? Everything gets twisted to fit the picture? I didn't dump Emily and I didn't go straight from her to Jan. Emily and I are friends. We went to bed a couple of times, it didn't work out, and we called it quits—nice but no cigar. Emily's not out to get me. That's total bullshit."

"She was in this house. Was anyone else?"

He merely rolled his eyes.

"Did she ever use the bathroom, or have access to it when you couldn't see her?"

He still didn't answer.

"That's how we have to think, Brian," I said. "Not that Emily stuck it to you, but that she had the opportunity. Which means we can't rule her out—same with Jan."

He returned to his chair, suddenly eager to talk. "Look, Lieutenant. I know you're a good guy. And I know you don't screw other cops. But this is all crazy. I'm just starting out and I got a lot to learn, but I am pretty good. Ask Sergeant Davis. I can figure out when people're pulling my chain. Emily Doyle is a nice kid. She's got a chip on her shoulder and she comes on too strong, but that's because she's scared of screwing up. She wants to make it so bad as a cop it hurts. There is no way in hell she'd go after me because we didn't have a good time in bed. I mean, Jesus, I'm about the only one in the department who can put up with her shit half the time."

"Why the chip on the shoulder?"

He shook his head impatiently. "Family junk. Her father wanted a boy, gave her shit as a kid, said she'd never measure up. She overcompensates."

"What about Jan Bouch?"

He hesitated at the sudden change in direction. "That's different."

I waited for more and finally had to prompt him. "Starting with the fact that you love her?"

His discomfort came off him like smoke.

"I love somebody, too," I said. "It's not something to be embarrassed about. Tell me what kind of person she is—objectively, as a cop."

"She has her problems," he admitted. "Her son-of-a-bitch husband for starters. He hooked her on coke to tie her to him. But she's working on kicking that." His voice became wistful. "She was, at least."

"Is she a strong person?" I asked.

"She's not Emily—God knows. She's got strong feelings, though. But she's no fighter."

"What do you like about her?"

Padget shifted uncomfortably in his seat. "She makes me feel good. The things she says are kind of dumb, but they put me right on top...I guess that sounds stupid."

Not stupid, I thought, but disarmingly flattering. "What kind of influence do you think Norm has on her, besides the drugs?"

He looked at me in wonder. "I hadn't thought about it till just now, but he reminds me of Emily's father—the two of them are real domineering."

"But where Emily ended up fighting back..." I left the thought dangling on purpose.

"Yeah," he agreed. "Maybe Jan does kind of cave in too much."

"She pretty much do what you ask her to when you're together?"

"Yeah."

I let him think about the significance of that for a moment before continuing. To make him useful—to both of us—I wanted him to begin thinking analytically again. "Brian, how did you two meet?"

He blinked a couple of times, as if clearing away a lingering doubt. "Oh, it was just an accident. I guess I got called to their house for a disturbance. Things started rolling from that."

"Norm was there, too?"

"We wouldn't've been called otherwise."

"You called her up afterwards?"

He sensed the inappropriateness of that. "No, no. I don't know. I guess we bumped into each other around town, got to talking..."

"And she started unloading her problems on you?"

Padget began fidgeting again. "I don't know, Lieutenant. We just started talking, you know? Like people do. We connected."

"Who stepped up the relationship to more than talking?"

That seemed safer to him. "She did. I knew it was wrong, or that people would think it was, but she made things pretty hard to resist. I thought I could help her out—get rid of Norm, maybe fix things so she could get her life straight."

"Maybe be a part of that life?" I suggested.

He paused for a long time. "Maybe."

I hesitated before asking my next question. "Remember what I said about thinking like a cop? Is it possible, putting your personal feelings aside, that Jan might've been manipulated by Norm, even while she was talking about a future with you?"

I was expecting a blowup, so I was surprised by his bland response. "The way things're going now, I guess anything's possible."

It wasn't lacking in fatalism, but at least he was open to suggestion. I rose and crossed to the front door. "I'll get out of your hair. Did you follow my advice about seeing a counselor, by the way? I guarantee it'll help."

"No."

I'd expected that. Cops tend to steer clear of analysts, not only because of a built-in reticence, but also out of fear their confessions will leak back to their superiors and be held against them. It had been known to happen.

I tried once more anyhow. "It doesn't have to be the department-sanctioned shrink. See someone on your own."

But he merely shook his head. "Thanks anyway, Lieutenant. I'm feeling better, knowing you're out there working for me. I wasn't so sure before."

I kept my mouth shut. What did it hurt for him to think my job was that clear-cut? And wasn't it to lend him support that I'd come here in the first place? What I said instead was, "Keep trying to remember what's been going on recently. Maybe you'll think of something helpful."

Unfortunately, he already had mentioned something relevant, which I didn't think was going to help him in the least. After I pulled out of his driveway, I didn't head for home as I'd originally planned, but north toward the Bellows Falls police station to find out if I was right. The evening shift was just coming on when I pulled into the parking lot. I could see their silhouettes gathered in the radio room, no doubt sampling the cookies I'd heard were regularly supplied by one of the officer's wives. As I entered the building, however, all conversation died as if cut with an ax, and the small group filed out the door, eyes averted. Only the dispatcher remained, now buried in paperwork, and Greg Davis, looking embarrassed.

"Don't worry about it," I said softly. "Part of the turf."

"Doesn't make it any more pleasant. What's up?"

"I was wondering if your call log indexed responding officers."

He led me over to the same computer I'd used earlier. "Sure. What case?"

"Everything involving the Bouch residence."

He cut me a look but remained silent, typing his instructions into the machine. Moments later, a list appeared on screen. I read it, nodded to him to scroll down, read again. I rubbed the back of my neck, disappointed.

"Get what you wanted?" he asked.

"That's all of it, right? There're no other records that might show Brian responding to at least one of those calls?" I thought further as he shook his head. "How 'bout if he was off-duty and just showed up to help?"

"It'd still be in here."

So Brian had lied. I sighed with disappointment. "That's what Emile remembered, too. First time we talked, he said he didn't think Bouch and Padget had ever met."

Davis glanced back at the screen. "He was right—officially at least. Looks like Emily Doyle showed up at the Bouches more'n anyone. Luck of the draw, I suppose."

"Yeah," I agreed, but I didn't believe it for a second.

14

It was late at night when my phone buzzed me back to the present. I'd been sitting half-conscious in my office, the paperwork I'd hoped to complete still littering my desk, victim of a seriously distracted mind.

The voice on the other end belonged to Jonathon Michael, and I could tell from its wavy clarity that he was speaking on a cell phone. "Joe, you up for a small drive? Steve Kiley would like to meet with you, me, and Kathy at the Rockingham barracks in about a half-hour."

I looked at my watch. It was closing in on midnight. "I take it this is not a social gathering?"

"You got that. Turns out he just found out about our little project. Kathy left a message for him a couple of days ago but never followed up on it."

"Swell. I'll be there."

I hung up, longing for the distracted state I'd just left. What Jonathon Michael had just reported meant that we now had the supervising officer of the drug task force worked up enough to demand a reckoning in the middle of the night.

Kiley was a strong-willed, ambitious man, who as head of this elite team had gained a stature rare among the State Police. It hadn't inflated his ego—he was a better cop than that—but it had given him power and independence in a system known to be tightfisted with both. The result was a man who was used to more respect than he obviously felt he'd just received from us—and respect was a touchy item for both him and his crew. The "drug police," to use the vernacular of some of his colleagues, conspicuously marched to a different drummer. Casually dressed, often bearded and long-haired, task force members kept their own hours, ignored the spit-and-polish of their peers, and some-times behaved more like the people they were after than the ones they depended upon for backup. This led to a good deal of ribbing, some of it ill-natured, along with a few suspicions that all that exposure to money and dope could lead to unhealthy habits. Being in the trenches of drug enforcement, far from the ranks and often away from one's family for long stretches, Kiley and his people became hypersensitive to such innuendos. Respect and courtesy from colleagues became unstated prerequisites for good morale, and slights were not ignored.

I had no doubts about the nature of the conversation I'd just been invited to join. The surprise was who I met after pulling into the barracks parking lot forty-five minutes later.

A small, compact man wearing a beard, T-shirt, and faded jeans stepped away from the shadows of a pickup truck as I emerged from my car.

"You Gunther?" he asked.

I kept my eyes on his hands. His tone of voice was neutral, but the time and setting were far from it. "Who's asking?"

"Bill Deets. I'm on assignment with the task force from Bellows Falls."

I stuck out my hand, which he shook after a slight hesitation. "Glad to meet you. I'm just about to have a powwow with your boss. You coming in?"

He shook his head. "You need to know you're barking up the wrong tree with Brian and Emily."

I raised my eyebrows. Padget was common knowledge, especially to someone with this man's connections. Doyle was another matter. "I'm going after Emily?"

His face hardened. "You looked her up in the computer a few hours ago. You think she's tied into Norm Bouch and put the screws to Brian. All that's so full of shit it's not funny."

I remembered the quiet dispatcher hovering in the background when Davis and I had done exactly what Deets had described. Unless, of course, Davis himself had spilled the beans. The mere thought of that gave birth to a small headache.

"I guess this means you've got a better idea about what's going on," I told him.

"I know you're about to ruin two good reputations for nothing." I considered several responses to that, including trying to allay his fears. But I didn't know the truth myself and was suspicious enough at his approach to question his motives. So far in this case, I'd found only surprises where I'd expected the mundane, and I didn't feel like adding to the confusion by taking Bill Deets into my confidence.

I decided instead to feed him some of his own attitude. "Ruining reputations is something I'll leave to the rumor mill. Talk to Kiley after we're done. If he thinks it's appropriate, he'll tell you what's going on. My advice either way would be to tell your colleagues on the PD to lighten up on Padget and give him their support. Right now, they're the ones acting like he's already been tried and convicted."

I didn't wait for him to answer but made my way quickly to the building's front door.

The Rockingham barracks of the Vermont State Police was the same nondescript, single-story, brick and cement design that had been used for every barracks in the state. It was, like its clones, too small, unimaginatively designed, and oppressive to work in. It fit my mood perfectly.

I stepped into the small lobby and presented myself to the dispatcher behind the thick glass panel in the wall. A minute later, Kiley, tall and broad, in cowboy boots and a ponytail, threw open the door to the interior. His smile looked sutured in place at great cost. "Joe. The others just got here. Glad you could make it." I bit my tongue and merely shook his hand.

He took me down the long central hallway to an office at the far end. "I heard what you were up to," he said without looking back, "and asked Kathy Bartlett for an update. She thought it might be helpful if we all got together at one meeting to sort things out."

Despite my irritation, I didn't really fault his testiness. His job was among the more dangerous in law enforcement, much of it undercover, all of it dealing with people whose trustworthiness could be doubted by their own mothers. If I'd discovered that a statewide investigation involving my turf had been launched behind my back, I would've been irritable, too.

"Nice of you to pick a time we were all free," was all I said under my breath.

Jonathon Michael and Kathy Bartlett were standing in the room we entered, Jon on his tiptoes, trying to peer out of one of those too-high windows at the gloominess beyond, Kathy in a sweatshirt and loose-fitting jeans, looking as if she'd just been tossed out of bed. Grim-faced, she merely nodded at me as I walked in.

"Grab some seats," Kiley said like a genial host, pulling a chair from under the large central table and making himself comfortable. "We might be here a while."

Bartlett gave him a deadly look. "All right. You're pissed and I'm sorry. It'd be nice to progress beyond that."

Kiley leaned forward and tapped the tabletop gently with his finger. "The task force reports to your office, Kathy. Was it so goddamn difficult to drop me a line?"

She sat, too, but in a chair against the wall, her hands buried in her pockets. "We've been over that. I screwed up. But we had good cause for not involving the task force in the first place, so none of what's said tonight is going to change anything—except that I promise not to drop the ball again. I mean, Jesus, Steve, we've worked well together for years."

But his concern, as we already knew, had little to do with bureaucratic mix-ups. "We were formed by general agreement," he said, "so local PDs and the State Police could clear their books of exactly this kind of case. I'd like to know what good cause it was that made you go behind my back." He looked hard at me and continued, "Joe's got a criminal case against a cop. Is there something about my own squad I should know?"

I opened my mouth to answer, but Kathy cut me off. "No. Absolutely not. It was pure and simple a conflict of interest, as I already told you. Your Bill Deets is buddy-buddy with his old department, and in particular Brian Padget, and I personally didn't want to put you in a tight spot. If things had worked out more smoothly, we would have talked about it calmly and at a more civilized hour and settled the matter then and there. I realize paranoia can be a life-saving instinct, but there is absolutely nothing else going on here."

But Kiley was shaking his head like a disappointed father. "I have officers from half a dozen departments—"

Kathy interrupted. "You ever targeted one of those departments when one of their officers was working for you?"

She'd done her homework, like the lawyer she was. Kiley shrugged defensively. "It wouldn't have caused a problem. I've got enough guys that I could've isolated the one to maintain the case's integrity."

I hadn't planned on mentioning my meeting with Bill Deets. Allowing that his motives had been genuine, I'd been willing to forget his combative approach. But I owed him no favors, while I was beholden to Kathy Bartlett. Steve Kiley was no neophyte—he knew half of what he was saying was simple posturing. But he was also human, was feeling self-righteous, and had taken the opportunity to pound us on the head with our own transgressions.

Given the hour, therefore, I felt enough was enough. "I just had a chat with Deets outside in the parking lot."

It had the desired effect. The tennis match between Bartlett and Kiley disintegrated into open stares.

"Now?" Kiley asked.

"Yeah. Just before I knocked on your door. I invited him to join us. He wasn't interested."

Kathy fought hard to suppress a smile. Kiley openly scowled.

"Look," I continued, finally sitting down myself. "That doesn't matter, either. He just wanted me to know Padget and Doyle are straight shooters and I was barking up the wrong tree."

"Who's Doyle?"

I waved that away. "One of Padget's fellow officers. The point is, he not only knew I was looking into Doyle within hours after I started, but he knew where and when you were meeting with us. This is Vermont—everybody knows what everybody else is doing. That's why I asked Jack Derby and then Kathy if we could bypass the task force, that and the fact that my department is becoming increasingly invested in whatever's going on."

"That homicide you found this afternoon?" he asked.

"Right—one of Bouch's runners."

Kiley was still looking unhappy. "I'm not going to argue the conflict of interest thing. You might even have a point. But have you done a lot of drug cases? It can be like wandering around a minefield without a map, and some of those mines might be cases we *are* working on, or at least snitches we're using."

Jonathon Michael spoke up for the first time, still leaning in the corner near the windows. "We'll run the names by you, Steve, same as always. You can help keep our noses clean."

"And if we get our hands on anything valuable after it's all done," Bartlett added, "cars, houses, cash, whatever, I'll try for the federal forfeiture route so the government will cut us each a check for our good deeds."

Kiley gave her a sour look. "Christ. That's not what this was about, Kathy."

She held up both her hands. "I know, I know. It's also not what I meant—you know that, too."

Mollified nevertheless—as Bartlett knew he would be—Kiley shrugged and stood up. "All right, what the hell. I guess I had my little temper tantrum. Getting sensitive in my old age."

Kathy and I joined him and began herding toward the door. "No," she said. "I had it coming. Lesson learned. Jon and Joe'll keep in touch, and if you feel things are going off track again, let me know. Just do it between eight and five, okay?"

Having left Kiley behind, Bartlett, Michael, and I stood in the warm breeze of the parking lot, bathed in the colorless glow of a full moon.

"Don't take that keeping in touch too literally," Kathy said softly, as if the parked cruisers nearby might report back to their masters. "There are lots of drug investigations that happen in this state without task force blessing or involvement. Right, Jon?"

He merely nodded, his eyes on the invisible horizon.

"Is that true what you said about forfeiting any assets federally?" I asked, "even though this is a state case?"

"Sure," she answered. "They're separate issues. The forfeiture's a civil matter. If we pitched it to a state judge, whatever money we got would probably end up in the General Fund. The feds work on the incentive system." She jerked a thumb at the barracks behind us. "People like Steve can be thin-skinned, but they're as broke as the rest of us."

"And as open to legal bribes," Jonathon added, as if to himself.

"What I'd like to know," Kathy said to me, her face coming closer and her voice flattening slightly, "is what you were doing digging into Doyle openly enough that Deets found out about it three seconds later. I thought we were putting the Padget case on the back burner for a couple of days 'til we got more background."

"I yielded to impulse," I admitted. "After we found where Jasper was killed, or probably killed, I went to see Padget. I kept thinking of him twisting in the wind..."

I was surprised by her reaction. "How is he?"

"Not good, and he'll probably get worse. His real problem is he's not being straight with us. He said he first met Jan Bouch through a domestic call to their house. I checked the log. He never went on any such call. Emily did, though, more than any other officer."

There was a long pause. Jonathon brought his gaze from the night sky to me. "Which tells you what?"

"That maybe we won't be going to Burlington quite as soon as I thought."

I drove home in the morning's early hours, the only car on the road for the entire trip, my brain struggling with the dozens of loose threads we'd identified so far, many of which didn't even look like they came from the same fabric.

By the time I crept into the bedroom, the various scenarios had started bleeding into one another like wet inkblots, and with about as much clarity. I dumped my clothes on the floor and slipped in under the sheet, fully expecting to spend the night's remaining hours staring at the moon in the skylight overhead.

"Been having fun?" Gail's voice floated in the air like a comforting caress.

I reached over and kissed her cheek. "Non-stop. Sorry I woke you up."

"That's okay. I got to bed early tonight. What were you doing?"

"Smoothing political feathers…I wish I could start answering questions instead. They're beginning to breed like gerbils."

She rolled over and draped one arm across my chest. "Tell me."

Normally, I would have begged off, for her sake if nothing else. It wasn't like she didn't need all the rest she could get. But her interest was genuine, and she was one of the best sounding boards I had. I gave her a guided tour of the tangled mess we were confronting.

After a few moments' reflection, she commented, "Sounds like you need to find out what those two young cops are up to."

"And how Jan Bouch plays into it."

Gail punched the pillows behind her head and slid to a semi-sitting position. "I know Anne Murphy."

It was more than a statement of fact. "Does this have anything to do with what you said a few days ago, about how 'we' needed to do something about all this?"

"I have a background that could be useful here—outside the SA's office."

I knew what she was referring to—two decades of counseling women at the local crisis center, being on the boards of half the social welfare organizations in town, even heading the town's board of selectmen for a stretch. She had the political and social bloodlines of a thoroughbred. "What're you thinking?" I asked.

"That maybe Anne will tell me things she wouldn't share with you."

"Which we might be able to use to slip through Norm's back door?"

She laid a hand on my forearm. "Maybe. I'm going to do this strictly by the rules, briefing Derby if necessary. But I'm hoping a man of Norm's ego wouldn't think his wife could betray him, even inadvertently, which in my book makes her a good way to get at him."

"God, how you've wandered from your days in the commune."

She slugged me in the shoulder. "Lucky for you."

15

When I walked into the squad room the next morning, Harriet Fritter gave me a broad smile and a slip of paper that said, "Call Greg Davis ASAP." She also told me I should get more sleep.

I closed the door to my small corner office and sat, exhausted, looking at the note from Davis. The urge to follow Harriet's advice and rest my head on the tabletop was suddenly hard to resist. I sensed only bad news lurking behind the "ASAP" in the note.

Reluctant to stir up the anxiety and despair that clung to this case like ground fog, I dialed his home phone number, suddenly worried that I hadn't voiced my concerns about Brian Padget by telling Davis the young cop needed counseling—and wondering if I was about to be told the consequences of that oversight.

"We've got a small problem," he said after I'd identified myself.

"Your connecting Emily Doyle to those calls to Bouch's place has spread like wildfire. There's all sorts of rumors you're investigating her, too. What's going on?"

I remembered wondering whether Davis or that quiet dispatcher had been the one to spill the beans. Davis's obvious irritation seemed to clear that up. Nevertheless, I kept my response tactfully vague. "Too many people are shooting their mouths off. Bill Deets was in my face last night about Doyle and Padget both, not long after you and I were seen fiddling with the computer."

In the brief silence following, I could hear him connecting the dots. Only then, and only briefly, did I feel sorry for the dispatcher's coming fate. "Can you tell me about Doyle?" he finally said.

"Only that we have a whole lot less than what her supposed friends are dishing out. She's come up on the radar screen a few times, and we are checking those events out. That's standard procedure..."

I stopped, hearing his weary, "I know, I know," echoing in the background. I volunteered, "Would it help if I came up there and talked to them?"

He was hesitant. "Probably not. The chief and the town manager have already gotten hold of this. I don't think anything you could say now would make any difference."

"What have they done?" I asked, stunned that things could get so bad so fast.

"Nothing yet. I just know they're keeping an eye on us. They haven't called a press conference or anything, but it won't be long before Shippee caves in and briefs at least the president of the village trustees. After that, it'll be public knowledge in about five minutes."

"Is the department even vaguely functional right now?" He sounded faintly insulted. "Of course it is. Morale stinks, but the job's getting done. Christ, we don't have any choice with Deets at the task force and Brian out on leave. We're using the part-timers more, so that's helping a little—it disperses some of the depression. But I'd be lying if I didn't say this whole thing's put Emily in a pretty tight spot."

"I'm going to have to talk to her, you know."

"When?"

"Could be as early as today. Depends on some other things I have going."

"Could that take place outside the building?"

"Sure. You name it. And I'll give you some warning on the timing. How's Brian doing? He seemed a little better when I left him yesterday, but I meant to tell you, I think he ought to find a coun- selor soon. He doesn't seem to realize what kind of freight train he's facing."

Davis's voice was grim. "He's finding out. I dropped by last night and found him passed out drunk on his living room floor. He's drying out in my guest bedroom right now."

I hoped Bellows Falls knew what they had in Greg Davis. "All right. I'll do what I can to wrap things up, for everyone's sake, but it's starting to get complicated."

"I read the paper," he said sympathetically.

That sat me up straight. "I haven't. What did it say?"

"Just that a presumed homicide had been discovered at an abandoned motel, and that Lavoie's gun probably played a part. I take it that was Jasper Morgan?"

"We think so, but it does up the ante on finding out who killed him. Our forensics guy thinks it was an acquaintance killing. He was on the bed when he caught the first bullet."

"Well, if it was Norm Bouch, I'll do anything I can to help. Just let me know."

"I appreciate that." I was about to hang up when I suddenly remembered a question that had been rattling around my head for days. "There is something, since you've got Brian nearby. When he wakes up, ask him who his mechanic is."

Breakfast at Dunkin' Donuts is something I enjoy all too rarely nowadays, with Gail's constant mutterings about the sanctity of a healthy body. So when Harriet told me Willy Kunkle was stopping there on his way to the office, I jogged down the block to catch him before he left.

Typically, he was positioned at the far end of the curved counter, his back against the wall and his eye on the front door. I took the stool next to his and ordered the largest cinnamon roll they sold, along with a cup of coffee to help ease it down.

"The old lady out of town?" he asked with a sarcastic smile.

"Business breakfast. I'm allowed. What've you found out about Jasper Morgan?"

"That why you're here? You'll get more out of that doughnut. From what I could find out, Jasper Morgan came, raised hell, sold dope, and then disappeared. Nobody knows who his contacts were, where he got his stuff, or what he did with the money."

"How 'bout his runners? You talk to any of them?"

"Sure, and they're pretty chatty, too. But they got zip to offer. Morgan dealt with them one on one, never in groups. He did the contacting and always met at a location of his own choosing. He'd give 'em the dope and an address and strict orders not to take any money—their cut of the profits always came in the mail later—cash only."

"How'd he get paid, then?"

"I went to a couple of the addresses myself. The people weren't too thrilled to see me, but I got 'em to open up." He paused to take a swig from his coffee mug, obviously hoping I'd ask how he'd pulled that off. I kept silent.

"He collected the money himself," he continued. "He'd phone and tell whatever customers to carry the cash at all times for the next few days, and then he'd appear out of the blue—on the street, at their jobs, wherever—and hit 'em up for it. Very cagey."

"Very trusting. Wasn't he ever ripped off?"

"I heard he was once—but only once. One of his little rug rats tested him and was never seen again."

I stopped chewing and gave him an incredulous look. "He knocked off a kid? And we didn't hear about it?"

Willy rolled his eyes. "Oh, come on. There's a ton of shit we never hear about. Some back-alley kid gets whacked and buried. His parents, if they care, take a six-second break from the bottle to look around and assume he's split town. End of story. His buddies got the message, though, and Jasper Morgan could trust 'em with the crown jewels from then on."

Cynical, but unarguable. "None of the runners ever saw him make a phone call or get a letter or hang out with his boss? Sounds a little unlikely."

Willy tilted his head meditatively. "Normally, I'd agree with you. Little bastards can't wait to squeal on each other, especially to us. But that's where Morgan's system really stood out. He kept switching runners—use one for a little while, give him a bonus, and kiss him off.

He stayed away from the gang bit. It meant using more people overall, but no one person got too ambitious, and Morgan could keep the details to himself. I think he was making a killing—for this town—with nobody the wiser 'cause he kept a low profile and let 'em all think he was playing for peanuts. Smart."

"Or well trained," I said. "Rumor has it that exact same type of operation is working in Burlington right now."

I finished my coffee, wiped my mouth, and stood up. "You coming?"

His own cup was empty, and his doughnut long gone, but his answer didn't surprise me. "Later."

My next stop was Sammie Martens, whom I found with Ron Klesczewski in the squad's conference room, using its long table to lay out a series of labeled folders. The precise methodology clearly spoke of Ron's influence.

"That the Morgan case?" I asked, sitting on a nearby filing cabinet to stay out of the way.

"Yeah," Sammie said glumly, "although I think we'll end up with more folders than paper to fill 'em, the way things're going."

"I know. I just talked with Kunkle. What did you find out about Emily Doyle?"

She made a face and turned to Ron. "You okay with the rest of this? I gotta dig that out of my desk."

"Sure. Go," he said.

She spoke over her shoulder as we walked to her cubicle in the next room. "I really hated doing that, poking into another cop's life. Gave me the creeps."

I didn't answer. Such sensitivities were the least of my concerns now.

She sat in her chair, unlocked a drawer, and removed a thin file. "Here," she said, handing it over.

"Thanks." I leaned against the partition facing her desk. "Run it down for me."

I wasn't being a hardnose—not entirely. A verbal report is usually preferable to its written equivalent, since you can immediately expand it with questions. On the other hand, I was making a small point—you can't always choose the kind of police work you do.

She let out a sigh. "Emily Doyle was born in St. Albans. Father Quebecois, mother American. Dad was a hardheaded, heavy-handed construction worker, moved around southern Canada and the U.S. border states for years before settling down in Burlington. He drank a lot and beat on his wife and kid—Emily was an only child. She uses her mother's maiden name as her own. The cops used to drop by the house regularly to sort things out. From what I heard, she began hanging out with them as a result—they sort of tucked her under their wing."

"The Burlington PD?"

"Right. She was about ten when they hit town. In school she showed a preference for structured organizations—team sports, the Girl Scouts, the PD's Junior program—and she turned into a wicked jock. Super aggressive, super competitive, and not real good at accepting defeat or criticism. When she finally applied to join the department, they turned her down, as did Rutland. That's how she ended up in Bellows Falls. The people I talked to thought she went there for the action and to build up a good résumé so she could reapply to Burlington."

"How was she in school?"

"Indifferent student, terrific athlete, and an on-again, off-again discipline problem. Far as I know, she never did drugs or alcohol, but she got into fights all the time, and always with boys."

"Padget told me her father wanted a son."

"Well, she's done everything in her power to satisfy him there."

"He's still alive?"

"Yeah. He migrates between the bar and whatever job he's working. His wife still lives with him, what's left of her. She's not too outgoing socially—surprise, surprise."

I ignored the bitterness. Sammie had her own struggles with aggression and competition with men. "But she never did anything crooked, right?"

"Not that I could find. 'Course, I was treading lightly here, calling in favors, telling people to keep it under their hat."

"It's interesting, though," I mused. "A woman with that background, responding time after time to the residence of a submissive woman and her abusive husband. It must've been like stepping into her own family movie, only this time as the authority figure."

Sammie watched me carefully. "Which leads you where?"

I pushed away from the partition and began moving toward my office. "Eventually, to a conversation with the lady herself. Thanks. I know that wasn't much fun."

After weeks of warm, dry weather, the forecast was warning of a major rainstorm, which prophecy proved true as Jonathon Michael and I approached Bellows Falls early that afternoon. The lead gray sky pressed low upon the broad interstate, making me feel I was racing between two immovable masses—a bug running like hell to escape a descending shoe. The rain was heavy enough to overtake the wipers and made me wary of hydroplaning the tires.

"You get anything on that computer search of Bouch's assets?" I asked Michael, more to ease the tension than to learn what he would have told me hours earlier had it been relevant.

"Nothing beyond what we already knew," he said. "No big surprise, of course—if he has any brains, he's got half a dozen dummy fronts to hide behind. I did get the report back on Padget's urinalysis. It doesn't match the sample you found in the toilet tank. What he was carrying around inside him shows no cutting agent whatsoever."

"It was pure coke?" I asked.

"So they said. What I know about chemistry you could feed to a tick. The bagged stuff was supposedly cut with procaine, and there was none of that in his system. It's too bad, in a way. Sometimes what they use is exotic enough to trace, but procaine's pretty common. It's unregulated and you can buy it through any vet supplies outlet—it's a topical anesthetic."

"Huh," I muttered. "The paper's informant implied it was all one and the same. I don't know how or why, but this could be good news for Mr. Padget."

I entered Bellows Falls from Route 5 and continued on to Atkinson Street. About halfway to the police station at the town's north end, I turned left onto a rough, dead-end street lined with small, scabby-looking old warehouses. The road was so full of water-filled potholes and patches, it was like driving across a rock-filled pond. At the far end, we stopped next to a cobbled-together, one-story building with a rusting metal roof. A hand-lettered sign over sagging garage doors read "Al's Auto."

Jon gave me a questioning glance.

"Quick stop," I said. "Davis told me this is where Padget had his car fixed when Emily Doyle was taking him to work."

We got out and ran, hunched over, toward a narrow entrance next to the garage doors. It was no more than a ten-yard dash, but we were drenched by the time we ducked inside.

On a normal day, the building's interior would have felt dark and hazardous—an evil-smelling hospital for decrepit, oil-bleeding cars. Today, it was almost embracing, its quirkily placed bare bulbs and the thundering rain on the roof giving a sensation of domestic warmth and protection.

We glanced around, seeing no signs of life and hearing nothing over the sound of the rain. I finally made a megaphone of my hands and called out, "Is anybody here?"

The answer came from disturbingly close by. "Yeah."

We both instinctively stepped back in alarm as two legs appeared from under a pickup I'd been near enough to touch. A man dressed in filthy blue overalls rolled out on a creeper and lay looking up at us. He was holding a flashlight in one hand and a wrench in the other.

"What can I do you for?"

I showed him my badge. "We're police officers. I was wondering if you could answer a couple of questions."

The man scowled. "M'I in trouble?"

"Not with us. It's about a car you serviced—for Brian Padget."

He pursed his lips, rolled off the creeper onto his hands and knees, and slowly rose to his feet. With blackened fingers, he groped in his breast pocket for a pack of cigarettes and lit his selection from a book of paper matches. I let him take his time.

"What about it?"

"You told Padget there was water in the gas tank. You know how it got there?"

He scratched his cheek, looking from one of us to the other, transparently pondering his best approach. "They say sometimes dealers spike the gas with water to stretch a buck."

"From what we could find out, Padget buys most of his gas from the same place. There've been no other complaints."

He tilted his head slightly, putting on a philosophical air. "I'll tell you what I tell some of my customers about that. I warn 'em to stay away from any gas station—even their regular one—when there's a gas truck filling up the underground tanks. People don't realize, every one of those storage units has some water in it. Just the nature of the beast. And it's no big deal as long as nobody stirs it up, 'cause water sinks like lead and stays on the bottom. But you get a big tanker dumping all that gas in there, mixing everything up, and you put that stuff into your car two minutes later, you're going to be takin' on some serious water."

Jonathon spoke from just behind me. "Do you *know* that's why the water was in the tank?"

The man pushed out his lower lip and shook his head. "Nope. I dropped it out of the car, emptied it, dried it, bled the lines, and hooked her back up. I checked the container where I poured the gas and saw there was water mixed in. She ran good afterwards, so I told Padget that's what the problem was."

"Is this common?"

"It happens, usually when the tank starts to rust through, or after a tanker truck refill, like I told you. But it's not too often it gets so bad you notice it."

Jonathon looked around the large room. "What kind of container do you empty the gas into?"

"Big plastic see-through thing. I got it around here somewhere." But he did no more than glance over his shoulder, as if to summon the container by magnetism.

Jon pressed on. "So you saw exactly how much water there was."

"Yeah, sure. Maybe a gallon, maybe more."

"Isn't that a lot?" I asked.

"Enough to mess things up. The feeder line to the engine comes off the bottom. You get a little water sitting there, no big deal. Maybe you hear a ping now and then, maybe not even that. More water, more of a problem. When you get into a couple of gallons or more, then you're sucking water and nothin' else, so the engine doesn't even fire."

I looked at Michael and raised my eyebrows. He shook his head slightly. "Okay," I told the mechanic, "thanks for the help."

We were almost back to the narrow door when his voice caught up to us. "He in big trouble, Padget?"

"That's what we're trying to find out," I told him.

Back in the car, the dampness rising from our clothes like a mist, I began driving toward the Island, between the canal and the bend in the river.

"What'd you think?" Jonathon asked.

"By itself, not much. Combined with everything else, it makes for one hell of a handy way to get Emily Doyle into Padget's house."

The directions Greg Davis had given me led us past where we'd parked to see the petroglyphs, and down a narrow, tree-choked lane that dead-ended at an enormous, ancient red-brick building that loomed out of the surrounding rain-soaked woods like an ominous vision from a fairy tale.

Jon craned his neck to see the roofline high above us. "I take it this is one of the famous mills? It's creepy enough."

I turned left down an embankment, picking my way through the weeds, and rounded the building's corner. There, the lane widened to a broad, grassy parking area, opposite a row of enormous wooden doors, one of which swung back on its hinges as we stopped.

Backlit by a string of bare light bulbs hanging from the ceiling behind him, Greg Davis gestured me right into the mill's embrace. Like Jonah entering the whale, I drove past him, and saw the grayness of the day vanish as the ponderous door slammed shut with a reverberating echo.

Michael and I emerged from the car slowly, taking in the shadowy archways looping high overhead, the broad, blackened, iron-hard oak floors, and the massive ribbons of ceiling-mounted conveyor belts, once linked to the river's thunderous power, now as silent and still as sleeping juggernauts. Everywhere we looked, there were electrical lights strung like Christmas ornaments, each one bright individually but cumulatively smothered by the sheer weight of the surrounding gloom. Incongruously small, as well as out of place, a dusty 1930s firetruck sat parked to one side.

"Boy," Jonathon said softly as Greg approached us. "You sure know how to pick your spots."

Greg shook hands. “I’m friends with the owner. It was the one place I could think of where no one would walk in on us. Emily’s waiting upstairs.” He gestured toward a broad flight of worn wooden steps.

Jon was still looking around like a star-struck tourist. “Your friend like paying utility bills?”

Greg laughed. “It’s free. Years back, when the power company bought the land, the man who owned this building demanded that part of the deal be free utilities in perpetuity. The lights burn day and night. It’s not a bad security system, although I know the guy would like to see the place put to better use. He’s tried to interest people in starting a business here, maybe a small manufacturer, but it’s been like moving a mountain with a spoon.”

We reached the top of the stairs and stood in a gigantic empty room, the size of a football field. It was clear of debris or obstacles apart from an orderly forest of regularly spaced steel pillars supporting the flat wooden ceiling. Every wall save one was covered with enormous paned windows, making the room as washed with light as its predecessor had been dark. Near one of these banks of windows was a small cluster of chairs, and sitting in one of them was the compact shape of Emily Doyle. She rose nervously as we approached.

Jonathon stepped ahead of me, as we’d agreed earlier. Given the mood of my previous encounter with Emily, I saw no advantage in being the point man. “I’m with the attorney general’s office, Officer Doyle. My name is Jonathon Michael. You’ve already met Lieutenant Gunther.”

She nodded, but made no comment. The fire I’d seen in her earlier had ebbed now that she felt herself in Padget’s shoes—a loss of spirit I took no joy in seeing.

Jon gestured for everyone to sit. Outside, mingling with the rain’s steady hiss was the throaty growl of the nearby river, visible at the bottom of the gorge as a frothing, lethal tumult. Fall Mountain opposite was lost in a veil of colorless mist.

“Before we begin,” he said, “I want to make one thing very clear. Despite what you might feel, you are under no obligation to be here, nor to speak with any one of us. Sergeant Davis is here so he can testify to that later if need be. You are absolutely free to walk away right now, and nothing will be made of the fact.”

A bit of the old Emily flashed across her face. “I doubt that.”

Jonathon didn’t let it pass. “You doubt what, Officer Doyle?”

“That if I walk out of here, it won’t be held against me. You guys’ll think I’m hiding something.”

Jonathon leaned forward, resting his elbows on his knees, his low, calm voice barely containing a sudden passion. "Your name has come up enough times that we wanted to talk with you. If you don't want to be part of that process, fine, but don't start thinking you know what's going on in my head. I happen to know what it's like being hung out to dry. I know you get distrustful and isolated. I know how conversations die when you enter a room. I won't be wondering what you're hiding if you hightail it out of here, because to me that would be the most natural thing in the world. Are we straight on that?"

I had to hand it to him. She merely nodded and said, "I'm sorry." I did wonder, however, at the allusion he'd made, and the implication that so many of us had at one time or another found ourselves on the outside of a demanding, often stratified system.

He sat back and crossed his legs. "Don't be. Now—do you want to be here or not? Simple yes or no."

Now Emily Doyle surprised me. She smiled lopsidedly and said, "No and yes."

Jon matched her smile and shook his head. "Point taken." He paused a moment, as if gathering his thoughts, and continued. "One last technicality. As Sergeant Davis is your immediate superior, you might feel more comfortable with him out of earshot. That would also not be held against you."

Here she was unequivocal. "No. I'd like him to stay."

"All right. We'll get started, but keep in mind that we're groping for answers here, not trading accusations, so try not to get your back up. It is our understanding that you and Brian Padget were intimately involved with one another. When you broke up, was it amicable or were there bad feelings?"

The kaleidoscope of emotions that swept across her suddenly red face was painful to watch. Given the emotional strain this woman had endured, and her inexperience in dealing with it, I was half surprised she didn't yield to her famous physical prowess and deck Jonathon Michael where he sat.

In fact, once her shock and anger had settled back down, like a suddenly disturbed flock of birds, her response, while tense, was delivered calmly. "We were friends before, and we still are."

"Did you know early on about his affair with Jan Bouch?"

She pursed her lips briefly. "Soon enough, I guess—town this size."

"How did you feel about that?"

"It wasn't any of my business."

Jon shifted in his chair, becoming slightly more pointed in his body language. "Let's try that one again."

"We'd already broken up. It was his choice." She paused. No one else filled the silence. "I thought he was nuts, risking his career."

I sensed in a slight widening of her eyes that she wanted to add something. But the moment was so quickly overtaken by Jon's next question, I wasn't even sure what I'd seen.

"Did other members of the department feel likewise? Was it a topic of conversation?"

"I knew they were talking about it, but not around me, since Brian and me had been going together. Sergeant Davis approached Brian unofficially, not that it did any good."

Davis moved slightly, his eyes on the floor. He hadn't told me of any such conversation and was no doubt feeling awkward. Unnecessarily, I thought—the talk had been confidential, and he'd honored that promise.

"You know Brian pretty well," Jonathon went on, "and you seem to think highly of him, even if his relationship with Mrs. Bouch was perhaps poorly thought out. Were there other times he might've acted inappropriately?"

Her expression darkened. "Did he do dope, you mean? No fucking way...I'm sorry. I mean, he's like a regular straight arrow. He won't even drink a beer because he doesn't want alcohol in his system just in case there's an emergency."

"How about his dealings with Norm Bouch?"

Again, I thought I saw that desire to say more, but all she said was, "I didn't know he had any."

Jonathon Michael frowned. "If he didn't have any contact with Norm Bouch, how did he meet Jan?"

This time, the body language was more eloquent. Her eyes swept across all three of us, and she wet her lips before answering, "I guess it was just around town."

"Not during a domestic to the house? The log shows the PD went over there pretty regularly."

She nodded emphatically. "Sure. They could've met during a call."

"Except that Brian's name doesn't appear in the log once, not as a primary, not even as backup."

There was a long, awkward silence. Her voice, when it came, sounded tinny in the vast empty space around us. "Then I guess they didn't."

Jon continued as if nothing had happened. "Do you and Brian talk shop a lot?"

"As much as anybody."

"But you implied you didn't discuss the risks he was running by dating Mrs. Bouch, despite your friendship."

Her eyes narrowed angrily. "That was personal. It wasn't shop."

"What do you think of Norm Bouch? You were on more calls to his house than anyone."

She crossed her arms defensively. "So?"

Jon made a show of raising his eyebrows in surprise. "Surely that's a reasonable question. Dominating husband, abused wife who won't ever file charges, kids left to fend for themselves. What did you think of all that?"

What I thought was that Jonathon Michael had made a quick study of my briefing about Emily Doyle. He'd painted an approximation of Emily's own household as a child.

"I think it stinks," she answered him. "Not that it matters. We're paid to pick up the pieces after the wife's been beaten to death, or the kids have been pounded on so bad their bodies are walking proof of it. Even then, the son of a bitch who caused it ends up with a pat on the ass from some judge who doesn't know shit from Shinola about what's really going on."

Jonathon avoided the debate, keeping on course. "Is that what you see happening in the Bouch home?"

"Worse, since we all know Norm deals drugs, too, and got his wife hooked on 'em."

Jon turned philosophical. "Why do you think that's been allowed to continue?"

She was animated by now, her suspicions blunted by his drawing her out. "Look at this whole town, for Christ's sake. It's full of people like Norm. Maybe not on his scale, but people who live by their own rules, playing the system for all it's worth. They get paid for their rent, their food, their kids' education. And then they get tax-free jobs under the counter, buy and sell dope, fuck themselves brainless, and think that's A-okay. How can we do anything about all that when the same system we're working for started it in the first place?"

It was a textbook simplification, the embodiment of what I'd been told upon entering Bellows Falls. The hopes and hard work of the citizens struggling against Emily's complaints were all but lost on her—reduced to occasional articles in a newspaper she barely glanced at.

"But if as you suggest," Jon prompted her further, "the Norm Bouches of the world are the worst of the bunch, what would you propose for them?"

"The same as for any tactical threat. Target 'em and take 'em out. You can't do much for most of the rest, but bringing Bouch down would send a big message." Her face soured. "Unfortunately, not everyone agrees with that approach."

Jon feigned ignorance. "Who do you mean?"

She looked at us all belligerently. "I know you're trying to get me to stick my neck out on the chopping block. But the Chief wimped out on this, and I don't care who knows it. I told him what I told you, but he just wants to retire nice and peaceful. And we're supposed to keep things quiet in the meantime. Might as well give Bouch a license to operate."

Jonathon nodded like a psychoanalyst taking notes. "You and Brian talk a lot about this?"

Her face shut down after a quick glimmer of surprise. "Not much."

He let out a small sigh, feeling he'd circled this spot before. "Thank you, Officer Doyle. We appreciate your time and cooperation."

She looked confused for a minute, then surprisingly disappointed. She rose awkwardly from her chair, muttered, "Sure," and walked toward the distant stairs. Greg Davis hesitated and then followed her.

Jonathon Michael and I waited until we could no longer hear their footsteps echoing below us. I rose and went to the old, wavy-glass windows and looked out. The rain cut across the scenery in diagonal sheets, sprinkling the glass with tear-shaped drops.

"What do you think?" I asked.

"Something's going on," he admitted, "but I'm damned if I know what."

"Or what to do about it," I added.

"Maybe nothing for the moment. Your squad is handling the homicide investigation in Brattleboro all right, aren't they?"

"Yeah."

"Then let's drop this for the moment and go to Burlington."

16

A trip from Bellows Falls to Burlington takes about two hours by interstate. It also involves a sweeping natural tour of the state, from the low, rolling piedmont of eastern Vermont, across the dramatic, forested, fortress-like Green Mountains that form the spine of the state and give it its primary identity, to the glacier-carved Champlain Lowlands, from which Lake Champlain stretches, cold and turbulent, to the Adirondacks beyond.

Burlington is the state's sole metropolis, its largest conglomeration of arts, medicine, education, and commerce, and in the previous century a major freshwater port for materials being shipped to and from nearby Canada. Including the satellite towns dependent upon it, one hundred thousand people live in the area, a fifth of Vermont's entire population.

It's been accurately described as a junior Boston—erudite, stimulating, culturally rich, and, with Montreal a short drive away, truly cosmopolitan. Spread over a descending series of low hills leading down to the shores of Lake Champlain, it has an Old World feel to it, accentuated by a preponderance of antique wooden buildings, pedestrian-only market streets, and the occasional governmental monolith. Dominating it all, since the city tilts toward it, is the lake—mysterious, deep, and at the best of times faintly ominous.

Our first stop, fittingly for a city with stylish ambitions, was a restaurant not far from the new police department headquarters—a favorite hangout of that building's occupants. Spanning the buffer zone between the city's commercial heart and its rougher, darker, more dangerous Old North End, Bove's was a supplier of hearty, well-spiced, time-tested food.

A long, high-ceilinged hallway of a building, it had a narrow door and two windows at one end, a serving bar at the other, and ranks of tables and booths in between. The kitchen lay tucked out of sight to the rear.

As Jonathon Michael and I stepped in from the damp outdoors and stood blinking in the relative gloom, we saw the dim outline of an arm waving to us from one of the booths, and heard our names called out in greeting.

The man behind the voice was Paul O'Leary, chief of the Burlington police force, a thirty-year veteran who gave networking its most positive meaning. From the upper echelons of virtually every PD in the state, and many outside it, to the bureaucrats and politicians who controlled all our purse strings, O'Leary knew everyone of consequence. He swam these crowded waters as an informed, friendly presence, working for the betterment of all departments and often interceding when he thought his help could be useful. While some in our profession maligned his sunny enthusiasm as cynical self-service, I'd seen his integrity and intelligence in action more than once and recognized his good humor as genuine. It was reflective of his style that we representatives of three different agencies were meeting in a neutral, convivial setting instead of his office just a few blocks away. This was someone who knew his way around in a turf-conscious business.

He rose as we approached—a small, wiry, animated man with short white hair—and ushered us into the booth, introducing the serious young woman seated opposite him. "Audrey McGowen, Joe Gunther and Jonathon Michael. I figured it was too early for dinner, so I just ordered coffee. That okay?"

The waitress appeared as if by mental telepathy, and we both followed O'Leary's suggestion. Our host waited until she'd retreated before folding his hands around his cup and looking at us both eagerly. "So, I hear we're on a chase."

In a role reversal of a few hours earlier, I began the briefing while Jon silently sipped coffee. O'Leary took it in with nods and occasional smiles; McGowen—Sammie's friend from the Academy—took notes in a small pad she'd pulled from her pocket.

"So we basically have two priority items that're relevant to our department," O'Leary summed up when I'd finished. "Locate Lenny and see if and/or how he connects to Norm Bouch, and discreetly dig into Emily Doyle's background to check out the same thing. Is that about it?"

To silent agreement from both of us, he continued, "I asked Audrey to be in on this, not only because your folks, Joe, have already started her going, but because she's well suited to this anyhow. She's been on our detective squad three years, after an impressive start on Patrol, and she's been running cases that overlap both juvie and drug-related crime, so she's familiar with the field and the players. She's also sharp as a tack."

Audrey McGowen gave us an embarrassed half-smile, as familiar as we were with her boss's cheerleader ways. "I thought we could start at the computer," she said. "See if Lenny crops up anywhere. Assuming that suits you."

"Absolutely," I said.

O'Leary gave a friendly wave to the waitress behind the counter and slid from the booth, dropping five dollars on the table. He led us outside to the drenched parking lot, from which we formed a two-car caravan and drove west toward Battery Street.

The Burlington Police Department used to occupy two overstuffed ancient buildings downtown, finally rendered so confusing through countless remodelings that once, after a prisoner had broken away from his handlers, he was relocated wandering around, fruitlessly looking for an exit.

The PD's new home is a 30,000-square-foot converted factory building dating back to the twenties, half of which later housed an auto dealership in which a murder took place—a bit of karma O'Leary was regularly moved to explain. It is modern, well organized, well equipped, and designed for a twenty-percent expansion—the largest, most up-to-date station house in the state, and a monument to the diminutive dreamer who'd made it happen amid tight budgets and low expectations.

That same man now led us to one of the parking lots near the building and, tucked under an oversized umbrella, escorted us through the front doors. In the lobby, he turned with a big smile and said, "Well, I'll get out of your hair. I hope you find what you're after. I know you'll be in good hands with Audrey, and if anything comes up where I can lend a hand, don't hesitate to let me know." He shook hands all around and was gone, leaving Jonathon shaking his head with a smile.

"Amazing," he said. "Welcome to my house. Have fun, but I gotta go. Every other chief I know would be on us like we were recruiters from a motorcycle gang, wondering what we were *really* up to."

Audrey McGowen laughed as she took us through a white-walled maze of hallways, crisscrossed high overhead by exposed piping and electrical conduits. "Don't sell him short. One way or the other, he'll know everything you've done in here before you hit the sidewalk. He just doesn't get in your face like a lot of them do."

We entered a small room with several computers stationed against the walls and gathered three chairs before one of them, with Audrey at the keyboard. She spoke as she typed her way to where we wanted to be. "After Sammie contacted me about all this, I poked around a bit after hours. Norm Bouch has been renting that apartment on North Street for about three years. I found only one neighbor who'd ever set eyes on him, and he said he was a real nice guy. Nobody local seemed to know him—I checked the bar at the end of the block, and a nearby grocery store. In that neighborhood especially, that's unusual. I wasn't sure what to make of it, except that he either keeps a super-low profile, or never uses the place."

She hit a final couple of keys and then paused. "Okay. These are the Intel files. We'll start with just 'Lenny,' and see if we get lucky. It's not that common a name."

The screen rewarded us immediately, identifying Lenny Markham, age twenty-eight, living on Cedar Street. Audrey studied the few coded entries below his name and sat back in her chair, her hands in her lap.

"We may've stepped into something here. There's an indicator to go through the chief of detectives before establishing contact."

Michael and I exchanged glances, the satisfaction of moments ago suddenly losing its flavor.

Burlington's chief of detectives was Timothy Giordi, Jr. He'd been a child when I first met him. His father worked for the Barre PD, just east of Montpelier. Tim, Sr., would drive his young straw-haired son around in the front seat of the town's sole patrol car, tutoring the boy in the ways of law and order. The kid never had a chance. From elementary school on up, all he talked about was becoming a cop. Every course he took, every summer job he considered, and finally, every college he applied to were solely to enhance his progress to that end. And to be a local cop at that. Where other people with his motivation might have aimed at some federal agency or at least the State Police, the other legacy left to him by his father was a love of the neighborhood. Tim Giordi applied to the Burlington PD fresh out of college and had been with them ever since, receiving his present assignment just a few months before his father died of a heart attack, the result, his son had once wistfully said, of bad coffee, worse food, and a lifetime of sitting behind the wheel of that patrol car.

The three of us found Tim driving a computer instead, hunched forward in his office chair, staring at the screen as if willing it to confess.

He looked up at us with obvious relief as Audrey knocked on his open door.

He rose to his feet, a wide smile on his face. "Hey, look who's here. Jonathon, Joe, good to see you. Christ, it's been a year or more. What've you been up to?"

While he spoke, he circled his desk, shook our hands, pulled chairs from the corners, and generally fussed enough to make his Italian-born mother proud. As soon as we were all seated, Audrey brought the mood to a focus by handing him a printout of what we'd found.

Tim read its contents and raised his eyebrows. "Ah," was all he said at first, with the kind of enthusiasm one reserves for unpleasant discoveries. He placed the sheet face down on his desk and asked me, "What's up with this guy?"

"We think he's working for a dope dealer in Bellows Falls—part of a network. Jon and I were hoping to talk to him."

"You're running that crooked cop case, right? Does this tie in?"

"We think so," Jon said. "But we're not sure yet."

Giordi steepled his fingers in front of his chin. "The reason Audrey brought this to me is because Lenny Markham is an informant."

He didn't need to say much more. I now understood both his and Audrey's reactions. Confidential informants—CIs in police jargon—ran the gamut from the vaguely reliable bum on the corner to the shifty-eyed undercover operatives so popular in the movies. Regardless of where they are in the pecking order, however, they are jealously kept by their individual police handlers. The breaking of a case often hinges on the availability and reliability of a CI, so the officer with the most or best of them does well to tend his or her flock. Unfortunately, this attitude isn't entirely altruistic. In a competitive market with limited upward mobility, officers see their sources as money in the bank. What everyone in that room understood was that we wanted access to someone whose handler was likely to voice a very strong objection.

Giordi checked his watch and picked up the phone, muttering, "Excuse me a second," as he did so. He dialed an internal number and said to whoever answered, "It's Tim Giordi. We need to talk. I just got an interagency cooperation request involving Lenny Markham. Give me five minutes to clear out my office, okay? Thanks."

He hung up and looked at us apologetically. "I hate to do this, but I better run this by Lenny's contact. Audrey, why don't you introduce these two to the soda machine or something? I'll page you in a bit."

We filed out and followed his advice, silently marching toward the refreshment machines to stare at the offerings. There was no question that we'd eventually get access to Lenny Markham. The attorney general of the state of Vermont wasn't likely to let a case be derailed because of some cop's desire to keep his sources to himself. But it was a delicate matter. The spirit of interagency cooperation was still in its infancy, with everyone paying it lip service, and many privately fighting it tooth and nail. And while the AG's jurisdiction extended to the state's borders, his success was often linked to the vagaries of local politics.

"I wonder who he's talking to," Audrey mused, her eyes fixed on a small bag of corn chips with a suspiciously fluorescent glow to them. Fifteen minutes later, we trooped back into Giordi's office, summoned by a disembodied voice over the building's P.A. system. As we crossed the threshold, I just barely heard Audrey groan and knew right then we were in for some negotiating.

The man sitting opposite the chief of detectives wasn't happy. He didn't get up as we entered, didn't offer to shake hands, and generally regarded us as if we'd just doubled his mortgage payments.

Giordi nodded in his direction as soon as we'd settled down. "This is Duncan Fasca, Lenny Markham's contact inside the department. Given the sensitive relationship between a contact and his CI, Duncan had a few questions about your interest in Lenny."

I glanced from Fasca to Tim and back again, picking up on Giordi's almost stilted manner. Not only had the conversation obviously not gone well between them, but they clearly didn't like one another in the first place. I gave Fasca an apologetic smile. "I'm sorry we stepped right into the middle of things. We had no idea Lenny had ties to the PD. We heard about him through visits he used to make to a Lawrence, Mass, guy named Norm Bouch—*he's* actually the one we're after. At first, we just wanted to find out what Lenny could tell us about Bouch, but I got to admit, it's starting to look like Lenny and him're working together. You hear about the homicide in Brattleboro—the blood in the abandoned motel and no body?"

Fasca spoke for the first time. "What of it?"

"We're pretty sure the dead man worked for Bouch, too—was Lenny's Brattleboro counterpart. We think Bouch runs a juvenile drug ring using regional lieutenants."

Fasca looked at me incredulously. "Markham's running a dope ring? Here in town? What kind of evidence do you have?"

"Witnesses to conversations between Bouch and him," I said vaguely. "But that's why we want to talk to him. To nail a few things down."

"A fishing expedition," Fasca said. He looked at his boss. "I expose Lenny to other cops, he'll stop working for me. Just 'cause his name came up in a conversation."

"When you set up Lenny as a CI, you knew he was no choirboy," Giordi answered stiffly. "Isn't it possible he could be doing this without your knowledge?"

That put Duncan in a corner. If he said no and we proved him wrong, he'd look like an idiot. If he said yes, then all room for objection evaporated. My mention of Jasper's homicide hadn't been anecdotal. I'd brought it up to show that Lenny could be tied to a capital case—and that Duncan Fasca should tread carefully. He steered for middle ground. "Maybe."

I saw the hint of a smile appear on Jonathon's face, which made me careful not to gloat. "Duncan, look. I know what a pain in the ass this is. But by your own admission, Lenny could be dirty, which means his time may be up anyhow. Why don't you come on board with us and show these guys the price of playing both ends against the middle? We could go after him ourselves, but it would be a lot easier with your help."

Fasca shook his head, his face an angry scowl. "That's easy for you. If it turns out to be a wild-goose chase, you haven't lost a thing. I end up with a snitch who never talks to me again. This guy's good. He's been real useful to me. You know that, Chief. I don't want to be run over by a bunch of hotshots from out of town who could give a shit what they leave behind."

"I don't think that's the case here," Giordi said, his voice carrying a veiled warning.

Reluctantly, Fasca had all but conceded. "Yeah, well, like I said, easy to say."

"You join us, you can find out for yourself," I suggested. "If you're interested, I'd like you in on the initial meet. You can steer the conversation yourself. That way, if we all agree we're barking up the wrong tree, maybe you won't lose him."

Fasca didn't answer immediately, but by now his resistance was purely for show. "He might not play if he knows I'm bringing someone."

The answer to that was too obvious to mention. The room remained silent a few moments longer, until Fasca finally threw in the glove. "All right, I'm screwed either way, so I might as well go along."

He suddenly leaned forward and stared at Tim Giordi. "But I want it known I'm doing it under protest, okay?"

Tim kept a straight face. "You got it, Duncan. Why don't you pull what you've got on Lenny?" He jerked a thumb at Jonathon and me. "They'll be wanting a full profile on him prior to any meeting. I'll send them your way as soon as I'm through."

Fasca heaved himself out of his chair and nodded sharply in our direction. He left without saying a word.

The mood in the air instantly lightened. Jonathon raised his eyebrows at me. "You sure giving him that much clout was a good idea?"

Giordi answered for me. "He's not much on manners, but Duncan's a hard worker. You point him in the right direction, and he'll chew through walls. He just has to feel he's got some element of control. I appreciate what you did, Joe, and I think you'll be happy with the results."

Duncan Fasca was as good as Tim Giordi's word. He took Jonathon, Audrey, and me to a small conference room and briefed us for over an hour on everything he knew of Lenny Markham, which, as it turned out, left ample room for Lenny to be functioning as we suspected he was. To my eyes, he was a classic hustler, working every angle, faithful to no one. Reviewing Fasca's limited perspective on him, I thought back to the context in which we'd first heard Lenny's name. Molly Bremmer had described him not as Norm's trainee but more as a colleague. Given the insight I had now, I wondered if Norm had recruited Lenny, or if Lenny had smelled an opportunity. If the latter were true, then the relationship between the two of them became more complex—and possibly more dangerous.

The briefing was valuable for another reason. It allowed us to see Duncan in his element, showing off his work, sharing his insights.

I could see Jonathon Michael getting used to the man and growing to accept him. He was as Giordi had described him—tenacious, persistent, and not very appealing—but he was also insightful in his way, and certainly knowledgeable about his beat. What he told us of Lenny was at least as useful for what it revealed about Burlington, which unfortunately for me resulted in a slight dampening of my admiration for the town. As eclectic and appealing as it remained, the Queen City's tattered petticoats were now exposed, and I found them depressingly familiar.

Nevertheless, by the time Duncan Fasca finally reached for the phone and called Lenny Markham for a meeting—"one on one"—I felt I knew enough about our target to be comfortable talking with him.

The phone call didn't last long. Both speakers were used to the routine. Duncan hung up after a couple of minutes and announced, "Flynn Theatre, tomorrow morning, ten o'clock, on the grid. He's got a job there."

Jon looked at him quizzically.

"The grid," Audrey explained, surprising us all, "is like a huge metal catwalk, 'bout forty feet over the stage. It's a good way to get around, and to see without being seen, but it's not a place for people who don't like heights."

In the silence that greeted her explanation, she added, "I had a summer job at the Flynn once. It's a beautiful old place—lots of nooks and crannies."

"Which is probably why he chose it," Jonathon said unhappily. "Is it safe?"

Duncan waved his concern away. "The Vermont Symphony Orchestra'll be practicing at the same time, for Christ's sake. It's not like it's the North End at midnight. He chose it 'cause he's there anyway, and none of his cronies would be caught dead in a real theater, that's all. He doesn't want to blow his cover."

A young woman poked her head through the doorway. "Is there a Joe Gunther in here?"

I raised my hand. "Yeah."

"You have a call on line three."

I thanked her and picked up the phone on the conference table.

"Gunther."

"It's J.P. I think we found Jasper Morgan."

17

It was dark by the time Jon and I reached Brattleboro, and raining harder than I would have thought possible outside a movie set. The water fell in a torrent, pouring off roofs of cars and buildings in hundreds of cascades, gathering in the streets like a diverted river.

I pulled into the abandoned motel's parking lot, now staked out with yellow "Police" barrier tape and occupied by a number of official vehicles. My shoes vanished underwater as soon as I stepped from the car, and I instantly felt the first cool, wet trickles of rain slipping in between my raincoat and neck.

Wearing high boots and slickers, and opening umbrellas over their heads, J.P. Tyler and Gail emerged from the lobby entrance to greet us.

"Christ," I told them, "has it been raining like this for long? I've felt like I needed gills since we hit this side of the state."

"About an hour," Gail answered, slipping her arm through mine so we could better share her umbrella. "It just opened up. From Bellows Falls north they've been getting hammered all afternoon. It wasn't even sprinkling here till this hit."

"That's what prompted me to use the dogs now," J.P. almost shouted over the sound of the water. "The weather's supposed to be bad for days, and I didn't want to wait."

Jon asked the obvious. "What dogs?"

"J.P. had cadaver dogs brought in from Maine," Gail explained.

"I thought with the huge amount of blood," he added, "and the relative freshness of the scene, we might get lucky." He gestured around to the side of the building. "It's over here. I'll tell you on the way."

We waded over to the side of the parking lot and down a slippery grass embankment, heading for the rear of the old motel and an overgrown, scrub-choked wasteland similar to much of what lurks behind the Putney Road's storefronts.

"Of course," Tyler continued, "freshness isn't that big a deal. These dogs have found bodies up to twenty-one years postmortem. But the weather—before this shit hit us—was ideal for a search. Not too hot, nice gentle breezes at both ends of the day, open land for the most part. Dogs need to locate and trace what they call the cone of the scent, and everything I could see looked good for that. I also really liked the layout of the scene." He waved his arm at the soaking darkness around us. "Dead adult body, quasi-urban environment, the shooter and probably one other with him...It was likely the corpse hadn't been carried too far, and buried fast and not too deep.

"Anyhow," he summed up, "it worked. The handler arrived with two dogs, started with just one, and inside an hour we had what we were looking for."

Following his powerful flashlight's beam, which sparkled madly from the millions of prismatic raindrops in its path, we crested a small rise and came to a narrow field in front of a solid wall of trees. Before us was a large tent, spilling brilliant light like a huge overturned cup of milk, and sheltering a half dozen people clustered around a dismally familiar excavation.

"They got the tent up just before the rain," Gail said quietly. "Even before they started digging for real."

"I didn't want to take any chances," Tyler added.

The group parted as we ducked under the tent flaps, revealing a carefully exposed, shallow rectangular trench. Mercifully, it was empty, its contents zipped into a black body bag resting alongside.

I crouched between the hole and the body, feeling the water squish out of my shoes. I had to speak loudly over the thrumming on the canvas above us. "What's the rundown?"

"Outside of the grave itself," Tyler answered, "we didn't find anything. We crawled around, used metal detectors, ran the whole routine. In daylight you can't see any buildings except the motel from here—at least none with any windows facing this direction. Sammie had Kunkle and Ron and a bunch of patrol officers canvass the area, like we did when we found the blood, but nothing's come up yet. They're still at it—that's why they're not here now—but it doesn't look good for witnesses."

I nodded my head toward the black bag. "And him?"

"We just zipped him in before you got here. The assistant ME was about to take him up to Burlington."

I glanced up, surprised, and saw Alfred Gould standing in the group. "Sorry, Al. Didn't see you there." I looked around at everyone. "Sorry to all of you, in fact—should've said hi. You know Jonathon Michael from the AG's office?"

The men were mostly our patrol officers. One worked with Al. Another I took to be the dog handler. They all nodded their greetings without comment.

"Any preliminary findings?" I asked Al Gould.

He squatted by the body's other side and pulled the zipper down a couple of feet, revealing a badly decomposed, musty-smelling remnant of a human being, its wildly mussed, dirty hair contrasting starkly with the neat skeletal grin just below it. Any remaining skin was dark and gelatinous, sloughed off entirely in places.

"It's better than it looks," he said, pointing at the skull. "The clothing retarded decomposition, so under his T-shirt the skin's pretty much intact. He's also wearing a pair of jockey briefs, but nothing else, so the notion that he was in bed looks good. The two bullet wounds seem to be through and through—one just under the ribs, the other in the neck. From the projectory angles and what J.P. told me of the scene, I'd say the abdominal wound came first, exiting just below the left scapula. That would be consistent with someone lying supine on a bed, his feet toward the killer, and with the killer also being low down, as if sitting on the dresser opposite. The second wound caused most of the bleeding, of course. I'd guess it pretty much tore away the carotid."

He straightened and redid the zipper. "Hillstrom'll give you all the details, probably by late tomorrow, and there'll be more to go on then, but those're the basics."

Beverly Hillstrom was the state's medical examiner, famous for her detailed analyses. "Thanks, Al." I looked up at Tyler. "And you're sure it's Morgan?"

J.P. shook his head. "Not scientifically. We contacted his dentist, so X-rays'll be sent up north, too. But we found his name stenciled in the back of his Retreat-issue T-shirt. Nothing we've found yet says it's not him."

Tyler hesitated, and then said, "We do have another problem, though, and none of us is real sure what to make of it."

He gestured to me to follow him. I rose, circumvented the open grave, and walked some twenty feet to the other end of the tent, where a large sheet of cardboard lay covering the ground.

"The dog picked up on this, too," Tyler said, and slid the cardboard over to one side. At first, I couldn't tell what he was showing me, other than a slight depression in the earth. Then I noticed a smaller, dirtier, more disintegrated version of the skeletal leer I'd just left.

"Jesus Christ."

"Al guesses it's a kid, but that's about it. Those few teeth and some bone fragments are all we found. The grave's a lot shallower, so we're thinking animals made a meal out of it, pulling most of the skeleton apart like they usually do. It's obviously been here a long time."

He looked up at the tent fabric above us, which was shimmering from the pounding outside. "Once this mess clears up, we can take this whole field apart, section by section. There might be more like this one. That's why I asked the dog handler if he could stay over. Sammie said it was okay."

"You talk to Willy about this one?" I asked.

"No. We found it by accident. We were putting up the tent and working on the other grave, when the dog alerted to the second one. We had to shift things a bit to protect them both, but that's all we had time to do. Willy had already left to help with the canvass."

"He told me Jasper had made an example out of a runner who ripped him off. The kid disappeared, the point was made, and things went smoothly from then on. We never heard a thing about it."

Tyler was staring at me incredulously. "What about the parents?"

"I asked the same thing. Apparently you and I are living in a dream world. They figured he'd run off—never thought twice about it. That's why I asked about Willy. If he can locate them, and the crime lab can extract some DNA from what's here, maybe we can put a headstone over this little guy. Is Al going to take care of him, too?"

"In a day or so. This hasn't been properly excavated yet, and I figured Morgan had priority."

"You did right," I said to his unasked question. "Take your time, do it by the numbers. It's not going to make any difference if we let him sleep a little longer."

The water poured across our skylight as if a hose were poised just out of sight above it. The noise on the roof, though much more muted, reminded me of the excavation we'd left a few hours earlier. Gail and I were in bed, the lights out, entangled in one another's arms. We were still slightly damp from having made love with an almost desperate passion, driven by a need to avoid the images we'd so recently witnessed.

The reprieve had been purely temporary, however, and I knew her thoughts, like mine, were back in the tent filled with too much light and sadness.

"Can I ask you something?" she said after a while.

"Sure."

"What's it like for you, seeing that?"

I paused a long time before answering. "I can't remember the first combat death I saw in Asia, or the first dead body I saw as a cop. They've all sort of blurred together. But I've wondered sometimes if with each exposure, I haven't come away with a small piece of that person's soul. It makes me think that one of these days I'll hit overload. Probably not, though. People get used to worse things than I've ever seen."

"So you don't feel tears, or anger, or even depressed?"

I was uneasy with the question, although not for myself. I was worried I hadn't paid attention to her under the tent, that some momentous spiritual shift had occurred inside her that my carelessness had allowed to run rampant. When Gail had returned to law school and later become a deputy state's attorney, I'd been pleased and flattered by the process, even though it had been taxing on us both. I'd felt her moving toward me philosophically and emotionally and had responded in kind, making of our buying a home together a symbolic act. Now, in this one question, I feared the threat of a tremor and wondered if it all hadn't happened too fast, with too many assumptions taken arrogantly in stride.

But I kept this to myself and merely answered as honestly as I could. "No. Sadness sometimes, probably born of frustration. Mostly, I just feel I'm on the outside looking in."

The rain filled the silence that followed, oddly reinforcing our sense of security in this house—the shelter we'd built over our shared life.

"This might be a little corny," I added. "But you're a big factor in making a lot of it easier to take."

She let out a deep sigh.

"How 'bout you?" I finally asked, the simplicity of the words belying the concern tucked beneath them.

She turned her face toward mine. "I was worried it wasn't right to feel that way—that I was missing something. Or turning cold."

I laughed, greatly relieved. "I don't think you'll ever have to worry about that."

We kissed, and she resettled herself and gradually went to sleep. But the conversation stayed with me long into the night. I'd spent a lifetime pursuing, controlling, or arresting people who frequently either got killed or killed themselves. But the further back I reached to see their faces, the more I realized my comment about what a stabilizer Gail's love had become for me went deeper than I'd thought. One of the biggest differences between those bodies and me, in a spiritual sense, was that they were alone, and I was not. It was a revelation a good many other cops could claim, too, of course, but as I'd been finding out recently, not all of them.

In the end, that thought gave me comfort, and—as I too fell off to sleep—a reawakening hopefulness.

18

From the sidewalk, Burlington's Flynn Theatre on Main Street is at best unprepossessing. One and a half stories high, it is by all appearances solid and well built, with a white stone facade demurely but elegantly carved with its name, but in that it is no different from an old bank building or a pretentious post office. The striking thing about it is the marquee crowning its bank of front doors like a jester's gaudy hat. Multi-hued, ornate, and speckled with hundreds of flashing colored bulbs, at night it draws in theatergoers like moths to a flame.

It was not at night that we gathered under that marquee, however, but shortly before ten o'clock the next morning, the time specified by Lenny Markham for his meeting with Duncan Fasca. We'd never considered making this a one-on-one affair, of course, but with the discovery of Jasper's body, and of what we were presuming was one of his runners, our wariness of Lenny's role had ratcheted up several notches. No longer were we content with merely stacking the meeting in our favor numerically. Now we were going to stake out the whole building, curious to learn what Lenny might do following our talk.

Unfortunately, our team had not grown much in size, the Burlington PD not being in a position to supply us reinforcements for a case they didn't own. Our adjusted plan of attack, therefore, was for Fasca and me to meet with Lenny, while Audrey McGowen, Jonathon, and a single plainclothes officer Audrey had begged from Patrol kept watch on the various exits around the building. We all had portable radios, turned off until needed so Lenny wouldn't be spooked by an inadvertent transmission.

Following some last-minute detailing, therefore, Duncan Fasca and I separated from the others and entered the lobby. Like the exterior, it was tastefully low-key—terrazzo floor tiles, antique marble half walls, niched display cases, alternating with mirrors and gentle lighting. The farther we walked, the more that lighting lit the way, allowing for an elegant transition from the glare off the sidewalk. The first sign that the theater's muted facade was in fact a charade surfaced as we passed from the lobby to the foyer. It soared overhead well in excess of two stories, dwarfing us physically and injecting an element of wonder. The back of the building was not only taller than its entrance but, being sited on the slope of a hill, extended downward as well.

The effect of this architectural slyness reached completion upon entering the performance hall itself. Even warned of something grand by the foyer's sneak preview, I was totally unprepared for the enormity of what we encountered. Huge, dark, cavernous, and as resonant as a tomb, the hall seemed more grotto than man-made structure. The orchestra seats swept down and away toward the enormous distant stage, taking full advantage of the site's natural incline, while the walls, ornate in lavish Art Deco, hurtled skyward to meet in an elaborate, graceful curved ceiling some forty feet above our heads. It had been like entering a modest house, discovering an impressive living room, and then proceeding into a cathedral at the rear. I was so taken with the effect that despite our reason for being here, I tilted back my head, let out a quiet laugh, and said, "Jesus. This is wonderful."

Fasca glanced at the ceiling, muttered, "Yeah, I guess," and pointed to a staircase along the side wall. "Let's head up and see if we can find him."

We didn't look far. As we reached the mezzanine, we were stopped by a teenager lounging by the guardrail, watching some eighty musicians tuning their instruments.

"You want to see Lenny?" the boy asked, visibly uncomfortable with the setting, obviously not an employee.

"Yeah," Fasca answered.

"Follow me."

He took us past an "employees only" sign up another set of stairs, to a landing with a steel ladder leading to a small, square opening some eight feet off the ground. "He's up there—on the grid. Make sure you don't got nothin' in your pockets that'll fall out—pens, pads, stuff like that."

The boy stood there, waiting for us to go on without him. Fasca hesitated, struck as I'd been by the meaning behind his instructions, remembering what Audrey had said about it being no place for those with vertigo.

"Where will he be?" Fasca finally asked.

"Over the stage. I gotta go." The boy bolted downstairs and vanished.

“This setup bother you?” I asked Fasca, “knowing Lenny?”

He shrugged and grabbed the first rung of the ladder. “He’s used rug rats before.”

Beyond the square hole at the top of the ladder, there was a tiny landing, a flight of three steps, and a broad wooden catwalk running from one side of the theater to the other, high above the mezzanine, and parallel to the stage. Not that any of this was clearly visible. The lighting allowed for only occasional glimmers, casting the vaguest of shadows.

I pulled a penlight from my pocket, having ignored the boy’s warning, and turned it on.

We were enmeshed in a spider’s web of enormous steel girders, crisscrossing the air space between the roof overhead and the ceiling I’d admired from below. Shooting off from our catwalk were two others, each at a ninety-degree angle, leading to the grid over the stage. Killing my penlight for a moment, I could see the barest outline of a man, far in the distance, moving around a large, dark piece of equipment.

“I think that’s him,” Fasca muttered and headed gingerly in that direction, as conscious as I was that a fall off the narrow plank bridge would take us right through the ceiling to the seats far below. None of the catwalks had railings.

As we got nearer, I returned the penlight to my pocket. The glow from the cavern beneath us filtered up around the feet of the man ahead, revealing the source of his attention to be a large, extinguished spotlight, sharply angled to pinpoint objects on stage. It was bolted to a thick stanchion, which was attached to an open-mesh steel grate. Its dark, tapered head—an oversized parody of a monk’s cowl—peered down through an open rectangular hole in the grid, also without a rail.

The man, whom I could now see was wearing black pants and a black long-sleeved turtleneck, turned and straightened as we reached him. In the light from below, his features were sharply highlighted, making him look like a silent-movie Dracula. “Who the fuck is this, Duncan?”

His voice was an urgent whisper, incredulous that the sacrament of a cop and his snitch was being so cavalierly breached. Under our feet, through the mesh of the grid and the hole at the base of the light, a crowd of small figures, casually dressed, sat in a large semicircle of chairs, instruments in hand. The familiar sweet jumble of their tuning up revived an instant mental snapshot of the first time my mother took me and my brother to a concert. We’d both thought that initial swelling of incoherent sound was the start of the program, and we'd been entranced.

From this height, I felt like I was looking down from a low-flying airplane.

Fasca's voice brought me back to the present. "This is Joe Gunther, Lenny. He's from the AG's office."

Lenny Markham glared at me. "My pleasure. Now get the hell out of here. It's a restricted area. No tourists allowed."

"He knows you're my CI."

Markham looked at both of us in stunned silence.

"The reason I'm here," I put in, "is that I think your life may be in danger."

Lenny rolled his eyes heavenward. "No shit, Sherlock." He pointed at Fasca. "You come sailing in here with a cop from Montpelier, say, 'He knows you're my CI, Lenny,' and you tell me my ass is up for grabs? What kind of fucking idiot do you take me for?" He suddenly stabbed Fasca in the chest with his finger. "You being straight with me?"

Fasca looked confused. "Sure, Lenny. That's why we came."

"Then tell me: is this bozo the only one who knows about me?"

The answer should have been an immediate and unequivocal "Yes." Instead, Duncan hesitated a split second and glanced at me. His "Sure," came too late.

Markham stepped back as if we'd just exposed him to the plague. "You cocksucker. I take care of your fucking career, and you run me up the flagpole." He shifted to me abruptly. "So who's out to kill me, besides you two assholes?"

"Norm Bouch."

Mimicking a bad melodrama, a sudden burst of orchestral music filled the air, causing both Fasca and me to instinctively look down. Lenny's reaction was more original. He grabbed the narrow end of the spotlight and swung it with all his strength. It spun around, smacked me on the side of the head, and sent me sprawling against Fasca.

Fasca fell back against one of the steel girders. I continued past him, and stepped through the open hole in the grid.

I have often wondered at the written accounts of people in times of peril. Does time slow down? Do you suddenly reminisce? As my feet slipped past the comforting plane of the grid, and I felt the sudden lurch of abrupt acceleration, neither of those impressions struck me. All I thought, and all I managed to say, was "Shit."

But that may have been because I wasn't given more time. Instead of having the full distance of the drop to come up with something more satisfying, I was jarringly interrupted by my right hand grabbing onto the edge of the hole as it went by.

There was a near-mystical feeling to it all in the end, however. Hanging there by one hand, the raised teeth of the grid's mesh cutting into my fingers, the pain from my shoulder just starting to set in, I did enjoy a moment of almost weightless euphoria. The music that had distracted me now filled the air in which I was suspended, sliding off the curved ceiling and hitting me with a wonderful, swelling vibration. I even knew the tune—the "Infernal Dance," from Stravinsky's *Firebird*—which my mother had exposed us to as children on the record player, another example of her campaign to bring us culture.

Between my dangling feet, the orchestra was hard at work, laboring over their instruments in perfect synchrony, their heads bent over the music. The conductor, in jeans and a colorful shirt, cut the air with her baton, which from here looked as large as a single shaft of straw. I felt warm, and stimulated, and washed with beauty. I could also feel my hand getting very tired.

"Joe?"

I tilted my head back to look up, half resentful of the intrusion. The movement made me dizzy, and I suddenly remembered how the spotlight had smacked my temple. Seeing Duncan's terror-filled eyes, I realized for the first time that I was in real trouble. Falling through a hole half-conscious hadn't seemed all that terrifying at the time. Having interrupted the process, however, and regained an element of focus, I was now all too aware of what was about to happen. A surge of panic hit me. "I can't hang on much longer."

He reached down tentatively and touched my forearm.

"You won't be able to hold me," I grunted, the pain in my hand becoming excruciating.

"Right, right," he muttered. "Can you get your other hand up?"

"I don't dare try. I can't feel my right one anymore."

"Shit," he said loudly, echoing my own thoughts precisely. Then, "Hang on," and he vanished from view.

I took that last comment as literally as possible.

I no longer wanted to look down, no longer thought the music beautiful and soothing. I was drowning in it now, felt it pulling at my legs. I shut my eyes briefly and thought about letting go. The relief from the pain, even though brief, might be worth it.

Fasca's excited voice brought me back. "I found something, it's like a safety strap. I'll try to get it around you."

It looked like an oversized leash with a heavy clasp at one end. He quickly slung it around my arm, clipped it to itself, forming a lasso, and then lowered the loop to the middle of my chest.

"Put your left arm through it, so I can snug it up to your armpit."

I did as he asked and felt the comforting bite of the strap against my body. Still looking up, I saw Fasca stand and straddle the hole, his legs braced for my weight, the strap snaking across the back of his neck and shoulders.

"Okay, now listen. When I tell you, let go with your right hand and lower that arm—fast. I don't want this thing slipping off. Ready?"

I was, intellectually, but nothing happened with my hand. I could no longer feel it, much less control it. My whole body was given over to pain and exhaustion. I shut my eyes.

"Now."

It worked, although I don't recall how. There was a sudden drop, a great tightening around my chest. Fasca grunted once, loudly, as if he'd been hit by a branch, and I remember swaying, as I'd enjoyed doing as a child from high in a tree.

Fasca's strangled voice barked out, "Grab on," moments later, and I reopened my eyes to see the edge of the hole at eye level. My right arm throbbing, I hooked my left onto the grid and began hefting myself on board. Duncan stopped pulling on the strap and quickly grabbed the back of my belt. With a final heave, he dumped me like a duffel bag at his feet.

He collapsed sprawling onto the catwalk. "Jesus H. Christ. That was close."

"Radio," I whispered weakly.

He shook his head in anger. "Damn," and grabbed a portable from his pocket. As soon as he turned it on, we heard Audrey saying, "He's gone back in. Joe? Duncan? You there? Come in."

Fasca keyed the mike. "Audrey. You see Lenny? He clobbered us and split."

Still flexing my right hand, I turned on my own radio and added, "Call for backup. Aggravated assault of an officer. Is he still in the building?"

"Yeah," Audrey answered. "He came barreling out the front door, saw me, and ducked back in."

"Okay. Stay put 'til reinforcements come, then check out the lobby and foyer. Duncan and I'll start working down from the grid."

I directed Duncan to the nearby ladder running down to the stage below, while I returned the way we'd come, sweeping the area as I went with my penlight. By the time I reached the short ladder to the staircase, my arm, though painful, had regained its feeling and mobility.

I first checked out the control room at the top of the stairs, where I found people manning computers and lighting equipment, and from where the stage could be seen through a row of thick glass windows. No one there had seen Lenny go by.

Returning to the mezzanine, I quickly ran up the aisle alongside the deserted seats, looking for anybody who might be curled up on the floor. After finding myself alone, I used the radio again. "Audrey, it's Joe."

"Go ahead. The lobby and foyer are clear."

"Same with the grid, the control room, and the mezzanine. Is the building sealed off?"

"People're coming from all over. I have an idea, though. Meet me just inside the performance hall doors."

I quickly descended the last flight of stairs and found her standing by a small hatch, much like the one we'd taken to the grid, mounted halfway up the wall.

"Where's this lead?" I asked.

"It's like the grid in reverse—they call it the plenum. It's a crawl space between the floor and the dirt, used to circulate air—1930s ventilation technology. It's got fans big enough to replace all the air in the building in three minutes."

She pulled on the handle and swung it open. Immediately, I heard and felt the rush of a steady wind sucking by the door. "And it's unlocked, which it shouldn't be."

She hopped up onto the threshold, reached inside and hit a light switch. Before me was an enormous concrete chamber, gray, feature-less, and about four feet high, stretching away in a downward curve as far as I could see. The dirt floor, covered in thick plastic sheets, alternated between broad avenues leading in the direction of the stage, and six-foot-deep trenches that ran alongside.

"Those are for any water runoff," Audrey explained, "in case of flood or whatever. I bet my butt he went through here. There's a door connecting it to the fan room."

I hesitated, although I liked the notion that I couldn't fall any distance from here. "Are the two of us going to be enough?"

She was already swinging her legs inside. "Sure. It's wide open and well lit."

I climbed up beside her as she updated the others by radio. It was true that by simply walking the entire breadth of the building stooped over, we could check on the ditches just as I had the rows of seats in the mezzanine—and with similar results. The difference in environment, however, was considerable. Where the first had been lofty, dark, elegant, and filled with music, the plenum was claustrophobic, starkly lit, and energized by a dry, odorless, virtually soundless wind. I felt I'd stepped from an opulent prior century into the vision of a lifeless future.

Audrey eventually led the way downslope to the chamber's back wall, and to another door next to a large wire-mesh window. Here the wind was at its most powerful, being sucked from around us in a steady, dull cyclone, lifting our hair and riffling our clothes, drawn through the opening by an enormous, ancient impeller fan that moved in a blur, but emitted no more sound than the element it was consuming.

Audrey drew open the door, ushered me through, and followed me into a bare cement room dominated by the fan. Over our heads, in place of a ceiling, was a louvered panel through which the air was pushed around the rest of the building. We left the room via a solid steel door and found ourselves standing, incongruously disheveled, in a brightly lit, silent, cement-walled hallway.

Audrey spoke in a whisper. "The way things stand now, the top, the bottom, and the front of the building have been checked. I've sent people in to clear the main hall and business offices. Duncan and Jonathon're covering the area above and behind the stage. That leaves this area." She gestured around us. "Three floors of hallways, dressing areas, utility rooms, and Christ knows what else, all tucked under the stage. We're at the bottom now. I figure if we just head up floor by floor, room by room, we can squeeze him between us and the people up top."

I merely nodded as she radioed the others, enjoying being a part of someone else's attack plan. I assumed the pain in my shoulder would disappear in time, but I was happy to be one of the soldiers for once.

Audrey's strategy worked well for the floor we were on. It had a single staircase heading up at the far end of the hallway, so we were able to cover one another during the room-to-room search. The next floor, however, proved another matter.

Reaching it, Audrey explained, "Two halls, two staircases, a shitload of rooms. This and the one above are where most of the action is when things are up and running. I'll take the far end and work this way. You start from here and meet me. Keep your radio handy."

I was too slow reacting. I didn't like her proposal and knew it wasn't necessary. If Lenny was stuck between us and the others, it meant time and patience were on our side. Flooding the next two floors with people as they became available was the prudent course. But fatigue had kicked in, creating a numbing submissiveness. I merely watched her trot down the hall and vanish through a fire door without saying a word.

Once she was gone, however, doubt became apprehension. All the standard protocols had been overwhelmed by spontaneity and a crisis mentality. I knew that with extra personnel already spreading throughout the building, calm would soon be restored, probably with the arrival of a senior officer. I'd been beaned by Lenny's spotlight barely fifteen minutes ago, after all, not long in the life of an emergency. I could even hear the music still reverberating throughout the building. But as I began going from door to door, my discomfort grew. I was pulling open the third door along the hallway when I heard a distant thump, dull enough to be barely noticeable. I stood stock-still, waiting for something more. Then I tried the radio. "Audrey? You okay?"

The dead silence sent me running.

I found her struggling to get to her feet in the hallway beyond the fire door. "You all right?"

She pushed me away, already staggering toward the distant staircase. "Son of a bitch jumped me. Went up."

I grabbed her arm to steady her, noticing a smear of blood and a large swelling by her temple, along with a look of determined rage. It never occurred to me to try to get her to sit down. I did, however, update everyone by radio.

The stairs led straight up to stage level, dark, grandiose, and reverberating with music. After the bright, bland corridors below, the contrast was disorienting. Stepping onto the stage itself, I saw people with flashlights running down the aisles from the front of the theater and heard, for the first time, the orchestra begin to falter.

A sonorous crash indicated why. Springing from beneath the scaffold-like risers on which the rearmost musicians were seated, Lenny Markham made a dash for the opposite side of the stage, using the middle tier of the orchestra as a shortcut. Like a football player with the crowd cheering him on, he pushed and shoved his way along, scattering bodies and instruments to an accompaniment of shouts and curses, with Audrey and me in close pursuit.

But Lenny had the advantage. Following in his destructive wake proved slow going, and by the time we reached the other side, he'd disappeared into the wings.

By now, people were converging from every corner. Audrey ignored them all. With her knowledge of the building's details and her passion to nail the man who'd made her look bad, she steamrolled her way past everybody and disappeared through a door in the far wall. The most I could do was ride shotgun.

We descended another set of stairs to a hallway like the one we'd just left—well lit, empty, and utterly quiet. "You sure he came down here?" I asked.

"He didn't have a choice," she answered, checking the first door.

It led to a large, dark, ghostly room with two oversized furnaces squatting in its middle like prehistoric monsters. We walked around them, sweeping the corners with my small light.

I was headed back out when Audrey stopped me. "Hang on. There's one other place."

She stepped up to a door I hadn't noticed, about three feet tall, mounted flush to the building's exterior wall. "It's the old coal bin," she explained. "Used to feed the furnaces before they converted to oil."

She crouched and grabbed the door's handle. At that moment, it flew back and smacked her in the forehead, sending her spread-eagled to the floor. I glanced at her quickly as I stepped past and saw her weakly reach for her head. I huddled by the side of the door and pushed it wide open with my foot, gun in hand. "Lenny, this is the police. Come out with your hands up."

I heard a frantic scrambling, as from a huge rodent struggling to run up a gravel hill. Gun and penlight held as a unit, I swung around the corner to look inside.

What confronted me was a room so vast and dark, and so filled with cloying dust, it virtually swallowed what little glimmer my small light could put out. I could barely discern, as if through a fog, a slight, pale, distant blur, at which I shouted, "Stop," to predictable results.

I stepped inside the room, aiming to give chase.

It was then the meaning of the strange noise I'd heard became clear. My ankles disappeared into a crunchy quicksand of loose coal, throwing me off balance and pitching me forward. The bin, long abandoned, still housed a half load of fuel, probably dating back decades, and it was through this that I had to pursue the pale figure up ahead, stumbling, slipping, and choking on a cloud undisturbed for years.

Halfway across the bin, a sudden flash of light made me instinctively leap to one side. The acrid, dust-choked tomb was abruptly filled with diffused sunshine, sparkling off millions of dark airborne particles like a perverse parody of a religious revelation. I squinted at its source and briefly saw the haloed outline of Lenny Markham as he scrambled into the light and escaped to freedom.

My headache returning with a vengeance, I slowly reholstered my gun.

19

Tim Giordi looked at us with open contempt. It was an hour after Lenny Markham had made good his escape from the Flynn Theatre, during which time Giordi had pieced together the string of poor decisions that had aided Lenny's escape. My sole comfort was that in that same period of time, I'd been able to take a shower and an aspirin and beg a change of clothes.

Filling Giordi's office were Audrey McGowen, a bandage around her head, Duncan Fasca, Jonathon Michael, and myself.

"I won't go into details now," Giordi began. "I still have more to investigate, and more apologies to make to a lot of pissed-off people. I did want it known, however, that this is not being considered a minor lapse of protocol. What happened out there was human, but it was not forgivable. You turned the routine stakeout of a nonviolent suspect into a circus by ignoring the precise procedures created to avoid just such an escalation. You people are goddamn lucky Lenny Markham wasn't armed or didn't choose to use his weapon. And you, Joe," he added, pointing at me, "it's a miracle you're not dead."

"For which I'd like Duncan officially commended," I said. "Nothing would have altered that part of this fiasco. Neither one of us had any reason to think Lenny would turn violent. I know things could've been done better later on, but I'd like his quick thinking reflected on the record."

Giordi sighed softly. "So noted. You did all right, Duncan. Which," and here he stared at Audrey, "is more than I can say for others."

Audrey didn't react, so I opened my mouth to fend for her, too.

Giordi stopped me with an upheld hand. "I know, I know. Officer McGowen is a monument of rectitude, decisiveness, and honor. And I am keeping in mind her obvious perseverance. But we all know there was a major screw-up here, and I am not going to let a bunch of smoke-screen testimonials disguise that fact. From what I've gathered so far, nobody's job is threatened, but this will be dealt with in such a fashion that you'll never pull a similar stunt again. Is that clear?"

He wasn't looking for an answer, so we all filed out without comment. In the hallway, Duncan Fasca, whom I'd written off earlier as a throwback to the hardheaded cops of yore, shook my hand. "Thanks."

"It was the truth. You saved my butt."

He shook his head. "I was scared shitless."

Audrey was looking at the ground. "I'm sorry I let you down."

I started to say something soothing, but Duncan surprised me again. "You did what you thought was right, and we all went along with it. You're not alone on this, even if they single you out—don't worry about that. There's not one of them that hasn't screwed up one time or another in their career, and they're the head guys. This'll pass. What pisses me off is that Lenny's not getting nailed for it."

"You have any idea where he is?" I asked.

Fasca shrugged without comment.

Jonathon, having weathered the storm without a scratch, suggested, "Maybe we could go over his files again—check his habits."

We headed toward the detective bureau and Fasca's desk.

"Why do you think he ran for it?" I asked no one in particular.

"You told him his life was being threatened," Duncan said.

"I said Bouch was threatening it," I corrected.

"But you didn't say how or why," Jonathon joined in, having been briefed on the conversation earlier.

"Implying he already knew," I said.

Fasca sat at his desk and began rummaging through its drawers. "Which brings us back to nowhere."

I gently fingered the bruise on my temple. "Maybe not. It could be my showing up with Duncan was what pushed him over the edge. Lenny plays both ends against the middle. Talking to you is one thing—predictable, safe, mutually beneficial, as is working with Bouch on the other side. But bringing me in implied the cat had been let out of the bag, just like you feared. He had to have heard we'd discovered Jasper's body—and assumed that Bouch had killed him. Seeing me was proof it was time to jump ship. He didn't want to be grabbed by us as some sort of co-conspirator, and he sure as hell didn't want to be whacked by Norm Bouch."

"Which means he's probably running around now tying up loose ends, if he hasn't already left town," Jonathon said.

Fasca was poring over the contents of one of his files. "Duncan," I asked him, "if Jon's right, Lenny's meeting with people. Not at his apartment or the local bar or wherever else you and he used to meet—he'd figure all those are covered—but someplace where he feels in control. You got any suggestions?"

Fasca began flipping through pages as I spoke, searching for something in particular. A minute later, he looked up, a small smile on his face. "It sounds a little nuts, but I think we ought to stake out the ferry. He and I never met there, but he mentioned it once a couple of years ago as the best place to meet if you're in a jam. You can check out everybody on board, it's hard to be bugged or photographed, and you got all the time in the world to conduct business."

A dead silence settled between us.

"I like it," Jonathon finally said. Sharing no small amount of dread, we rose to our feet and filed back into Tim Giordi's office.

"What's he doing now?" I asked.

Audrey's voice came over the earpiece in a whisper, making her hard to hear over the throaty rumbling below decks. "They're both at the bow, looking at the water, still talking."

"You there, Jon?" I asked.

There was a brief pause, I imagined so Jonathon could casually turn his back and speak into the mike hidden under his jacket. "I'm here. They're not looking too happy with each other."

"All set down there, Duncan?"

"All set," Fasca replied, the huge diesels bellowing behind him. I put the radio back on the pilothouse map table and stared out at the horizon, as I imagined the two below were doing on the car ramp. Between the low clouds and the vast gray expanse of the lake before us, I might as well have been looking at a huge pool of cement. The Adirondack Mountains of New York, usually Lake Champlain's most dominant feature, were barely a smudge beyond the murkiness.

We were on board *The Champlain,* a double-ended, 148-foot-long, 725-ton ferry, built the same year as the Flynn Theatre—1930. This I'd learned from the captain, who now stood glumly beside me, having run out of conversation in the face of my distracted silence.

I was dressed in khakis and a work shirt, wearing a watch cap of vaguely nautical appearance. Jonathon was part of the deck crew, openly walking around the boat, tending lines and looking innocuous. Audrey, with bandaged head, was wrapped in a blanket, confined to a rented wheelchair near the stern ramp, accompanied by the oldest police officer Giordi could supply, big-bellied, white-haired, and avuncular, who was making a great show of being the doting nurse. Duncan and three others were confined to the engine room, since one glimpse of him would tip Lenny to our presence.

Lenny Markham, in the meantime, having appeared as we'd hoped at the ferry that same afternoon, was keeping company with the nervous boy who'd escorted Duncan and me to the grid at the Flynn. Neither one had showed up in a vehicle, but Lenny—significantly, I thought—was carrying a heavy-looking duffel bag.

I leaned forward and tried unsuccessfully to see the leading edge of the bow ramp beyond the upper-deck railing—as I had ten times before. I was in Duncan's predicament in a sense, having met Lenny face-to-face, but we'd all agreed the lighting had been too poor to make it count, and that standing in the pilothouse I'd be virtually invisible—a member of the crew people noticed but did not see.

Frustrated, I switched my gaze to the starboard window and looked back toward the Vermont shore, now barely visible. A mere dot in the distance, the Burlington PD's boat ran a parallel course, waiting to be called in if needed.

"They're on the move," Audrey reported at last. "Coming toward me through the central parking area. I can't see them too well with all the cars in between."

"Jon. Got 'em?" I asked.

"Getting there," he answered. "I'm opposite the stairwell to the engine room. I don't have them in sight yet."

"Don't rush," I cautioned, instinctively moving to the side I knew Lenny and the boy were on, one level below.

"I just caught a glimpse of them," Audrey came back on. "They're moving toward one of the openings on the side of the boat, where all the smaller cars are parked."

I left the confining pilothouse, crossed the deck, and looked over the rail. Flush with the ferry's exterior steel hull were the large oval holes supplying fresh air and a view to those below. Skirting the length of the boat, just under these windows, was a continuous, foot-wide fender of steel pipe, attached to the hull by angle irons. For an instant, I considered lowering myself to it, just above the rushing water, so I could crouch beneath the opening and eavesdrop on Lenny's conversation.

"Okay, I see them now," Jonathon reported. "They're between two cars, still talking."

"Anyone in the cars?" I asked, stepping back from the rail.

"As far as I can see, they're empty. And there's nobody nearby. Oh, oh…" There was a pause. "Sorry. Had to duck. Lenny was looking around."

I didn't like the sound of that. "Keep a close—"

But I was cut off. Jonathon suddenly started shouting, "Go, go, go. Man overboard. Lenny just knifed the other guy."

The radio exploded with voices, each drowning the other. As I turned back to the pilothouse, I heard shouts of, "Freeze. Police," echoing out over the water. I tore open the door and shouted to the captain, "Man overboard, this side."

My ear still ringing with disembodied chaos, I ran to the stern and began scanning the water, searching for anything bobbing on the surface. What with the gray, choppy surface and the ferry's own wake, I couldn't see a thing. All too slowly, I felt the boat shifting underfoot and saw the previously straight line of froth behind us begin to twist into a curve. I changed channels on my radio and called on the Burlington PD boat to swing in behind our original course and see if they could find the young boy's body.

By that time, I was heading toward the stairs to confront Lenny in cuffs. I was stopped by Audrey's voice. "Joe?"

"On my way."

"You might not want to do that. Lenny's grabbed a hostage. Some old lady was asleep in one of the cars he was near. Jon didn't see her."

I froze in place. "What's the layout?"

"Lenny's where he was, near one of those window-type things. We're fanned out in a semicircle behind all the cars. He's got a knife to her throat."

"No gun?"

"None visible. What's your location?"

"Still up top. Keep him talking. I might be able to flank him."

I looked over the railing again at the narrow steel fender fifteen feet below. I checked the bulkhead nearby and found a traditional orange life ring on a hook with a coil of rope attached.

Unraveling the rope, I quickly tied it to the railing, threw the rest overboard so it trailed in our wake, and returned to the pilothouse. "Got a pair of gloves?"

The captain, still in the midst of making his circle, merely pointed to a pair by the window. I grabbed them and ran back to my rope, putting them on while I swung one leg over the side.

My toes parked on the outer edge of the deck, I looped the rope across my shoulders and brought my gloved hands together in front of me. Slowly, I paid out line until my body was parallel with the blur of water. Ignoring the pain that leapt back to life in my damaged right arm, I began stepping backwards down the hull.

I'd positioned myself well aft of where Lenny was holding the others at bay, but as I worked my way between two of the window openings, I came into full view of some two dozen people. Nobody commented or pointed, either riveted by the action or cognizant of my intentions. Still, it was with a sigh of relief that I reached the fender, ducked out of sight, and let go of the rope.

Now I was on the equivalent of a narrow ledge at the foot of a sheer cliff, with water rushing by so close I could almost touch it. As long as I was under one of the large windows, this wasn't a problem, since I could hook my fingertips onto the bottom edge for stability. But moving from opening to opening was something else. The dividers were five to six feet wide—enough to force me to take at least two long side steps without any handhold at all. In addition, the closer I got to Lenny, the more likely it was he would hear me. Any noise on my part and he'd be able to lean outside, still holding his hostage, and merely pitch me into the water. Too late I remembered Tim Giordi's admonition against yielding to impulse and thought of how much easier it would have been to wait for the police boat to come alongside and show Lenny he was surrounded. On the other hand, I told myself, with one murder to his credit, he was possibly no longer in the mood for debate.

The first window divider proved pretty easy. I was still far enough away that I could use my momentum to help me along. Crawling toward the second, however, I began to have doubts. I could clearly hear Duncan negotiating and, as I got closer, could see the back of Lenny's head showing just beyond the next divider. Bridging that second gap would have to be like walking a tightrope—slow, easy, and with absolute balance. And with a gun in one hand.

Perhaps it was the will to succeed, or a slight tilting of the boat in my favor, or probably, as I still think, pure dumb luck, but that last, short, perilous journey was made without mishap. I slid along the fender, my feet flat and perpendicular to the bulkhead, my arms spread out to either side, and my cheek pressed against the damp steel, until I was so close to Lenny, I could smell him. At that point, I closed the fingers of my free hand firmly onto the window ledge and gently pressed the barrel of my gun under his ear. He froze as if I'd hit him with a tranquilizer.

"This is a gun, Lenny. Do you understand?"

His voice was barely audible above the water's rush. "Yeah."

"I want you to drop the knife and let the lady go. Okay?"

His hand opened, and the knife dropped out of sight, landing with a clatter. The old woman almost messed things up, twisting around and nearly knocking me off my perch, but by then the others had closed in, encircling Lenny and pulling me on board.

After a few congratulatory backslaps, I moved away to the ferry's bow, now pointed back toward Burlington and the nearby police boat, which was lying dead in the water.

I changed channels on my radio and called on them to answer.

"Go ahead," came the response.

"Any luck finding the body?"

"We've got it on board. He didn't make it."

I thanked them and asked that they stand ready to receive us, in exchange for additional people to process a crime scene. I then slipped the radio into my pocket and stood staring out at the slate-colored water.

Audrey McGowen's voice mingled with the breeze around my head. "You okay?"

I turned to look at her, noticing her injuries had spread to include a semicircle of bruises across her eyes and cheek. I thought back to an earlier conversation I'd had with Gail, whom I was missing terribly just then.

"I don't know."

20

Why'd he kill him?" Duncan asked, of no one in particular.

" Jonathon was sitting on the police boat's gunwale, his feet planted on the bench running across the stern. "He probably represented a threat. He's the only one who saw you and Joe meeting with Lenny."

"And maybe because for every lieutenant you often have a sergeant," I said. "Could be this kid knew more than was good for him. The duffel bag was packed for a long trip. Lenny might've been heading for someplace only he and the kid knew about."

Jonathon, Duncan, and I formed a semicircle on the fantail. Audrey had stayed on the ferry to help the crime scene team. Lenny was under guard below deck, having refused to say a word since surrendering. The body bag containing the subject of our conversation lay at our feet like a misshapen ottoman.

"Either way," Jonathon resumed, "it sure makes you think twice about old Norm Bouch. That is some fear to instill in a guy, to make him kill a kid just so he won't be traced."

The muffled bleating of a pager floated into the air among us. Instinctively, we all checked our own units, found nothing, and returned to staring out across the featureless water. It was Jonathon who finally asked, "So whose was that?"

We looked at one another and then, as if pulled by a common string, stared at the bag in our midst.

"I'll be a son of a bitch," Duncan exclaimed, and fell to his knees.

He pulled open the zipper, revealing a pale, wet, blue-tinted version of the young man we'd met that morning. He peeled back the flaps of the bag and slightly rolled the body to one side. Reaching under, he extracted a beeper and held it up.

Jonathon took it and checked the display. "This was it, all right."

"You got your cell phone?" I asked him.

He pulled it out of his inside pocket and handed it to me. I gave it to Duncan. "Call your office, get an address on that number, and let's see if we can get a search warrant."

Duncan pushed the appropriate numbers, passed along the request, and waited. A minute later, he looked up at us, grinning broadly. "It's Norm Bouch's apartment on North Street."

North Street looks like a transplant from another city. Unlike Burlington's college-influenced, commercialized downtown, or the residential areas of old Greek Revival architecture with dime-sized backyards, North Street looks like something out of turn-of-the-century, down-at-the-heels Chicago. It is a gray, featureless, ruler-straight avenue filled with bland, worn, flat-faced buildings. The effect is of pure utility—cheap houses built to shelter, and nothing more. It is also pervasive—even the occasional exception seems tainted by the whole, as if all the fancy architecture in the world couldn't alter the reality tucked behind those peeling wooden walls. Of the visible businesses, bars and junk food convenience stores predominate.

Norm Bouch's apartment was located next to a lawyer's office, its windows protected by Plexiglas since, as Duncan explained, every time the lawyer had lost a case, the client had paid him with a brick on the wing. The building was square, flat-roofed, wrapped in scalloped asbestos siding, with doors and windows so flush with the surface they looked painted on. Two patrol units were on guard by the time we arrived, a search warrant in hand.

"Any movement?" Audrey asked one of the uniformed officers. He shook his head. "Not in or out. Someone's pretty nervous at the window, though. Checks on us every five minutes."

We entered the building by the front door, climbed a set of narrow, dingy steps, precariously equipped with a loose railing, and arrived at a door on the top landing with a shiny new peephole in its center. Jonathon pointed at it and raised his eyebrows before Duncan pounded on the door.

We heard soft footsteps approach the other side and hesitate. Duncan held his badge up to the peephole. "Knock, knock," he said in a loud voice, "Police."

The door opened slowly, revealing a pimply-faced teenager weighing ninety pounds fully clothed. "What do you want?" he asked, his voice cracking.

Fasca pushed the warrant at him. "To search this place. Belongs to Norm Bouch, right?"

"Who?" The boy stepped aside to let us enter.

"What's your name?" I asked him.

"Randy Haskins."

"You live here, Randy?"

The others had spread throughout the small, dark, shabbily furnished apartment. Haskins eyed them nervously. "No. I come to visit."

"Where do you live, then?"

"On Archibald."

"And who do you visit when you come here?" I steered him over to a lumpy sofa covered with a dirty electric blanket with the wires hanging out. I took the armchair opposite.

"Lenny Markham. I thought he owned it." He looked around nervously. "Are you sure you have the right place? I never heard of the other guy."

"You used the phone to call a beeper number about two hours ago, didn't you?"

His mouth opened. "How'd you know that?"

"Who were you calling?"

"Robbie Moore."

"Why?"

"Just to hang out—you know."

"What do you and Robbie and Lenny have in common?"

Randy Haskins swallowed hard. "Nothing. We're just friends. We do stuff together."

"Then why are you here and they're not?"

"Lenny lets us use this as a crash pad. We all drop by when we want. It doesn't have to be to meet anybody."

"So there are more than just Robbie and yourself."

His face reddened. "A few." He began absentmindedly picking at a dark rectangular patch sewn into the middle of the blanket.

"What are their names?"

He hesitated, chewing his lip.

I leaned forward. "Randy. Our being here should tell you it's all gone up in smoke. A judge doesn't sign a search warrant unless there's a very good reason for it. You and I both know what that reason is, right?"

I gave him enough time to nod.

"Then you probably also know your best bet is to be as cooperative as you've been so far."

He grimaced as if in pain. "I don't want to get in trouble."

"From Lenny? He can be nasty, can't he?"

Again, he nodded.

"Well, here's the deal, then. Lenny met with Robbie on the ferry earlier today, and before we could stop him, he stuck a knife into Robbie's heart and threw him overboard. Robbie's dead, and Lenny's in jail, and he's never getting out."

Randy's mouth opened and closed several times. "Robbie's dead?"

"I'm afraid so. Why do you think Lenny killed him?"

He rubbed his forehead, shaking his head. "He was stupid. I told him to keep quiet. *Lenny* even warned him, but he didn't take it seriously. I was scared of Lenny. I knew he didn't kid around."

"Keep quiet about what?" I asked gently.

"Running dope. That's what we did so Lenny would take care of us. But it was supposed to be secret. That was the one big rule. Lenny said he'd kill anyone who squealed—that he'd done it before and would do it again."

"And what was Robbie's problem?"

The patch on the blanket was almost totally detached, what with Randy's nagging it. "He liked to brag. Made him feel bigger. He did everything he could to suck up to Lenny, but then he'd shoot his mouth off to complete strangers—ask them if they wanted some dope, that he could put together a big score if they'd pay."

"He was working behind Lenny's back?"

Randy shook his head sharply. "No, no. That's how Lenny found out about it. Robbie came to him and said he'd set up a deal—all Lenny had to do was produce the dope and collect the cash. Lenny almost took his head off, but he still didn't get the message."

"Why didn't Lenny get rid of him? Wasn't there a regular turnover of kids?"

At that Randy seemed genuinely baffled. "There was...But it didn't affect Robbie. Even with all their fights, they really liked each other."

I placed the list of names Randy Haskins had eventually given me on the conference table. "He didn't know Norm Bouch, has never been to Bellows Falls, didn't know if Lenny had either...There doesn't seem to be any connection at all between Norm and Lenny, except for the use of the apartment."

"Which was clean as a whistle," Kathleen Bartlett said.

"Right."

We were back at the Burlington Police Department's headquarters—Bartlett, Jonathon, Audrey and myself—sitting around a small table near the coffee machine.

Kathy Bartlett sighed. "Well, maybe it's just as well. It would've complicated things if you had found something. What about phone records?"

"We got 'em. The long distance numbers are being checked right now, but I wouldn't hold my breath. There were none to Bellows Falls or Lawrence, Mass, or anywhere else connected to all this." I slid the Randy Haskins list across the table to Audrey. "Maybe you can get something out of this, but my guess is Lenny played it pretty close to the vest."

"Which is why we think he whacked Robbie Moore, by the way," Jonathon added.

"Why did you say it was just as well we didn't find anything in the apartment?" I asked Kathy, my spirits sinking still further. "Aren't we going to deal on this?"

She shook her head. "I've spent the last four hours in the ring with the Chittenden County SA. There is no way in hell he's going to piss away election-year bragging rights on a first-degree, premeditated murder of a minor, witnessed by a bunch of cops, just so we can get the goods on some penny-ante dope pusher in Bellows Falls. Those were his words, not mine."

She cupped her cheek in one hand and looked at us mournfully. "We might get a crack at Lenny in a year or more, after the SA's finished with him, and assuming his lawyer'll go along with it, but I doubt even that. We wouldn't have anything to offer him. He'd have to want to talk to us from the goodness of his heart."

There was a long, telling silence while we pondered the likelihood of that scenario.

"Where's that leave you?" Audrey asked, sensing her own involvement in the case was nearing an end.

"Up a creek," Jonathon answered, reflecting the general mood.

"Lenny was supposed to be our ticket to Norm Bouch."

I'd been staring at the tabletop, running through every angle I could think of, struggling with the feeling that we'd never get anywhere on this case. I finally looked up at Jonathon. "You staying here to sew up the odds and ends?"

He nodded. "A day at most."

"I'm heading back to Brattleboro," I told them. "I need to find out how things're going down there anyway, and maybe I can kick something loose that we missed."

In the dark of night, the trip between Burlington and Brattleboro is smooth, monotonous, and fast—interstates all the way. Beyond the reach of the headlights, the mountain ranges, sloping fields, and glacier-carved valleys tug at the mind's edge like half-forgotten memories, making the car's closed interior a comforting cocoon. It was a time and place I preferred for thinking, and I was moodily indulging myself when the cell phone cut it short.

"My God," Gail said, "You're a hard man to find. I've been calling all over."

"Why? What's up?"

"Greg Davis wants to see you. Brian Padget's in some sort of pickle."

"That's all he said? When did he call?"

"Over two hours ago."

I let out a sigh. I'd been looking forward to a good night's sleep. "And I suppose he wants to see me ASAP."

"You got it—at Padget's house."

I was forty-five minutes north of Westminster.

"There's something else," she added. "Remember I told you I knew Anne Murphy? After I cleared it with Derby, I called her up to see if she'd tell me more about Jan Bouch than she'd told you. What she said—unofficially of course—was that Jan suffers from dependent personality disorder. That's a clinical diagnosis."

"What's it mean?"

"They're like recipe titles, basically—this plus this plus this equals manic depression, or whatever. With Jan's problem, there are eight ingredients total, and she's got most of them: can't make everyday decisions without advice, depends on others to assume responsibility, doesn't argue out of fear of being rejected, can't stand being alone, clings to the people she quote-unquote loves, and—this is the one I thought you'd like—is so needy of attention she'll volunteer to do things she doesn't like or knows are wrong."

"Did Murphy go into specific details?"

Gail's laugh was made tinny by the phone. "Not a chance. She'd cross the line only so far. She knows what I do for a living, and she knows who I sleep with."

"Which probably won't happen tonight," I muttered sadly. "Did she say if Jan's being treated, and if so, how successfully?"

"One of the aspects of this disorder is that the patient is often in an abusive relationship, and that when the therapist suggests getting out of it, the patient regresses. In fact, in order for any detachment to begin to work, Anne said the counselor first shouldn't argue the contention that the abuser is a great guy. 'Course, Jan's not even close to that stage. As soon as Anne mentioned Norm might be part of Jan's problem, the discussion came to an end."

"So she's still under his thumb."

Gail's energy was pumping into my ear. "Right, which put me on another track. Anne also told me Jan's super-connected to her kids. She's not a great mother—you told me that much—but she's incredibly attached to them. It probably ties into the dependency thing. Anyhow, I was thinking *they* might be the way to get her to turn on Norm."

I furrowed my brow in the darkness. "How?"

"Use SRS to apply a little pressure. Let her think that unless she makes some serious changes—Norm above all—she could lose her kids."

I could hardly believe this was Gail. The state's Social and Rehabilitation Services were famously tough-minded when motivated and definitely had the power to do what she'd just suggested. "Jesus. That's hardball."

She picked up on the implied criticism. "Only if you don't give a damn. I'm not doing this to nail Norm—he's your problem. I want this woman and her kids free of him. She may have her kinks, but from what Anne told me, a little care and attention could get her straight. I don't mind playing hardball for that."

I smiled at the familiar passion. I should have known better. "All right. So what's your plan?"

"I contacted an SRS investigator friend of mine. She'll be visiting Jan tomorrow morning. Norm's supposed to be at work then."

"What if your friend finds the kids are doing fine?"

"It doesn't matter. After the visit's over, you can put whatever spin on it you want."

Up to now, I'd been hoping for a break along evidentiary lines—some clue we'd overlooked. But with Gail's strategy already underway, my horizons had been broadened, and with them possibilities I'd almost abandoned.

Slowly catching her enthusiasm, I muttered, "Since it looks like Norm used his wife to get to Padget, maybe we could pull the same scam in reverse."

She didn't respond, waiting for more.

But I didn't want to jinx my luck. "Gail, could you do me a favor? Find out what town Jan and Norm were married in. Maybe Anne knows."

She hesitated, obviously tempted to ask what I was up to. Instead, all she said was, "I'll see what I can do."

There were two cars parked in Brian Padget's driveway when I pulled up, one of which I assumed was Greg Davis's. Despite my initial disappointment on the phone with Gail, I was curious why I'd been summoned. I doubted, however, that it was because Padget had followed my advice and figured out how and why he'd landed in his present predicament. As promising as Latour thought him, Padget was also young and inexperienced, and more prone to wallow than to dig his way out.

Davis met me at the door, his weary expression confirming the worst. "Thanks for coming."

He stood aside, ushering me into a dense atmosphere of stale, fetid air, tinged in equal parts with sweat, booze, and vomit. A faint but refreshing tang of coffee struggled feebly in the background.

"Great," I commented. "When did this start?"

"I checked on him last night. He'd been drinking some, but I thought I'd shaken him out of it. A couple of hours ago was the first chance I had to drop by since. Looks like he's been at it all day."

I wandered past the small kitchen, down the hallway to the back bedroom, where the smell approached critical mass. In the dim light leaking in from behind me, I saw Padget lying face down on the bed.

"Brian. It's Joe."

"Fuck you." His voice was muffled by a pillow.

"Hear you've been having a rough time."

"Get the fuck outta here."

I picked my way carefully across the room, noticing a dry pool of vomit on the rug near the night table. I sat in a small rocking chair. "You've probably had enough of people getting out of your hair."

His head shifted. A pale half-moon of face appeared from out of the pillow. "What?"

"What's been going on, Brian?"

"What the hell do you think? I'm the crooked cop—might as well be a leper. The paper calls me that, the guys at the station're thinking it, that asshole Shippee wants me fired yesterday, and the chief's letting me cook in it."

"You talk to Emily?" The face vanished back into the pillow.

"You're not telling me she cut you off."

Silence.

"So you did it for her, right? Won't let her come by, won't talk to her on the phone?"

I could barely hear him. "No."

"She's the best friend you got."

"I messed her up enough already."

"You were used, Brian. Somebody put water in your gas tank so your car would malfunction and Emily would have to drive you to work. It was a double setup to taint you both."

"Then why'm I still going to court?"

It was a good question, and reflective of his thinking clearly despite the self-abuse. In fact, what I'd just said was speculative, absurdly optimistic, and procedurally inappropriate. Alleged dirty cops were supposed to stew on their own, not be comforted by the investigating officer.

But I didn't care much about the rules of protocol anymore.

"'Cause I can't prove it yet," I answered him. "I am getting closer, though. Did you do any thinking about how you got nailed, like I asked?"

He turned to face me again. "You think this is a crossword puzzle or something? Some bastard planted dope in my house—in my body, for Christ's sake. How the hell'm I going to figure how that happened?"

"The dope in the toilet tank and the stuff in your system don't match. They came from two different sources. You need to start thinking about that."

He raised himself up on his elbows so he could shout at me. "Fuck you. What the hell you think I been doing?"

"Feeling sorry for yourself."

He grabbed the pillow and tried to throw it at me, collapsing in the process and smacking his reading lamp, which I caught before it hit the floor. I heard Greg nervously shift his weight in the doorway.

"You know," I said, "it would help if you were straight with me."

"What's that mean?"

"That in the middle of all this shit, and with people like me and Greg and Emily all pulling for you, you've been holding back on the truth."

He didn't answer. I let the silence last as long as was necessary. The response, when it came, was predictably feeble. "I have not."

"You told me you'd first met Jan on a call to her house for a domestic dispute."

"So?"

"That was a lie. You were never on any of those calls."

He lapsed back into silence.

"Emily, on the other hand," I continued, "was on almost every one." I thought back to what I'd said about both of them having been framed, and wondered why they'd earned that much attention.

He rolled over and slowly began sitting up, swaying with the effort. I glanced at Greg. "Could you get a cold, wet towel?"

He disappeared without comment.

"You leave Emily alone," Padget finally gasped, fighting nausea. He swung his feet over the edge of the bed and held his head in his hands, breathing hard and deep.

"Why should I? She's the one who put you on to Norm Bouch in the first place."

He continued trying to keep his stomach under control. Davis returned with the towel and soundlessly placed it in his hand. Padget buried his face in it, rubbing it around. Through the material, he asked, "She tell you that?"

The phrasing of the question gave me hope I'd gotten lucky. "She told me Norm Bouch was the scum of the earth—to be taken out like a tactical threat and held up as an example."

Padget shook his head. "God, she hates his guts."

"What did she do?"

Suddenly, giving in to all his penned-up emotions, Brian Padget began to weep. Starting with a slight shaking of the shoulders, his grief spread until his entire body was racked by sobs. I shifted over next to him on the bed, rubbing his back and shoulders. Greg Davis moved into the room and sat opposite us.

For fifteen minutes, we let him dredge himself out. Then gradually, I began coaxing him back, telling him to breathe deeply, straighten up, open his eyes and look at us. Eventually, he took a final, shuddering gulp of air and wiped his eyes with the towel.

"Tell us the truth now," I urged.

His voice was barely audible. "Emily was running a covert investigation on Norm Bouch, but she refused to quit when I found out. I told her it could cost her her job—ruin everything she'd fought for her whole life—I finally said I'd do it instead, that if she didn't let me, I'd turn her in. She knew I was serious. We fought like hell—that's why we broke up—but she finally went along."

Greg and I exchanged looks. As irony had it, this admission put Padget in hotter water than he already was. If he were cleared of the drug charges, he'd end up battered but still employed. Running a clandestine investigation, however, put his career in the same jeopardy he'd been trying to spare Emily. Police officials do not take kindly to cops becoming freelancers.

"What about Jan?" I asked. "How did you two get together?"

He shook his head with embarrassment. "I was staking out their house one night when she walked right up to me and asked me what I was doing. She'd noticed me hanging around. She wasn't angry—just curious. And she was real sad. I could see it in her eyes—all the shit he pulls on her. She came to see me as someone who might help her and the kids to get free."

I listened quietly, fighting the urge to tell him I thought he'd been worked like a trout by an expert angler. Norm's fingerprints were all over this story, down to the unbelievable notion that Jan would notice someone hiding in the bushes and then go out to meet him without consulting her husband.

"You should've run the case by me," Greg finally said. "I might've okayed a surveillance."

Brian looked at him sadly. "We didn't believe that. We were sure the chief would give it thumbs down, him not wanting to make waves and all."

"Why not admit you and Emily wanted to score points," I said harshly, irritated by their arrogance and naiveté both. "Bring in a bad guy on your own? Emily's got a problem because Burlington wouldn't have her, and you're so hot to climb the ladder, you can barely stand it."

Greg gave me a warning look, and I softened my tone. "Look, I know it got away from you, but how did you think it was going to end? Even if you got the goods on Norm, people were going to ask how you'd done it. Being successful wouldn't have made you any less of a maverick. Why didn't you follow your own advice to Emily?"

He shook his head tiredly. "We didn't think it out. It was like a personal thing I got caught up in—first stopping Emily from getting fired, then trying to save Jan. I felt I could do it."

I shook my head silently. Any chastising by me was gratuitous compared to what he was facing. I patted his back instead, told him to try to get some sleep, and that for the rest of the night I'd stick around in case he needed me.

Davis and I retired to the living room after tucking Padget in. We left the lights off and settled in opposite corners of the sofa.

"You think he'll get to keep his job if he's cleared?" I asked quietly, already hearing the dull rumble of Padget's snoring down the hall.

In the reflected glow from the street light outside, he shrugged. "The chief likes him, or used to. He might get a month or two without pay if he's lucky. Politics could run him over—Shippee hates all this—and I doubt his career'll have much oomph, at least in the short run."

"Things improving any at the department?" I asked.

He sighed. "Not a whole lot. The job's getting done, but no one's heart is in it. This thing's like a group headache none of us can shake."

"Latour still seen as part of the problem?"

"He's not helping any."

"And you can't talk to him?"

There was a pause. "We don't have that kind of relationship."

Silence fell between us for quite a while. I finally stuck out my foot and prodded his own in the dark. "You've done your time here. Go home to your family. I'll bunk on the couch."

After a moment's thought, he rose to his feet. "Guess I will. Thanks."

I walked him to the front door. "Why did you call me, by the way?"

I jerked a thumb over my shoulder. "This wasn't anything you couldn't have handled."

He didn't answer at first, rubbing his hand along the door frame instead, as if checking it for splinters. He spoke slowly at first. "That was a mistake. I didn't know about Emily and him running a case on their own. That sort of changes things."

I tried interpreting that. "Meaning you were pissed and wanted me to see the damage I'd done."

He laughed softly, shaking his head. "That makes it sound mature. Guess I screwed that one up."

"I don't think so," I disagreed. "You're trying to take care of your people. I don't have a problem with that."

He nodded meditatively. "Silly impulse, though. I shouldn't have done it." He looked up then. "How do you think this'll wind up?"

"I've got my fingers crossed," I told him, at least guardedly optimistic. "By the way," I added, "something happened in Burlington today that might make Norm a little antsy. Is there any way you could keep an eye on him—enough to let me know if he leaves town, or changes habits radically?"

"Sure," he said. "Shouldn't be a problem." I watched him get into his car and drive off into the night. I hoped he was right. If Norm turned from puppet-master to loose cannon, there was no telling what might happen.

21

By the time I left Brian Padget the next morning, he'd showered, shaved, eaten a light breakfast, and made an appointment with a local counseling service. Given the condition I'd found him in, I wasn't begrudging a poor night's sleep.

It was perhaps that developing hopefulness that made me turn again toward the Bellows Falls police station instead of continuing home.

Emile Latour was in his awkwardly laid out office, sitting at his desk, staring into space.

He looked up when I tapped lightly on the door frame. "Hi, Joe. Come on in."

"I just spent the night babysitting Brian Padget. You been to see him since all this hit the fan?"

He frowned. "Babysitting him? Why?"

"Greg Davis called me. He's been dropping in on Padget, seeing how he's doing. He found him blind drunk and sick, feeling sorry for himself. He's better now." I sat in one of the guest chairs and studied him, watching a series of thoughts pass like shadows behind his eyes.

He seemed to absorb what I told him in slow motion, gradually lifting his hand to rub absentmindedly at his temple. Finally, he said, "I didn't realize."

I kept my voice neutral. "He's a kid—and an idealist. He hasn't acquired what we've got to fall back on."

"But what about the urinalysis?"

"I can't prove it yet, but I think the dope was put into him somehow. It doesn't match the stuff we found in the toilet tank, which is what the snitch told the paper they'd both been using."

Latour's gaze returned to his untouched paperwork.

"How're the others holding up, with Padget heading for arraignment?" I asked.

He sat back in his chair, his shoulders slumped. "The whole department's in a mess. I get, 'Yes, Chief,' 'No, Chief,' and 'Will you sign this, Chief?' And that's about it. I stuck my foot in it saying what I did at that news conference. I lost them."

"You disappointed them. That's different."

He looked slightly irritated. "The end result's the same. They won't talk to me. I don't know what to say to them. Half of them think Brian's dirty and Emily's in it with him. The other half have gone totally nuts, saying Shippee, me, Norm Bouch, the village trustees, and all the dirtbags in town have ganged up to screw them." He waved a hand feebly across his desk. "Coming to work is like going to a funeral every day."

"What about Shippee?" I asked. "What's his role?"

Latour's face darkened. "That son of a bitch. He doesn't give a good goddamn. He wants it solved, period. He sees this new group in town trying to make things better, and his contribution is to tell me to fire any troublemakers I find in my department. To him it's all whitewash and flowers—cater to the do-gooders, buy yourself some political mileage, and then watch them disappear in six months, wiped out by their own disappointment—just like before."

I was impressed by his anger and tried stoking it a little. "You told me earlier you thought they had more on the ball than that."

"They do. I know it started with flowers and name changes, but they've moved beyond that. They're talking about taking care of the kids that just hang around the streets now. They invited them to their meetings and asked them for suggestions, for crying out loud. You don't see Shippee at those. For the first time, there's a sense these folks aren't going to be happy till something improves. I looked around the room at their last get-together, and I saw people who can't stand each other trying to find some middle ground. It was amazing."

"They approach you yet?" I asked.

He blinked, as if coming out of a daydream. "Sure they have, with the usual complaints—loitering kids, open drinking, cars speeding, too many drugs…I'm two guys down and the rest are in the dumps. I'm really going to hold my breath, keep my fingers crossed, and make everything better."

I got up and headed for the door, not wanting to feed his bitterness. "You're not in a position to do that, which may be part of your problem. You ever think you might've outgrown your job, Emile—that you could do more if you weren't Chief of Police? Maybe you're more frustrated than burned out."

I half expected an angry comeback, but as I looked over my shoulder, he was merely staring into space again. I thought I saw a difference, though—an intensity in his expression, as if in reviewing his own words—or mine—he might have found something deserving a second look.

"I'll see you around," I said in parting.

He didn't respond.

Gail called me at the office shortly before noon. I'd been going over our double homicide and finding little of use. Nothing new had surfaced concerning Jasper Morgan, and we still hadn't put a name to the little guy in the adjoining grave. Willy had spent hours trying to trace the parents, but without success.

"Jan just got her visit from SRS," Gail reported.

"What did they find?" I asked.

"Not enough to warrant any action by them, but they didn't tell her that, and the effect was what we were after. If you want to chat with her before hubby comes home from work, now's the time."

"I'm on my way," I told her. "But before I go, did you find out where Norm and she were married?"

"Anne thought it was Bellows Falls, but she wasn't sure. I had our clerk check it out, and she couldn't find any record of it, so Anne must've been wrong. They probably went to Vegas or somewhere—that sounds like Norm's style. Why did you want to know, anyhow?"

I answered vaguely. "Legal question—trying to sort out any potential husband-wife problems we might run into. I'll let you know how I fare. Thanks for setting it up."

I dialed Brian Padget's house immediately after hanging up. "Hello?" The voice on the other end wasn't chipper, but it didn't sound drunk, either.

"It's Joe Gunther. How're you doing?"

"I went to the shrink, if that's what you mean."

"It wasn't, but how did it go?"

"All right, I guess. It makes me uncomfortable."

"That's probably good. Digging into yourself should hurt a little. I got a question for you—some legal paperwork I'm trying to clear up. Where were Jan and Norm married?"

"Here," he said immediately and then corrected himself. "I mean Bellows Falls. She told me one night they had a church wedding—white dress, tux, one of the kids as ring-bearer, the whole shootin' match."

"They didn't do a Vegas number?"

"I don't think so. She told me she's never been more than ten miles outside town her whole life."

"Thanks. Keep away from the bottle, and keep Greg and my phone numbers handy, okay? You hit the sauce again, I'll wring your neck."

His laugh was short and halfhearted, but reassuring anyway. "Okay, Lieutenant."

I made two more phone calls before dialing Kathy Bartlett. "You find anything hopeful down there?" she asked after we'd exchanged greetings. "I just hung up on Jonathon, and he's got nothing good to say."

"Could be. The SA's office here sicced SRS on Jan Bouch this morning. They didn't find anything, but she's biting her nails. I'm about to see if I can turn up the heat with a private visit of my own. How fast do you think you could pull an inquest together so you can really make her sweat?"

She had enough experience to quickly grasp what I was up to, and apparently enough trust in me not to play twenty questions, at least not at this point. "I'll have to call around—see what court or judge might be willing to play. You might have a problem, though."

"I know," I quoted, " 'the privilege of communications made within a marriage.' I don't think they are married. A records check in Bellows Falls revealed nothing. Jan's talked about a big church wedding to Brian, but I called the preacher and he knows nothing about it. I also found out Jan's suffering from a psychiatric dependency disorder. My guess is she made up the marriage to feel closer to Norm, and he played along because he didn't care either way."

"We're going to look pretty stupid if he whips out a marriage certificate at the last minute."

"Could be that fear is what he's counting on. We'll never know unless we call his bluff."

She only paused a moment. "Granted, but we're not there yet. You have your interview, and I'll make those calls. Talk to you later."

Jan Bouch looked at me as if I were a ghost, standing on her front stoop. "What do you want?" she asked, her voice trembling. "My husband's not here."

I made no effort to smile but spoke politely. "I know that. I'd like to talk to you, if that's okay."

She glanced around nervously. "I don't know. Maybe that's not such a great idea."

"You spoke to SRS this morning." Her eyes widened. "Are you here about that?"

"I think you know why I'm here, Mrs. Bouch."

She bit her lower lip, her eyes glistening. "Am I going to lose my kids?"

For an instant, I almost faltered, thinking of how I was about to become the latest of this woman's abusers. "That's pretty much up to you."

Her resistance weakening, she kneaded the doorknob and shifted her weight uncertainly, her distress paradoxically stiffening my resolve.

"Mrs. Bouch," I persisted. "Last time we talked, in the chief's office at the police department, I suggested you seek help. You decided otherwise. Do you really want to turn me away again?"

She backed up quickly, opening the door wider, suddenly afraid we might be caught in the open. "Okay. Come in."

I stepped inside, saw a few pieces of furniture placed haphazardly around the messy room off the hallway, and headed toward them, arranging two chairs so they faced each other. "Have a seat."

She followed me in, looking at the walls and ceiling like a tourist on her first visit. Hesitantly, she did as I asked, sitting on the chair's edge with her hands clenched in her lap.

"Mrs. Bouch, you must know things aren't going well for you. You've been having an affair with a man facing a drug charge, you're living with another against whom drug trafficking allegations have been made, the police department has a record of your chronic involvement in domestic abuse calls, you have an admitted history of repeated drug use, you're receiving mental counseling, and you've just been visited by SRS. Do you have any idea what all that looks like?"

Tears were flowing down her face. "I try my best. I really do."

"I know you do. Wasn't I the one who offered you help?"

She nodded silently. "What did I tell you?"

"That I should leave Norm. But I can't."

"Can't or won't?"

She gave me a pleading look.

I leaned forward, suddenly deciding to gamble on pure intuition. "I know you're in pain, but despite what you think, you still have some options. Do you feel that inside you—the desire not to be pushed around so much?"

"I don't know."

"How did it feel when Norm ordered you to have an affair with Brian?"

Her eyes widened. "How did…?"

"Or when he told you Brian was going to be hung out to dry—after you'd discovered you'd actually fallen in love with him?"

She rubbed her forehead. "I don't know."

"Jan," I said, using her Christian name for the first time, "when you and Norm were at the police station, telling us the sexual harassment charges were false, and that you'd actually been having an affair with Brian, do you remember how you felt when you were asked whether Brian was ever in uniform when the two of you were together?"

"I'm not sure."

"Norm opened his mouth to answer, and you beat him to it. Remember?"

Her face cleared suddenly. "I said, 'No.' I knew otherwise it would get Brian into trouble."

I matched her enthusiasm with my own. "That's right. You said, 'No.' But you did more than that. Why did you say it so fast, so clearly?"

She looked like she was concentrating for a final exam. "Because Norm was about to say, 'Yes'?"

"Don't ask me, Jan. Tell me. Was that the way it was?"

"Yes, it was. I didn't want him to do that."

"You stood up for yourself," I said, "and you helped a friend. You may've caught hell later, but it felt good, didn't it?"

"Yes," but her voice had lost some of its edge.

"Would you like to stop using drugs?"

She perked back up. "Oh yes, I would."

"Or live peacefully with your children, happy and in control and without fear?"

"I'd like that."

"What's the biggest barrier between you and those goals?"

Her eyes widened at the possibility of a single simple solution.

"The drugs?"

"That's pretty big," I agreed. "But what brought them into your life?"

"Norm?" she asked in a whisper.

I leaned forward. "What would change if he were out of the picture?"

"I could get my life back," she suggested, almost to herself. I wasn't sure how great she'd actually find that to be, but I wasn't about to quibble. While I was blatantly manipulating her with my own self-interest, there was also no way I didn't think Jan Bouch could stand an improvement in her life.

"Here's another one—what do you think will happen if you let things continue the way they're going?"

The tears began flowing again. "They'll take my kids away?"

I kept quiet, cautious about saying too much. Instead, I got to my feet and began walking around the room, dominating it with my presence, occasionally passing behind her to heighten her insecurity.

"Mrs. Bouch, I don't need to tell you that forces are at work right now that are bigger than anything you can do to fight them. You've gotten used to being pushed around by Norm, but that's nothing compared to this. There is a silver lining in that, though. You know what it is?"

I was behind her when I said this and paused long enough to force her to ask, "What?"

"It's that those larger forces are on your side. They want you to succeed, to live with your kids, to have a normal, happy life. They want to make sure Norm doesn't hurt any more people than he already has... Like he's hurt you."

Predictably, she wavered there. "He's not a bad man."

"You asked him for a favor when you first got together and began having children, didn't you?" I asked, my voice lowered, my head just behind hers. "You asked him for something that wouldn't have cost him a thing, but which meant everything to you—and to those same children."

Her head bent forward and her weeping increased.

"He forced you to live a lie because he wouldn't make this simple dream come true, didn't he?"

Her entire body was shaking by now, bent over almost double. I tried to use that grief to temper the adrenaline I felt coursing through me, but I couldn't resist seeing it as a measure of my success. The gap between me and Norm—at least regarding this one pathetic soul—had grown immeasurably close. His victim had become mine.

"He wouldn't even marry you, would he, Jan?" I ended in a whisper.

"No," she wailed. "I wanted my kids to be different from me, but he wouldn't do it. That's why I lied about being married."

At last, I put both my hands on her shoulders, bridging the gap I'd so cynically created. "It's okay, it's okay. You did it for good reason. You tried your best. And if Norm hadn't kept pushing, it might've worked."

I circled around to face her, crouching low so I could see her eyes. "It's fallen apart, and you know who's to blame. I know it's scary, and that you don't want to do it, but for your children, you're going to have to make some choices. You won't be alone this time. People will be there to help you, but you'll have to help them, too. Do you understand?"

She nodded dumbly. I knew she had no idea what I was talking about. That would come later, and at the hands of others—others, I comforted myself, who really would have her best interests at heart.

"Some people are going to want to talk to you about Norm," I resumed. "Ask you questions about his business dealings. You may not think you know anything, but your helping them in any way will be crucial. It'll be at a special meeting called an inquest, and the only people there will be a judge and a prosecutor—a friend of mine named Kathy. Are you willing to be a part of that?"

Again, she nodded.

"All right. I think it might be better if Norm doesn't find out about this. Remember the women I mentioned in the chief's office a few days ago, who take care of people like you and your kids?"

"The shelter?"

"Right. I can have all of you taken there right now, where Norm can't find you, so you can be safe until Kathy and the judge ask you those questions. Are you agreeable to that?"

"Okay," she said simply.

I straightened up, the tension draining out of me. The frustration I'd felt losing Lenny Markham to the legal system was finally dissipating in the face of new expectations.

"You stay here," I said to her. "I've got a few phone calls to make."

22

Jonathon Michael found me at the Women For Women shelter in Brattleboro, three hours after my conversation with Jan Bouch, and right after Gail and I had finally handed her and the kids over to the shelter's staff. Those few hours had seemed without end, since as soon as I'd gotten Jan to agree to an inquest, I was sure Norm would come waltzing through the front door and ruin everything.

"I just hung up on Kathy," Jonathon said, walking across the parking lot with me. "She's arranged a date here in town with Judge Rachael Aumand, at eight tomorrow morning."

I turned to stare at him. "Tomorrow morning? How the hell did she pull that off?"

He smiled. "The judge said she'd come to work ninety minutes early. Kathy can be very persuasive, especially after what happened in Burlington. 'Course, I don't think it hurt that Aumand and she went to law school together. Lucky, too, 'cause there isn't an opening in the court docket till next month."

"Thank God for living in a pea-sized state," I muttered.

"There's something else," Jon added. "I'm guessing you asked Greg Davis to keep an eye on Norm Bouch?"

"Yeah," I admitted. "Last night and this morning both. I didn't want Norm busting in on me."

"Well, he's been trying to get hold of you—left a message with Kathy. Norm's disappeared. He didn't show up at the site he's been working on, and no one's seen him around town."

"He must've heard about Lenny," I said.

"Maybe. I hope he didn't hear about you snatching his wife, too."

We reached my car and I pulled open the door. "You think we should issue a BOL?"

Jonathon shook his head emphatically. A BOL involved a lot of people all of a sudden, none of whom knew the details behind the request. It also had a way of leaking outside police circles, often to the press. "It might spook him more than we want," he said. "Push him underground. Right now, he's probably scrambling to make sure Lenny isn't the start of a major hemorrhage. What might be better is a selective BOL, to every unit with a specific interest in the drug business. If Norm is running around checking for damage, it's bound to cause a ripple somewhere."

"Time to mend fences with Steve Kiley?" I asked, raising my eyebrows.

"Say what you will about the task force," he answered, "they have better connections than anyone I know."

I swung in behind the steering wheel and looked up at him. "Let's meet up at the Municipal Building. We can call him from there."

There were two messages waiting for me at the office—one from Beverly Hillstrom, the state's medical examiner, the other from Brian Padget. After introducing Jonathon to Sammie, and asking her to show him what she had on our two homicides, I dialed Padget's number first. Given the time I'd spent trying to straighten him out, I wasn't about to let him dangle longer than necessary.

"Hi, Brian. It's Joe," I said after he'd picked up.

"I been doing what you asked, thinking back over everything. I thought of something that's probably pretty dumb, but I can't get it out of my head. You know how you got me to spruce up this morning? Shave, shower, and all that? Well, I use aftershave—always have. Could that be a way to get coke into my system?"

The simplicity of the idea was startling. "Do you feel any numbness after using it?"

"No. That's why I think it's probably wrong. But I bleed a little when I shave—my skin's not all that great—and it just seemed possible. It'd be like I was giving myself a dozen miniature injections, sort of. But I didn't feel anything, and I can't see or smell anything wrong with the stuff."

"You wouldn't," I said. "It's mostly alcohol, perfume, and coloring. It would cover anything. Stay where you are. I'm sending someone up to take the aftershave to be tested. And keep your fingers crossed. I don't think this sounds crazy at all."

I dialed Isador Gramm in Burlington next, the only board-certified forensic toxicologist in the state, and a man I'd consulted in the past to great advantage.

"Is it possible?" I asked him after explaining Padget's theory.

"I've never heard of it, but I suppose so. You say he bleeds as a result of shaving?"

"Yes."

There was a thoughtful pause at the other end. "I can't see where it wouldn't work, Joe. Alcohol would not only completely dissolve the cocaine, but it would work as a carrier taking it into the system. It would be tough for whoever spiked the aftershave to come up with just the right amount—enough to appear in the urinalysis, but not so much that your victim would notice—but that could be dumb luck. I think the coke, by the way, would have to be pure. Any cutting agent would mess things up—either make the aftershave cloudy or inhibit the effect of the cocaine."

"I know this is a little unusual, but if I had a courier hand-deliver this bottle to you in about three hours, could you run it through your machinery and bill it to the AG's office?"

"Moving up in the world, are we? Sure, I don't see why not. Send it on."

I called over to the Patrol Division and arranged for a courier. Then I dialed Beverly Hillstrom's number.

"You do send me the most curious packages," she told me minutes later. "Although I'll tell you right up front that I have nothing to report on the small skeletonized remains, other than it appears to have been a male Caucasian in his mid-teens. I found absolutely nothing on what might have killed him."

I was disappointed with that, less because it implied an investigative dead end, and more because I truly hated the idea of taking someone so young, and dumping him into the bureaucratic equivalent of a pauper's grave.

"What about Morgan?" I asked.

"There I can be more helpful. I'll be faxing you my full report later, but I know how you like a sneak preview. Also, I found something you might find interesting, which I'll tell about in a moment.

"Al Gould," she continued, "was right on the mark concerning cause of death. The first bullet caught him through the body at a sharply oblique angle, a wound which if treated within an hour or so need not have been lethal, although it did stimulate significant blood loss. The second bullet was fatal, removing the right carotid and part of the jugular and causing massive exsanguination. Both bullets passed without measurable residue or noticeable fragmentation, and both appeared to me to have been shot from far enough away not to leave any powder marks. Of course, I've sent the clothing and samples to the lab, but my guess—which will not appear in the report—is that your shooter was not overly skillful. I think the first shot was intended for the heart, missing it posteriorally, and the second was probably aimed at the head—the standard coup de grâce between the eyes—ending up in the throat. So unless you're dealing with someone very clever, you can eliminate any known crack shots.

"The body otherwise," she went on, "was unremarkable in presentation, typical of a young male in good condition. Toxicology hasn't reported back yet—they'll be sending you separate findings in any case—but I wouldn't be surprised to find both alcohol and drugs present. Mr. Morgan's inner workings showed typical signs of both, albeit not to the extent they're often present in older and/or more self-abusive people. I would say he got around without noticeable deficit.

"Now," she finally said, to my relief, "for the interesting anomaly I mentioned. Inside Morgan's body, along the path of the first bullet, I found a single, tiny filament of copper wire."

I frowned at the phone. "Could it have come from the bullet's jacketing?"

"No. I put it under the microscope. The size and shape of it suggest it was carried there by the bullet."

I thanked her after a few closing comments and sat back in my chair, my eyes shut. In the darkness of my memory, I flipped through a catalogue of mental snapshots, looking for the one I recalled that featured small electrical wiring.

Satisfied at last, I left my office and circled the cluster of desks in the squad room to find Sammie and Jonathon poring over her reports.

"Jon," I asked him, "did they find any prints belonging to Norm Bouch in that Burlington apartment, or anything else that proves without doubt he was ever there?"

"Yeah, along with three dozen other people's, plus the neighbor's statement who said he met him once."

"I just hung up on Hillstrom. She found a tiny piece of electrical wire inside Jasper Morgan's body. When I was interviewing Randy Haskins in that apartment, he was picking at a small patch sewn into an old electric blanket covering the sofa. I remember because I saw the wires dangling out one end of it." They both looked at me blankly.

"Bouch took the blanket off Morgan's bed and brought it to Burlington?" Sammie asked incredulously.

"Did you find anything personal belonging to Morgan in that motel room?" I countered.

"No."

"No pants or shirt or anything else, right? The place was cleaned out, just in case people like Marie Williams came snooping around later. Assuming Morgan ran for it right after he'd been shot, there probably wasn't much blood on the blanket. So why waste it, when all it needed was a small repair?"

Jonathon was smiling. "Might be a question to ask Jan tomorrow morning. She was probably asked to patch it."

"And in the meantime, we can get another search warrant and pick it up for a lab analysis."

He began moving away. "I'll call Kathy."

"I've got a courier going to Burlington in a few minutes if she needs something signed by either one of us."

He waved acknowledgement over his shoulder and vanished into my office.

"Even if Jan identifies it," Sammie warned me, "it won't take you far."

I smiled at her, sensing at long last the first spidery signs of a real break developing. "Every bit counts, Sam, even the little ones."

Early the following morning, Jonathon Michael and I were sitting on a bench in an inner hallway of the Windham County Courthouse, outside the spacious office of Judge Rachael Aumand. Inside were Jan Bouch, the judge, Kathy Bartlett, a stenographer, and the battered electric blanket we'd retrieved from the Burlington apartment.

When I'd picked her up just after sunrise, Jan had looked terrible—pale, nervous, teary, and obviously sleepless. She'd protested that she'd changed her mind, which I'd been expecting, and proclaimed Norm to be the victim of a miserable childhood. It had taken me an hour to turn her around, and I was by no means convinced the conversation would last three minutes into the inquest.

It had been over an hour, however, and we hadn't heard a peep yet. "If she does nail that blanket to Norm," I said quietly, my voice echoing off the bright, pristine walls, "maybe we should issue that BOL on him."

"Why?"

"Jasper's dead, Lenny's under wraps, Jan and the kids are in protective custody, Steve Kiley's got every task force CI working to find out where Norm is and what he's up to, and Greg Davis has the whole BFPD interviewing everyone who ever knew him. He'd have to be on another planet not to know we're after him. And if he did pop Jasper, he'll be twitchy as hell and prone to use a gun again. I don't want anyone approaching him without knowing all that."

"Works for me," Jonathon said after a short pause. "What did your toxicologist friend come up with?"

I'd told Jonathon of Padget's theory about the aftershave, but I hadn't heard back from Isador Gramm until early this morning. "Brian was right. It was laced with pure coke—a perfect match to what they found in his system, and nowhere close to the stuff in the toilet tank."

"Which makes it 'Good news, bad news'?" he asked.

"Yeah," I agreed. "A plausible scenario for how it got inside him, but not proof he didn't spike the aftershave later and pretend he suddenly had a bright idea. Still, it doesn't hurt him any."

A woman poked her head through a doorway halfway down the hall. "Phone for you, Joe."

I followed her into a large room with several desks scattered about. She ushered me into a glass-walled cubicle along the wall, told me to push the blinking button on the phone, and closed the door as she left.

I picked up the receiver. "Gunther."

"It's Kiley. We put feelers out as soon as you called last night. The only thing we got so far is some guy who sounds like he pulled the same stunt Bouch did. He dropped out of sight yesterday—totally. His name's Peter Neal, works mostly out of the Montpelier/Barre area. There's a chance he's one of Bouch's lieutenants. We heard he runs kids like the others did."

"Could he have left the state to make a buy or something?"

"That's what I asked, but disappearing without warning doesn't fit his routine. There's a buzz about it in his social circle."

"You think he might've been hit?" I asked.

"Things've been peaceful in that area. I called the local PDs to see what they had. They confirmed Neal's a probable dealer, but he's known to keep his cards to himself—neat and tidy. All I got is the coincidence of Bouch and this guy pulling a vanishing act at the same time."

I thought for a couple of seconds. It was interesting information— it was also payback in the subtlest of forms. In Steve Kiley's eyes, we'd run roughshod over his task force. His revenge had been to deliver the goods in a timely, effective manner. "Point taken," I thought. Out loud, however, I said, "It can't be coincidence. He must've cut and run."

"From us?"

"From us, from Bouch. From what we've found out, you don't want to be near Norm when things go sour. I don't guess the local PDs have bothered finding out where Neal might be."

"Nope."

"Could I ask you a big favor, then?"

I could almost hear him smiling at the phone. "You can try."

"If we're right about Neal, then he's probably run to neutral ground where he hopes nobody can find him—from either side. I'd love to get this one. You think you could squeeze his contacts till one of them fesses up? He has to have left a forwarding address somewhere."

"I think we can do that."

"Thanks Steve. I owe you a big one."

"Yes, you do."

I returned to join Jonathon on the bench, filling him in on Kiley's discovery, including the latter's satisfied sense of irony.

Twenty minutes later, the door to Judge Aumand's office opened, and Kathy emerged with a tear-stained Jan Bouch. Kathy caught my eye from behind Jan's back and gave me a thumbs-up. I rose and took Jan's hands in my own. "You feeling okay?"

Looking at the floor, she merely shook her head.

"You've done a harder thing than most people will ever have to do. We all appreciate it. It'll get easier from here on. You're with good people—they'll see you and the kids get what you need."

One of the Women For Women staffers appeared at the far end of the corridor to take Jan back to the shelter, apparently summoned by Kathy from inside the judge's chambers. I released Jan's hands and patted her on the shoulder. "Don't hesitate to call if you want, okay?"

She kept silent as the staffer gathered her up and escorted her back up the hallway. The three of us waited until she was gone.

"Arsene Gault. That name ring any bells?" Kathy asked immediately.

"It does with me," Jonathon answered. "We've nailed him before for fraudulent business dealings. He's a Realtor in Springfield."

Kathy Bartlett explained. "Jan said his was the one name she heard time and again in connection to Norm, either when he'd mention it in passing, or when Gault would leave phone messages. As far as she knows, he never came by the house, and she never saw Norm meet him when they were out and about together. But the phone calls were frequent."

"Money laundering?" I asked.

"It would fit," Jonathon answered. "Gault deals mostly in dumps, selling to people with no sense and less money. He's got the scruples of a cockroach."

"Did Jan ever see Norm dealing drugs?" I asked Kathy.

She rolled her eyes. "Not that she told me. I must admit, I've had better witnesses. Most of the time, I was handing her Kleenexes. I didn't get a hell of a lot more than what I just told you. The blanket was a home run, though. About the time Morgan disappeared, Norm dumped it in her lap and told her to wash and mend it. She said she didn't notice any blood on it at the time and had no idea where it came from or ended up. Still, a jury loves that kind of thing.

"I think Gault's the next domino to push over, in any case. I got the judge to grant an extension on this inquest, so the sooner you two can round him up—and all his paperwork—the better. My suggestion, Joe, since Jon and I do this all the time, is that he and I corral the legal forms and signatures, while you locate Gault so we can grab him when we want him. Is that agreeable?"

It was definitely that. With one amendment. "I think I might do more than just locate him," I said.

Jonathon instantly took my meaning. "A surveillance?"

I shrugged. "Norm's out there somewhere—maybe heading for Tijuana—but given what we think he did to Jasper, and how Lenny reacted to being exposed, chances are he's nearby, sharpening his claws. If Gault's as tied to Norm as we hope, he's probably a walking target."

Jonathon looked at me thoughtfully, too experienced to dismiss the idea. "Watch your back. We'll be as fast as we can."

23

Arsene Gault's weather-beaten office was located on Wall Street in Springfield, a town three times the size of Bellows Falls, and a mere sixteen miles north of it. Once an industrial powerhouse, and birthplace of everything from steam shovels to gravel roofing to the jointed doll and the mop wringer, Springfield, despite harsh economic times, had managed to keep its head more successfully above water than Bellows Falls, if barely, and had certainly avoided its smaller rival's bruised reputation.

Not that I could currently tell that I was in any kind of town. While Wall Street was fully within Springfield's municipal embrace, this stretch of it was only sparsely inhabited and boxed in by a tree-choked embankment, making it look like a rural road.

It was the morning following the inquest, I was fighting the effects of too little sleep, and it was raining again. I stretched and looked across the street at Gault's office. A product of the 1960s, it was one-storied, flat-roofed, clad in brick, and generally looked like a single floor of a New York tenement, except that it was much smaller.

I'd been parked here for three hours, having tailed Gault from his home that morning, and having babysat him most of the night. From what I could tell, he worked without associates or a secretary, and during the time I'd been watching, he hadn't received a single customer. If he wasn't wrapped up in crooked deals with Norm Bouch, I couldn't imagine how he made ends meet.

I straightened slightly in my seat. Ahead of me, where the road curved away to the south, I saw something move. There had been sporadic traffic during my vigil, but none of it unusual—until now. This hint of motion, which should have grown into an oncoming car, had stopped.

I strained to peer through the water coursing across the windshield. All I could see was grayness and mist.

I hit the wipers once.

A dark shadow emerged from the washed-out backdrop of the distant embankment.

I slid over to the passenger side of the car, eased the door open, and slipped out, keeping the car between me and the shape in the distance. The rain pounded me on the back, and I pulled an old baseball cap out of my pocket to shield my eyes. I also pulled my gun from its holster and kept it in my hand.

Still bent over double, I worked my way along the ditch, my shoes filling with water as they had when we'd found Jasper Morgan. The dark shadow ahead gradually emerged as a black van with tinted windows, parked so its driver could just see Gault's building from the corner. As I got nearer, I saw a misty plume feathering out from the exhaust pipe.

Fifty yards shy of my goal, the ditch became a culvert running under a driveway. I was on the other side of the road from the van, and there was no cover to be had anywhere.

Pausing to memorize the license plate, I rose from hiding and stepped onto the road, my gun tucked behind a fold in my raincoat.

The reaction was instantaneous. Its rear wheels spinning, the van leapt forward, making a halfhearted stab at running me over. I stepped aside like some urban toreador, the driver's side mirror barely missing my head, and watched it fishtail into the gray distance. The van's darkened windows had prevented me from seeing the driver.

I jogged back to my car, soaked and cold, and called Dispatch on the cell phone.

Maxine Paroddy answered on the first ring. "Brattleboro Police."

"Max, it's Joe. I need a Springfield area bulletin issued on a late-eighties black Ford van with tinted windows, possibly being driven by Norman Bouch. There's already a BOL out on him. Add a possible armed-and-dangerous to that." I recited the license number to her.

"You okay?" she quickly asked.

"Yeah."

"Okay. Stay put."

She put me on hold and issued my request. Chances were slim anyone would spot the van. With so few police officers covering the entire state, it was a miracle when one of these bulletins worked on an abandoned vehicle, much less one in motion whose driver knew we were after him. Still, it was the thought that counted. It also made me hope that if the driver had been Norm Bouch, he'd keep low at least long enough for Jonathon to reach me so we could put Gault under wraps.

Maxine came back on the line. "You want the registrant for that van? You better be sitting down."

In a puddle of water, I thought. "Fire away."

"Jasper Morgan."

I smiled grimly at Bouch's sense of humor. "Thanks, Max. Keep me informed."

The cell phone chirped a few seconds after I'd hung up. "Gunther."

"It's me," said Jonathon. "I've got all the paperwork and I'm coming into Springfield now. You got him in your sights?"

"Yeah, but I'm not alone." I gave him Gault's address and brought him up to date.

Jonathon appeared ten minutes later. I left my car, noticing the downpour was finally easing up, and crossed the road to meet him.

"Jesus," he said, checking me out, "Did Norm get away by boat?"

"Almost."

"How many're inside?" he asked, nodding toward the building.

"He's alone."

We went in together, Jonathon leading, entering a small waiting room with a couple of old armchairs, a dirty rug, and some calendar art on the walls. Arsene Gault, stooped, potbellied, and with a few strings of hair draped across an otherwise bald head, appeared at the only other door, a sour look on his face.

"Who're you?"

Not a man used to seeing customers.

Jonathon introduced us and proffered two documents. "We're from the attorney general's office, Mr. Gault, and these are subpoenas—one a Duces Tecum granting us access to all your business records, and the other requiring you to appear at an inquest at the time and date stated on the front."

Gault's expression didn't change. He continued looking at us distastefully from under bristling eyebrows.

"Swell," he said, and turned on his heel.

We followed him into a dingy, cluttered, mildew-smelling office. He tossed aside a newspaper spread across his desk and quickly dialed a number from memory.

"Mr. Gault?" I added. "I think you ought to know I found Norm Bouch parked in a van down the street just now, staking this place out. I probably don't need to tell you it's a lucky thing I scared him away."

He gave me a long, considered look and then returned to the phone. "Bob? It's Gault. Get your ass down here. I'm in deep shit this time."

It was Steve Kiley's voice. "Peter Neal has a great-uncle who owns a farm in Addison County, south of Vergennes, in Waltham township." He gave me precise directions out of Middlebury.

"You sure he's there?" I asked, the phone tucked under my chin as I struggled to pull on a pair of pants. I was standing in my office, having left Arsene Gault in Jonathon's care. Gault, after conferring with his lawyer, had demanded protective custody prior to appearing at the inquest the next morning.

Kiley sounded amused. "I thought we'd let you figure that out—least we could do."

I didn't begrudge him the dig. "Fair enough. Thanks for the help."

Addison County extends like a slightly wrinkled blanket from the western foothills of the Green Mountains to the shores of Lake Champlain, south of Burlington and north of Rutland. Addison's national claim to fame is Middlebury, home to the college of the same name. For Vermonters, however, it is the county's primary function that matters most. It is farmland—a vast, rolling, dark-earthed footprint of the ancient glacier that split the Greens from the Adirondacks, both of which loom on either border, as if resentful of the valley that keeps them apart. The sky in this part of the state—everywhere else blocked by hills and peaks—is a huge, arching dome, shimmering hot and blue as we drove beneath it, although the remnants of this morning's rain lingered as gray mist in the mountains, like soiled cotton caught on thorns.

Vermont, despite its reputation for cows and farms, is better represented by trees and stone, another contrast to Addison's unique features. Driving along the smooth, undulating, narrow black road north of Middlebury, I was struck yet again by the pure plenty of this patch of earth. Each treeless hilltop revealed another panorama of farm after farm stretching off into the distance, pinned in place by clusters of glistening silver and blue silos. The breeze was pungent with cow manure, cut grass, damp soil, and the fresh tang of the cold Champlain waters, forever shimmering like a mirage at the foot of the Adirondacks. The wildflowers scattered by the sides of the fields and ribbon-smooth roads echoed the perennials proudly coloring the window boxes of widely spaced neat white farmhouses.

There were three of us traveling this countryside, all but oblivious to its charms—Jonathon and I in the lead car, followed by a local deputy sheriff, loaned to us as a courtesy.

Jonathon was reading the faxes Steven Kiley had sent us on the heels of his phone call, holding them flat on his lap against the wind from the open window. "Mr. Neal certainly fits the Lenny Markham mold. I wonder how Bouch found these guys?"

It was a rhetorical question. We both knew people like Norm met one another both conventionally and by the good graces of the system Jon and I worked for. Be it through parole offices, prisons, or social rehab and counseling sessions, society had made it a point to bring these people into constant and continuous contact, from where—antisocial though they could be—they learned to network along with the best of the upwardly mobile.

"We're getting close," I warned him.

He looked up and gazed across the agricultural mosaic. To our right was a huge, gently sloping field, with a large farmhouse and a group of buildings at its bottom. Bordering the field's far edge, a narrow dirt lane connected the road we were traveling to the farm's dooryard. In between, as small as a Tonka toy and trailing a plume of ocher dust, a tractor slowly worked the field. Its driver, a tiny smudge of red shirt from this distance, was crowned with a mane of gleaming white hair, which glittered like a torch in the sun.

"That's him," Jonathon said, his voice terse.

"How do you know that?"

He tapped the paperwork in his lap. "It says he's almost an albino, with shoulder-length hair."

"Damn," I said. "It's not often this easy." I spoke too soon. As we neared the road to the farm, I saw the tractor stop, and its driver shield his eyes to peer in our direction. I suddenly rued our agreeing to have a marked police car as an escort.

"There he goes," Jon said.

Sure enough, Peter Neal abruptly started rolling again—fast this time—aiming directly for the lane.

"What's he doing?" Jon pondered.

I swung into the lane myself and hit the gas, trying to close the distance before he got there.

Neal beat me to it. The tractor lurched over the ditch, bounced onto the road and stopped, blocking the way as effectively as a dam. Neal leapt from his seat, his hair flying behind him like a flag, and began sprinting toward the distant buildings.

I sped right up to the roadblock and ground on the brakes, skidding to a halt before it. I climbed out and ran to the tractor, the heat from its cowling rippling the air above it. The keys were gone. I'd turned to shout to Jonathon, when I saw the sheriff's car leave the road in an attempt to go around and come to a shuddering stop in the soft earth of the ditch. The deputy staggered out, dazed and rubbing his chest from where his seat belt had bruised him.

Jonathon was out and running around the tractor, in hot pursuit.

"Call for backup," I shouted to the deputy and jumped down to follow Jon.

Ahead of us, more distinct as we neared the barn, the goal of Neal's flight became clear—a four-wheeler was parked to one side of a feeding pen, ready and able to take him cross-country and away.

"The ATV," I panted to Jonathon, still ahead.

"I see it."

A mere hundred yards before us, Neal straddled the machine. A cloud of blue smoke burst from its tailpipe and floated off in the breeze like a balloon. The vehicle lurched three feet forward and stalled. We could hear the starter motor grinding in impotent rage, trying to ignite a flooded engine.

All the while, Neal's pale face kept flashing in our direction as he checked on our progress.

Jonathon yelled as he ran. "*Police.* Stop where you are."

For a split second, Neal seemed to consider it. Then, with an angry kick at one of the tires, he bolted into the barn.

Without hesitation, Jon cut to the left and ran the length of the building to seal off the rear exit, leaving me to handle the front.

Gasping for air, I staggered up the cement apron before the two large sliding doors and tucked myself out of sight of the dark, cool, cavernous interior. Waiting for Jonathon to get in place, I studied the doors next to me, noticing they were equipped with a hasp and a long stick on a string.

"Peter Neal," I finally shouted into the gloom. "This is the police. We're not here to hassle you. We just want to talk. Come on out."

Aside from the sounds of a few animals shifting around, I heard nothing from within.

"Neal, we know you worked with Norm Bouch, and that you're more worried about him than about us. That's why we're here. We want to help you."

I looked back along the road. The young deputy was awkwardly jogging our way, his hands on his hips to keep his gun and stick from flopping around.

"Neal," I tried again. "There's no point to this. We're on the same side here. Come out so we can talk about it. There'll be no cuffs, no arrest, no nothing. Just talk."

The deputy reached me. I silently put him in my place and retreated to the dooryard, analyzing the building. Aside from the doors front and back, there were only several small windows running along the long walls. The silo was connected to one side. A short, low, roofed passage-way ran to what looked like an equipment garage on the other.

Hoping to encourage Neal like a mouse in a maze, I motioned to the deputy to shut the doors and lock them, and then follow me as I circled the neighboring garage, looking for an alternate entrance to the large closed door at its front.

I found it near the back—a disused narrow doorway, half blocked by a sheet of plywood hanging by a single hinge. Doubled over to avoid knocking anything loose, I slipped into the darkness, the deputy still close behind.

Almost totally blind, I was enveloped by the familiar smells of my childhood—oil, gas, and manure, against a background of hay dust and the distant sweet odor of silage filtering through from the barn next door. As my eyes adjusted, the disembodied shapes around me emerged into a harrow, a manure spreader, a baler, and assorted other machinery. Far to the front, as I'd hoped, was the outline of a pickup truck, its nose almost touching the front door.

I pulled my gun and gestured to the deputy to do likewise, motioning him to work his way forward along the near wall. I took the opposite side, nearer the barn, and slowly picked my way through a tangle of agricultural odds and ends, thinking back for a moment to when my father, my brother, and I spent long winter evenings servicing the equipment we'd use for spring planting.

There was a faint sound from the passageway leading to the locked barn. I crouched behind an empty oil drum and waited. I saw a shadow furtively flit past against a strip of sunlight through a crack in the wall, heading for the truck. I waited until I heard the slight squeal of the passenger door opening before I followed. With the click of the door quietly being pulled shut, I sidled up to the side of the truck, swung around to face the open window, and leveled my gun at the pale-haired shadow of the man sliding toward the steering wheel.

"Don't move, Peter," I said.

He froze instantly, his whole body coiled to react, and I suddenly knew in my gut this wasn't going to work, that he would yield to impulse and do the one thing I'd been hoping to avoid.

Then, just beyond him, the deputy appeared in the driver's window, pointing his gun, as I was, at Peter's head. It wasn't great tactics—had either one of us fired, we probably would have killed the other along with Neal. But fortunately, he didn't put us to the test. He dropped his hands to his lap and said, "Okay."

I opened the door and crooked a finger at him. "Come on out."

He slid over and I grabbed his arm, twisting him around as he came out so he was facing the truck. "Lean up against the cab, step way back, and spread your legs."

The deputy circled around and covered him as I carefully checked him for weapons. I then removed my cuffs and snapped them on his wrists.

"I thought you just wanted to talk. You said no arrest," he complained.

I ignored him and turned to the deputy. "You better call off the cavalry. And tell Jon where we are."

He nodded and left the way we'd come. I steered Neal toward the front door and slid it open a few feet, letting the bright sunlight knife into the darkness. "It's amazing what you'll say when you want something," I told him, and pushed him outside.

There were several hay bales stacked against the garage wall. I pointed to one of them. "Sit."

He did as I asked, tossing his white hair out of his face and staring at me belligerently. "Who the hell are you, anyway?"

Jonathon Michael rounded the far corner of the distant barn and approached us. I waited until he was within earshot before answering. "We're from the attorney general's office, Peter, which is some of the worst news you've ever had."

He gave us both a sneer. "I'm scared to death."

"We know that. That's why you're here. 'Course, it's not us you're scared of. It's Norm Bouch. And in your place, I would be, too."

"I don't know who you're talking about."

"Lenny Markham did," I said. "So did Jasper Morgan. As you know, we found one, and Norm found the other. And Lenny's not complaining. How long you been down on the farm, Peter? Twenty-four hours? Less? We got to you pretty quick, didn't we? And we have no idea how close behind us Norm might be. We just know he's out there, taking care of loose ends."

Neal didn't answer, but the anger had slipped from his face.

"I don't think Mr. Neal's interested," Jonathon said softly. "We might as well pack up and leave—let this brave young man with his trademark looks fend for himself. Maybe he can dye his hair and go live in New York or something."

I shrugged and pulled out my handcuff key. "Turn around."

Peter twisted on the hay bale and I undid the cuffs, but he remained sitting there, meditatively rubbing his wrists. His expression reminded me of one of my uncles', when he was deep in the middle of a late-night card game.

"What do you have on Bouch?"

I feigned surprise. "You know him?"

"Up yours."

"We're taking his operation apart, piece by piece," Jonathon answered.

I tried reading into Neal's question, thinking he had something specific in mind, and remembering how J.P. Tyler had thought two people had moved Morgan's corpse. "And we know you and he visited Jasper in that motel."

"You have proof?"

He might as well have confessed.

I smiled. "We have you."

He stared at the ground for a moment, weighing the odds. "What would I get out of the deal?"

"Did you kill Jasper?" Jonathon asked.

"No, but I saw Norm do it."

"Then," I answered, "I'd recommend you get immunity. You'd also get to live."

He paused a while longer. "You close to catching him?"

I understood his concern, having seen it mimicked by Arsene Gault. "We'll put you under lock and key till we do—protective custody."

He finally nodded and stood up. "Okay. It's in the barn."

He slid open the doors I'd had the deputy lock earlier and led us down the center feed passage. A couple of cows stood in their stanchions, noses shoved into troughs. Near the back wall was a wooden ladder leading up to the loft. Neal climbed it with practiced ease and returned us to the front of the barn, running a tall, dusty gauntlet of stacked bales. Just shy of the closed hay door, he stopped, reached above a thick overhead beam, and retrieved a manila envelope. He handed it to me without comment.

In a shaft of light from a small window tucked under the gable, I opened the envelope and peered inside. A nine-millimeter semi-automatic pistol gleamed back at me.

"It's that cop's gun," Neal explained. "I was supposed to get rid of it. It's got Norm's fingerprints on it."

24

I was standing at the second-floor window of the State's Attorney's reception area, my hands in my pockets, looking at Brattleboro's rush-hour traffic. I was lost in thought. An arm slipped through mine.

"How're you doing?"

I looked down into Gail's face. "Hey, there. I was just thinking I should be in an incredibly upbeat mood."

"Which you're not."

"I'm not complaining. Kathy Bartlett's down the hall cutting a deal with Gault's lawyer so he'll spill his guts about Norm Bouch. I got an eyewitness to Norm killing Jasper Morgan, a gun with his prints on it, and an electric blanket from Bouch's apartment with chemical traces of Morgan's blood. And Bartlett told me that at the inquest, Jan Bouch admitted the whole case against Brian Padget was a frame. She said Norm not only broke into Padget's place, spiked his aftershave, and dropped that bag of coke into the toilet tank, but that he watered Brian's gas tank so Emily Doyle would get sucked into the mess with him."

"Sounds Christmas wrapped."

"Except the box is empty." I pointed with my chin at the passing traffic. "I saw Bouch early this morning—I'm pretty sure it was him. He was staking out Gault's office, probably getting ready to knock him off. An hour ago, I heard they'd found the van he was driving, abandoned on some logging trail...It's hard to celebrate when the bad guy is still out there."

"If there's one thing I'm learning in this job," Gail said gently, "it's that you have to settle for what you can get. Brian's off the hook, and Jan and her kids are headed for a better life. Those are real accomplishments. Bouch will get what he deserves, even if you aren't the one to give it to him. That's the way it works out sometimes."

I smiled and kissed her.

Kathy Bartlett stepped into the corridor and joined us, speaking in a theatrical whisper. "I can't believe I'm locked in a room with two slimy chiselers, while you two are necking out here."

"Things going well, are they?" I asked.

Her voice returned to normal. "Actually, not too bad. We've gone from where Gault was going to take the fifth, to where he's going to give us everything we want."

I thought of the comments I'd just exchanged with Gail. "In return for...?"

Bartlett smiled. "Use and derivative use immunity, meaning we not only can't use his own testimony against him, we can't use anything we discover as a result of that testimony."

"So he walks away clean as a baby," I said unhappily.

Bartlett shrugged. "True, but about as poor, too. Steve Kiley'll love this part. It turns out we're talking about a lot of property—one to one-and-a-half million dollars' worth—including Norm's apartment in Burlington, since he was renting from himself. He's got apartments, houses, and small businesses all over the state. Once I channel it through federal forfeiture proceedings, we should all be a whole lot richer. It's been a particular pleasure reminding Mr. Gault of that fact, and that we'll be watching him like a hawk from now on."

"So you're all set?" I asked her.

"We'll still do the inquest, to formalize everything, but it looks pretty solid."

There was a small, awkward pause after she finished, all three of us thinking the same thing.

"Except for Norm," Kathy finally added.

"Right," I agreed.

I found Jonathon Michael back at the police department, working with Sammie and Ron Klesczewski to transfer all they had on the murders of Jasper Morgan and the mysterious skeleton to the AG's office. Peter Neal had only known the youngster as Billy and claimed he'd been beaten to death by Morgan and Bouch together, an accusation we all knew would probably never make it to court.

We were about an hour into this process when the phone rang and Ron handed it to me.

It was Gail. "I just got a call from Women For Women. Jan Bouch has disappeared."

"Damn." I waved my hand to catch Jonathon's attention.

"I'll meet you there," Gail said, and hung up before I could protest.

We drove over in silence, dreading that Norm Bouch had been at work. Gail was already in the parking lot, talking with Susan Raffner, the director and an old friend of hers.

"How long do you think she's been gone?" I asked Susan.

"It could be a couple of hours. We check on them periodically, but they aren't under lock and key."

"And you have no idea where she might've gone?"

Susan shook her head.

"Could she have been grabbed?" Jonathon asked.

"No," Susan said emphatically. "Not being incarcerated doesn't mean they wander around at will, and people don't come on these grounds without being noticed. Every door is monitored around the clock. She had to have actually snuck off, taking pains not to be seen."

"Are the kids still here?" I asked. "Maybe they can tell us something."

Probably embarrassed by the turn of events, Raffner didn't argue but urged that the interviewers be limited to Gail and me.

There were five children all told, of whom only two were actually Jan's, and this was the first time I'd actually been introduced to them. During my visits to the house—aside from the boy with the deflated ball—they'd either been peripheral bodies in blurred motion, or not there. They ranged in age from three to about seven, and were as dissimilar from one another as a pack of street urchins.

Gail, Susan, and I sat next to each other on the floor of a small room, a hollow-eyed TV set in the corner, with the children grouped around us.

Gail started off. "My name is Gail. This is Joe."

"I seen him," said one of the older boys.

"Where?"

"At my house."

"I remember you," I said. "You were almost tall enough to grab a doughnut out of your mom's hand, even though it was over her head."

He smiled with pride. "I got it, too," he lied, "two of 'em."

"You did not," the ball player said, punching him in the arm. "You got 'em after Dad threw 'em out the door, just like we all did."

Gail interrupted by pretending to glance around. "Speaking of your mom, where is she? I had something I wanted to ask her."

"She's gone," a little girl said.

The older boy cuffed the back of her head. "She'll be back."

Gail looked disappointed. "That's too bad. Where do you think she went?"

"Home," said one.

"To see the fireworks, I bet," said another.

"The fireworks?" I blurted.

"Yeah," the oldest answered, looking at me like I was brain dead. "It's Old Home Days tonight."

He didn't need to elaborate. The Rockingham Old Home Days fireworks display was the largest in the state, running for forty minutes and drawing over ten thousand people to Bellows Falls from all over Vermont. They lined the river and jammed the bridges and railroad yard, since the rockets were fired from the riverbank north of town.

"Did she tell you that?" I asked.

The boy didn't answer, having obviously supplanted his own desires with Jan's.

"Why did you say, 'home'?" Gail asked the small girl who'd spoken first.

"She told me, just before she climbed out the window."

I could feel Susan stiffen beside me, no doubt wondering, as I was, why Jan had suddenly chosen to leave. Phone calls were screened here, but I suspected Norm had found a way to lure her out. He had been manipulating her for years, forcing her to do things she wouldn't normally willingly do. It took no great stretch to imagine he'd used her guilt at betraying him to force her across a suicidal line.

Having seen the results of Norm's ruthlessness, I had no doubts he was going to repay Jan for her transgressions as he had Jasper Morgan, young Billy, and who knows how many others. But where those others might have come under Norm's concept of business expenses, Jan and his relationship was far more convoluted. She had climbed out that window as a martyr might journey to self-sacrifice, and he, rather than fleeing to parts unknown, had put domination above survival. They were like two halves of a pair of scissors about to snap shut.

I leaned forward slightly, my eyes on a level with that of the small child. "What exactly did she say?"

"She said, 'Don't worry, honey. Everything'll be fine. I just have to go home for a while.'"

"She didn't go home," the other small girl said, speaking for the first time. "That's not what she meant. She told me she was going to her thinking place."

At last, I thought. "And where's the thinking place?"

"The old milk plant. She took me there once. It's neat."

It was almost dusk, shortly before the fireworks were to begin. From all over the area, sheriff's deputies, State Police, and the Bellows Falls and Walpole police were converging either on Bellows Falls or the old creamery itself. This was not, I had stressed to everyone, to be a high-profile approach. Assuming a small child's guess was right, I didn't want people spooked, least of all Norm Bouch.

But even if I'd asked for the National Guard, it wasn't going to be an easy location to surround, much less contain. The plant, as I knew from Greg Davis's tour of the town days earlier, was at the bend of the river, between the two bridges leading to New Hampshire, just above where the falls turned from neck-breaking rapids into a precipitous drop. That much was actually a tactical advantage—normally. The so-called Island had an unbreachable boundary on three sides, limited access, and was covered mostly with abandoned factories, warehouses, and the open railroad yard. Tonight alone, however, this no-man's land became Times Square on New Year's Eve. Fully half the expected crowd of ten to twelve thousand people would be standing shoulder-to-shoulder on the Island, lining the river just above the milk plant. A dozen more would be illegally camped on its roof.

Gail, Jonathon, and I were in my car, heading toward Bellows Falls from the south, using blue lights only to quietly warn of our approach. Well shy of the town line, however, we hit heavy traffic, and from there on, I edged along at a steady five miles an hour. It stayed that way through downtown and onto the Island, where I finally gave up, pulled over, and killed the engine.

"Let's go on foot. Gail, I'll leave the radio on channel two so you can hear what's going on. If the need comes up, I might ask you to use the cell phone, so keep an ear out, okay?"

She slipped in behind the wheel, kissing me through the open window. "No heroics, please."

I gave her a thumbs-up and went to the trunk of the car, where I extracted two armored vests and a couple of flashlights. I handed one of the vests to Jonathon. "Better put this on under your shirt."

We jogged down the narrow dirt trail that followed the riverbank to the empty milk plant, looking, I hoped, like two latecomers heading for the show.

I keyed my portable radio. "This is Gunther, approaching from the south, along the river. Who's in place and in command?"

To my surprise, Latour's voice came back. "It's Emile, Joe. The cordon's still pretty thin. No one's gone in yet."

"Any signs of anything?"

"Nothing so far. I'm just ahead of you on the dirt road."

We reached him a few minutes later. Aside from several genuine spectators circling the building to gain access to the railroad yards, we were largely alone.

Emile explained the layout. "The north side's as crowded as this is empty, and there're people on the roof and at some of the upper windows, like every year. So far, I've got four people positioned at all corners of the building, a couple more along the north wall, pretending they're on crowd control, and Greg Davis and Emily Doyle standing by to go inside. I might be getting five or six more, but with the roads and bridges either closed or jammed with people, travel times're going to be lousy. Do you want to take over command?"

I did, but I kept it to myself. Latour was finally in movement, showing he knew what to do. If this was redemption in the making, I wasn't about to impede it. "No."

He gave me a surprised, appreciative look. "Thanks. Then if you don't mind the suggestion, I think we should just contain the building, wait till the crowd disperses after the show, and go at this nice and peaceful. The only problem is the people already inside—all potential hostages." He hesitated and then added, "How good is your information that Bouch or his wife are actually in there?"

That wasn't something I wanted to discuss. "Good enough. I also don't think we can wait, as reasonable as that sounds. If we do, all we're likely to find is Jan Bouch's body. We may anyhow…But I agree with you about the potential hostages."

Latour shook his head unhappily, and I immediately began reconsidering my decision to leave him in command. But he didn't disappoint. "All right. How 'bout you and Jonathon go in with Greg and Emily, and I'll send uniforms to cover the areas you clear as I get them."

"And if we find spectators, we'll herd them into secure rooms and post someone on the door," I added. "It'll be safer than escorting them through the building."

"Okay." He pointed to a far corner. "The entrance is around there. Davis and Doyle are already waiting. Good luck."

We found them pacing nervously before the front door, both wearing civilian clothes. I told them of Latour's plan.

Emily looked incredulous. "Jesus Christ. That place is huge. The four of us could be in there all week checking it out."

I ignored her complaint. "That's if we approached it conventionally, which we can't do. Jan's kid told us her hangout was a room on the top floor, facing the river. Jonathon and I will head there first, while you two and as many others that show up work the problem from below. Emile'll give us what he can when he can."

Greg Davis squatted down, picked up a thin stick, and drew an outline of the building's interior in the dust. "Three floors, more or less." He pointed at the double doors facing us. "The ground floor's a mess. Lots of rooms, junk, storage vats, equipment, hallways—a ton of places for someone to hide. The good news is it'll be totally empty—no windows facing the fireworks. There's a central corridor right down the middle, with a staircase at the far end. Get there without being ambushed, and it's almost home free."

He shifted slightly to sketch a second plan. "Next floor is the creamery proper. Wide-open, high ceilings, lots of windows, none of them facing where the fireworks'll be. The best viewing areas," he added a rectangle to the north of the square he'd just drawn, "are in three big rooms separated from the main floor by three doors. That's also where people are on the roof. Those rooms only have ten-foot ceilings, so from the outside, that whole part of the building's kind of stepped-down from the rest. Access to the roof is by fire escape on the north wall. The third floor is more like a mezzanine or catwalk. It's where the executive offices used to be, right over the factory floor, high against the ceiling. The corridor feeding the offices is only equipped with a railing, so from below, it's like the bridge of a ship, overlooking the deck. All the offices are on the side facing the river, away from the show."

I glanced at Jonathon. "That must be where we're headed."

Searches like this are always tense. No matter how many people you have keeping you company, the feeling is always one of total isolation. You become convinced that behind every door, lurking in every shadow, is the guy with the gun who's about to take you out. For a moment only, all three of us gazed at the enormous building before us, no doubt sharing those very thoughts.

"Okay," I finally murmured. "Let's get it over with."

Jon and I entered first, walking virtually back-to-back, a flashlight in one hand, a gun in the other, and our radios muted by earpieces. We walked slowly and quietly, pausing occasionally to listen and get our bearings. Greg's directions had been schematically accurate, but they hadn't prepared us for the mood of the place. Dark, cool, and crowded with industrial paraphernalia, to us it became a lethal house of horrors.

It was with considerable relief that we reached the stairs, gave our position on the radio, and headed up.

The next floor was in stark contrast to the threatening muddle of shadows below. As described, it was an enormous room, high-ceilinged, lined with ten-foot-tall windows, cluttered with old, dust-covered equipment clustered into regularly spaced workstations. Bundles of pipes and conduits shot up from each of these to the ceiling and spread out to all four corners like huge metal straws, crushed over against the inside cover of a too-small box. Bathed in the remnants of the departed day, and tinged by the glow of the town all around, the room looked like an abandoned movie set of some abstract, industrialist nightmare.

I immediately noticed the far wall with the three doors, behind which, even from where we stood, we could hear people talking and laughing, gathered together in excited anticipation.

Jon looked at me and pointed at the doors quizzically. I shook my head and indicated the gallery tucked up against the ceiling and running the length of one wall—the executive aerie Greg had likened to a ship's bridge.

Jon nodded and followed me silently up the metal staircase attached to the far end.

Flashlights now off, we paused at the top landing, taking in the catwalk ahead, a railing on one side, offices on the other. Aside from the muffled sounds from below, we couldn't hear a thing. The dull light seeping through the huge windows across the chasm made me feel I was in a tunnel instead of twenty feet in the air, and gave the whole setting a claustrophobic feeling.

We crept to the first office and found the door open. Normally, I would have had a long-handled mirror to safely check the room from around the corner. But circumstances were far from normal. Harking back to the old days, I stuck my head out into the doorway and instantly withdrew it, listening and waiting for any response. There was none. I repeated the gesture—more slowly this time—with similar results and finally did it again with my flashlight on. The room was bare—and empty.

Throughout this exercise, Jonathon stood back slightly, prepared for attack from either direction.

Room by room, we progressed in this stealthy manner, sometimes switching roles, but finding nothing until we reached our first closed door, three-quarters of the way down.

My back against the wall, I tried the doorknob gently. The door soundlessly loosened against the jamb. Switching on my light, I nodded to Jon opposite, who followed my example and prepared to enter low and fast. On a soundless count of three, I threw open the door. Jon barreled past me and rolled to the right, I half fell in after him and cut to the left. The halos from our lights dashed around the small room, desperately searching for a body in motion. They found one who would move no longer.

Confident the room was otherwise empty, Jonathon stepped back into the doorway to stand guard.

"That her?" he asked over his shoulder.

I was surprised he didn't know and then realized they'd never met.

"Yeah. Jan Bouch."

She was lying sprawled on the floor, her torso propped against the wall under the window. Her eyes were half open, seemingly lost in a daydream, her face, so tense in life, was slack and hopeless in death. As I approached her, there was a sudden, frightening explosion from outside, and the room filled with violent, shimmering color. I glanced out the window and saw blazing streamers falling from the sky like stars, plunging toward the ghostly froth of the river below. The colors played dimly on Jan's skin and hair as I turned my light away.

"Her son said she'd come here to watch the fireworks." Jonathon took a quick look in my direction. "What's her status?" he asked, not having heard me.

I felt for a carotid. Her skin was soft and warm, but in memory only. "She's dead."

Jon updated the others.

I played the light on her again. She was disheveled, her lips cut and swollen, one eye puffy. I saw a small hole in the front of her blouse and unbuttoned it enough to confirm the dark puncture in the skin beneath. There was no blood.

I thought back to all I'd learned about this couple, and all the warning signs I'd heeded but could do nothing about.

Latour's voice came over my earpiece. "Joe, do you advise changing tactics, now that she's dead?"

"Hang on a sec," I answered him. "Let's finish checking this top section. She hasn't been dead long, so if he is in the building, I don't want to rush him. We still have a potential hostage situation here."

Jon and I searched the rest of the gallery, room by room, the earlier quiet now replaced with raucous cracks, bangs, and strung-out screams from high overhead. The darkened, haunted corners flickered with garish rainbow colors.

When we returned to the top of the stairs, I radioed, "Top floor clear. Heading down."

Extending beneath us, the vast plant floor glimmered eerily in the dying colors, each one of which brought muted outbursts of appreciation from behind the doors at the room's north end, where the trespassers could see the fireworks we were missing.

"Emile?" I continued, "how many can you give us up here? We're on the main floor."

There was a pause. "How 'bout five?"

"That's good. He probably made it out, but I want to corral the spectators before we call it quits."

We descended the staircase and met Emily, another Bellows Falls officer, two state troopers, and, to my surprise, Emile himself. I gave him a smile. "Couldn't stay out of the action, huh?"

He looked slightly embarrassed. "Greg runs things better than I can anyway," he muttered. "Besides, I won't be able to do this too much longer."

I glanced over his shoulder and saw Emily roll her eyes, forever unforgiving.

"Here's the layout," I said. "This room looks empty, but we haven't checked around each of the workstations. There are seven of us, so let's break into teams of two, and work in a row, walking from here to the far wall. That," and I played my light on the distant doors, "is where our trespassers are enjoying the show."

We set out like grouse hunters in a twilight landscape, our movements punctuated by the jittery beams from our lights. We proceeded quietly, the sound of our progress supplanted by the noise outside. The cavernous room around us shifted alternately from one garish color to another.

At the far end, I turned to Emily and Latour. "Is there any difference between one room and the next in terms of size or layout?"

They both shook their heads.

"Then we might as well use whichever one has the most people to hold them all."

Using the same three teams, we entered the separate rooms without fanfare or noise, slipping inside like latecomers to a movie, our flashlights extinguished.

In my room, the center one, I could see the outline of almost ten people standing before a wide bank of multi-paned windows, gesturing and calling out excitedly with each new explosion. Occasionally, several of them would lift an arm and suck on what appeared to be a beer can. I spoke quietly into my radio. "This is Joe. I've got close to ten."

"Five for me," answered Emily.

"I only got three," said a voice I didn't recognize.

Latour came on. "Round them up and bring them to where Joe is, then. Tell 'em they're not in any trouble—just that we want 'em where we can find 'em."

I opened my door and motioned the two groups to enter. Aside from a few startled looks, no one seemed to care much about the sudden appearance of so many cops, and merely moved to the window to resume their enjoyment. We all gathered together near the door to consider our next move.

Still uneasy, however, I kept watching the spectators, the lifelike warmth of Jan Bouch's skin lingering on my fingertips—as palpable as a scent of Norm's proximity.

It was then, barely registering the muted conversation around me, that I focused on one particular silhouette. Yielding to instinct over good sense, I took aim with my flashlight and hit the switch.

Bouch's reaction was instantaneous. For a split second, I saw his pale face half turned toward us before it vanished like a ghost. In that same instant, I saw a familiar glimmer in his hand.

"*Gun,*" I shouted, and pushed at the others to scatter them. But there was no redeeming a bad situation. Having overlooked the obvious possibility that Norm, finding his escape blocked, had hidden among the spectators, I'd exposed us all to lethal danger.

The room exploded in a terrifying travesty of the fireworks outside, slashing flashlight beams and wild shouting replacing rockets and starbursts. In the kaleidoscopic result, I saw people either diving for cover, or frozen in place with their hands up, all to an orchestra of, "*Police*—nobody move."

In its midst, I saw Emily Doyle, half crouched, her gun and flashlight held in a classic shooter's stance, scanning the room for a target.

But the target, largely concealed, had already found her. Momentarily revealed in a red flash from outside, protruding from behind a large piece of equipment by the window, was a hand holding a gun. Norm was taking a careful bead on one of the thorns in his side.

I shouted a warning, to no avail in all that noise, and simultaneously saw Emile Latour break from the tattered darkness, hitting Emily like a car broadsiding a small pet. Just as their bodies commingled, they were caught in the fiery muzzle-flash of Norm's gun. I clearly heard Latour let out a surprised grunt of pain before they both vanished into the gloom that clung to the floor like fog.

In the split second in which this all took place, I aimed and fired quickly three times in Norm's direction. There was a second shout of pain, the sound of a gun skittering across the floor, and a sudden stunned silence in the room, now sharp with the smell of cordite.

"Norm Bouch," I shouted, "this is the police. Surrender immediately."

The response was a shattering of glass and the blur of a balled-up human shadow hurtling through the window.

I dropped my flashlight and reached for the radio at my belt. "All units. Suspect's left the building through a window—north wall. Shots have been fired. Possible officer down."

I ran, stumbling over scattered bodies still squirming for safety, and leaned out the jagged hole, half expecting to see Norm Bouch sprawling face down on the ground. Instead, I found a fire escape attached to the building's side.

I climbed gingerly out the window, hearing footsteps clanging on the metal steps below. Latour had said there were people on the roof, but I'd been so focused on finding Jan, and then Norm, that I'd not only forgotten about them but that Davis had specified the presence of the fire escape. My frustrated rage found new strength at my own continuing stupidity.

I began shouting again into the radio. "Suspect's heading down the north fire escape. Close off the bottom. He may still be armed."

The way down led to a small platform ten feet off the ground, from which a metal ladder had been lowered the rest of the way. As I began my own descent, I could feel the fire escape quivering under Bouch's weight. I also saw that there were no officers below waiting for him. Human to a fault, they'd bolted from their posts to render aid when I'd announced the downing of one of their own.

I almost fell to the platform below, again calling for help on the radio, and reached it just as Bouch hit the ground. He stumbled once and took off hobbling toward the rear of the nearby crowd. As I swung my leg over the ladder's top rung, I glimpsed the immensity of the scene before me, captured like an infrared photograph in the burst of a crimson rocket. There were thousands of people extending like an oil slick from within twenty yards of the creamery to the distant riverbank—a clotted mass of heads and shoulders as densely packed as commuters at a suburban train station. From the moment Bouch hit its outermost fringe, he became indistinguishable from his surroundings.

Of my two remaining hopes, one was that I could track him by the disturbance he'd leave in his wake, as I might a car driving through a corn field. The other was evidenced by the blood I found on every rung of the ladder. Norm Bouch was badly wounded, if only in the hand, so even if he got away this time, either the blood loss or the need for care would eventually force him to where we might find him.

My adrenaline, however, drove me to make the first option a reality. As soon as my feet touched the ground, I bolted for where I'd seen him disappear, telling the others the direction I was taking, and recommending that all exits from the Island be blocked immediately. Through my earpiece, I heard the tactical machinery switching gears; Greg Davis also thoughtfully let me know that Latour had received only a superficial wound. Emily Doyle, whose unprotected head had been in Norm's sights, would be hard put to proclaim her chief's uselessness in the future.

My pursuit through the crowd was like running underwater. As I'd hoped, I could track Bouch's progress by the effects of his passage—people complaining of being shoved aside, a few still regaining their footing, others noticing to their horror the blood he'd smeared on their clothes. I didn't endear myself to any of them with my barely gentler version of the same treatment, despite holding up my badge and muttering constant apologies. It became a chase made surreal by its molasses-slow movement, regularly pierced by strobe-like flashes of violent primary colors. My vision was reduced to a tight series of still pictures, each following the other by several seconds, and each tinged with a different hue.

Despite the pace, however, I could tell I was gaining, at times catching sight of people being jostled just a few dozen feet ahead of me. I also knew by now where we were headed. Steering up the middle of the jammed railroad yard, Norm had reduced his options to two, both of them train trestles. One was a short span over the mouth of the canal, leading directly into downtown Bellows Falls. The other, closer by, was the much longer bridge to North Walpole, parallel to and twenty feet downstream of the dam. It wasn't until we were almost at the top of the yard that I saw Bouch cut right and head for the latter.

Still pushing through the crowd, I brought the radio once more to my mouth. "Suspect's heading for North Walpole across the railroad br—"

I didn't get to finish. Easing by a huge bearded man, I was seized by the shirtfront and almost lifted off my feet. His whiskers tickled my chin and his beer-soaked breath enveloped my head as he bellowed, "Goddamn it, you assholes, stop pushin'," before tossing me away like a small discarded toy. He sent me piling up against a half dozen others, all of whom absorbed my fall with a chorus of angry yells. I lay sprawled on the ground as people milled about, trying not to step on me. Another man, smaller but just as irritated, finally bent over me and yelled, "What the fuck's your problem?"

In response, I merely shoved my badge in his face.

He backed up, said, "He's a cop," and a small clearing instantly formed around me. I regained my feet and took off toward the bridge.

The delay, though brief, had been crucial for Norm Bouch. By the time I reached the wooden police barricade blocking the bridge, all I could see was an empty steel trestle, its shiny metal rails glittering from the lights high above. I dropped my hand to the radio clipped to my belt and found it missing, a victim of my encounter with the bearded man.

I looked around frantically, seeing if Bouch could've taken another route. But the bridge, being just downstream of the dam, spanned a cauldron of lethally churning water, and the riverbank dropped straight into it.

I quickly turned to a woman sitting on the barricade. "I'm a police officer. Did you see a man go onto the bridge?"

She took her eyes off the fireworks to look at me angrily. "Sure I did. He almost knocked me over doing it. I told him he'd get busted."

"Where did he go?"

She looked over my shoulder, her eyes blank with surprise. Then her hand rose to her mouth. "Oh, my Lord. Did he fall in?"

It was a pertinent question. The recent rain had swollen the river almost to its crest, and the dam's taintor gates had been lifted to spare the canal upstream, and the hydroelectric plant it fed, from being totally overwhelmed. The tradeoff was that the bend around Bellows Falls' man-made island—the peaceful midsummer stream I'd visited just days earlier—was now a rampaging, heaving, tumultuous torrent. Survival in its throes, and especially over the falls, seemed impossible.

I thanked the woman and stepped out onto the trestle, keenly aware of the water crashing over the dam a few yards to my left. The farther I got from shore, the more the sound of water all but eclipsed the loudest explosions overhead.

I stuck to the middle of the tracks, mindful of how the bridge's intertwined superstructure afforded all too many hiding places, playing my flashlight into every dark corner I came to, my gun at the ready. Feeling increasingly exposed and isolated, I kept glancing ahead, hoping to see reinforcements approaching from the far shore.

But it didn't happen. As inevitably as fate, Norm Bouch emerged as from the metal itself, an instant transformation from angular shadow to seething bundle of human rage—punching, scratching, kicking, and gouging with a fury I'd never before encountered. In my efforts to simply stay on my feet, both my gun and light went flying. Locked together like boxers in a clinch, suddenly caught in a blinding flash from the heavens, we tumbled off the bridge into the steaming waters.

We landed in a bubble bath, the water so aerated it was more foam than liquid. It drew us deep under, not supplying any resistance to swim against, and twisted us about like laundry. But while the notion of air surrounded us, it was water nevertheless, filling my nose and mouth and wrapping me in a cool, smooth, smothering cocoon.

Bouch was unaffected. His dark outline still blocking my blurred vision, he kept his hands clamped around my neck and began trying to hook my legs with his own, as if hoping to suck me into himself, oblivious to his own need to survive. He was all revenge now, the manipulator out of tricks, his only remaining goal to make sure that in death, as in life, he didn't go alone or without making somebody pay. I ran my hands along the sides of his face and pressed both my thumbs as hard as I could into his eyes, feeling the heat expanding in my lungs as my oxygen neared depletion.

The effect of my efforts seemed negligible at first, and far, far too slow. Norm began to thrash, his head tossing from side to side, which only made me hang on tighter. The water was a swirling screen of whitewash, subtly highlighted by the muted colors of the fireworks display. But my vision began to dim as I ran out of air, and slowly I felt a numbness overtake me.

At which point, Bouch desperately released my throat to grab at my hands.

Stimulated by the sudden freedom, I placed one foot firmly against his chest and pushed with all my remaining strength, tearing myself loose of him.

The result was dramatic. From a crashing, twisting whirlwind of froth, I was thrust into solid fluid. The resistance all around me doubled, and I swam to the surface, searing my lungs with warm summer air. The noise of rushing water was overridden once more by the dizzying crash of exploding pyrotechnics.

The respite was short-lived. No sooner had I taken in one big restorative breath than I was dragged underwater again, this time by the weight of my waterlogged armored vest. Pulling at my shirt and fumbling with the clinging Velcro straps, I felt once more my brain closing down. With one final effort, I stripped the vest and pushed at the water around me with my hands. This time, when I broke to the surface, I stayed put.

I lay on my back for a few stunned seconds, the undulating stream rocking me gently, my vision—moments ago shot through with frantic pinpricks of fading neurons—now filled with wondrous flowers, starbursts, and radiating wheels of light.

All riding on the growing thunder of the falls just ahead. My mind clear at last, my heart pounding against the coming onslaught, I twisted about, looking for something to hang on to. But all around me, moving with ever growing speed, I could only see leaping, silky, multicolored water. Ahead, the twin portals of the bridge spanning the falls arched high overhead, doorways to oblivion. And above them, like marbles balanced on a wall, the shapes of spectators' heads all craned away from me, their eyes fixed on the sky.

I stared at them, my last glimpse of humanity, until I was sucked down into the cataract.

I'd been told years before that survival in fast water often depends on one's position—that if you keep flat on your back, with your arms spread out and your legs held before you, the descent of a rapids can approximate a sled run down a mountain.

It had seemed reasonable at the time—appealing to my human ego that helplessness could be defeated by mere proper positioning. The reality was I felt like a leaf in a torrent, and just as likely to be pulverized.

I was thrust about, tossed up, sucked under, and twisted around with no regard for my own efforts. The force controlling me was absolute. I breathed when I could, and otherwise gave in to whatever would decree my fate. I was aware of the rocks. They loomed enormously to all sides. I felt them gliding beneath and beside me, the slippery texture of them brushing my outstretched fingers. But the water, while trying to outlast the air I held tight, also buffered the blows and helped whisk me away from the sheer mass of solid granite. At one point, near the end, when I was thrown like a salmon from the water's embrace, it gathered me again into a deep pool, softening a two-story free fall with the yield of a down pillow. From there, I bobbed into gentle rapids, beside the outwash from the hydroelectric plant, and, more by instinct than with any remaining energy, I slowly paddled into the gravel-strewn shallows.

There, my hands and feet touching bottom like branches protruding from a log, I floated, barely conscious, and watched a parade of firefly-sized flashlights snake their way down the distant shore to the river's edge.

25

Greg Davis stopped near the entrance to the railroad trestle. It had been two days since my swim in the Connecticut River—and an overnight stay in the hospital for observation—and the water level had dropped back to where the hydroelectric plant could take everything the river had. The taintor gates were closed, and only a thin film of water coated the downstream side of the dam.

Davis pointed to where Norm Bouch and I fell in that night. "That's where we found him. Looks like a fun place to swim right now—under a small waterfall—but we couldn't grab hold of him till they lowered the gates a few minutes, and then we had to move fast. Before that, he just kept bobbing out of sight…I don't know how you made it."

I stared at the placid scene, no more dangerous now than a backyard pool. Sensitive as always, Davis didn't say any more but stared off with affection in the other direction, across the canal at the gritty, timeworn, ugly backside of his home town.

I broke away from my daydreaming and followed his gaze. A small group of carpenters was working on one of the buildings overlooking the canal, reinforcing a balcony the length of a city block.

"I hear congratulations are in order," I said.

He turned to me and smiled, embarrassment mixed with pride. "The Chief thing? Thanks. It's only a recommendation. The powers-that-be have still got to rule on it."

"Latour's backing can't hurt, especially now that he's the hero of the hour."

Davis went back to the view. "Yeah…He had that coming, though. He put his whole life into this town, and he did a good job. It wasn't his fault he got tired. Not that he's taking off…He told me yesterday he'll stick around to help the town rebuild itself, and that Shippee'll be his first project. He thinks he has enough on him to encourage him to go job hunting. So there may be light at the end of the tunnel."

"How's Emily doing?"

He laughed. "There's someone who learned a lot in a short time. You don't speak ill of the chief around her." He looked at his watch. "You want a ride back? I gotta get to work."

I shook my head. "It's a pretty day. I'll walk. Thanks."

I watched him drive slowly across the tracks and down the yard toward the road. Emily Doyle had been an easy fix. She was a young enthusiast, dealing with the world in black-and-white terms, unconcerned with such inconsistencies as a contradictory alliance with Emile Latour.

Brian Padget was another matter. I'd started today's pilgrimage to Bellows Falls with a visit to his home, to formally let him know that all charges had been dropped, and that the papers would be running a full explanation of the circumstances in a few days.

Not surprisingly, this had not affected him like the wave of a magic wand, eradicating the past and healing all wounds. He'd merely moved to the window and stood there, sightlessly staring out, fingering a curtain in one hand.

"What are you going to do now?" I'd asked. "Latour said you can pick up where you left off with the department, if you want, once you've paid the piper for playing maverick. Probably not a bad idea, at least for the short run. Give you time to think things over."

He hadn't answered, and I'd been forced to think of the differences between us. Despite the despair and the growing sense of futility that had nagged me early on, unconsciously I'd been bolstered throughout by stalwarts like Greg Davis and Jonathon Michael and even Emile Latour, who'd finally risen to the task at hand. I'd also had a lifetime of experience to call upon, and in Gail the backing of a friend on whose support I could count.

Padget had benefited from nothing like this. Manipulated into disgrace, he'd been just as passively extracted from it, and like any piece of manhandled baggage, while he'd survived the trip physically, he'd been forever scarred by the process. Watching him stare out into space, his options unknown, I'd mourned my inability to be of much use. I hoped he'd stay in law enforcement, but I knew that might be expecting too much.

I turned away from the river and walked toward the village, my reborn optimism attracted by the repair work being done on that old building.

Ignoring the clearly written sign not to do so, I crossed the canal using the short railroad trestle, and cut left along the opposite bank until I was standing at water's edge, in the grass, looking up at the imposing structure. From this side, it reached four stories to the sky—stained, rusting, disfigured by an ugly fire escape, and yet oddly regal. Beneath the grime were ornate cornices and fancy moldings—details of an ancient attention to care and pride—the murmurings of the old Bellows Falls.

One of the carpenters paused in his work to look down at me from the balcony. "How're you doin'?"

"Okay. Fixing the place up?"

"Yeah. Been empty longer than I been alive. Still in good shape, though. They want to turn it into a teen center, a restaurant, who the hell knows?"

"That's a good thing, though, right—instead of letting it rot?"

He shrugged and turned to peer at it again. "I guess. They might pull it off this time—God knows the town's due for some good luck. But if I had the money, I'd spend it somewhere else."

"You from around here?" I asked.

He looked down at me for a long time, his face finally breaking into a smile. "Yeah—probably die here, too…I see your point. Guess I better get back to work."